Men Among Giants

by

Kent Krause

Men Among Giants

Kodar Publishing
ISBN 13: 978-0-692-46484-7
ISBN 10: 0692464840

Cover photo by Matt Brown

Permissions

For Jill,

Mom & Dad,

Brenda,

and the friends of Dave King

Other books by Kent Krause:

The All-American King

Behind in the Count

Ninety Feet Away

Acknowledgements

Thank you to Shapato Publishing and Jean Tennant for publishing the first edition of *Men Among Giants*.

I am also grateful to several others who helped me with this novel: Richard Clarence for informing me about the history of Sherman Field in Lincoln; Mark Piro for answering my questions about medical issues relevant to the book; Benjamin Rader for writing an endorsement for the back cover; Jim Ballard and Hilary Sire for organizing book signings; and Cindy Conger, Patty Beutler, Keith Larsen, and Patrice Reynolds for writing/publishing book reviews of this novel.

Finally, a major league thank you to my wife Jill. Her advice, editing, and encouragement have not only improved my books, but made writing them more fun.

Chapter 1

"Will Eileen be there?"

"Yeah. Want me to ask her to bring a friend?"

"No … um, yeah sure. No, forget it. Not tonight."

Sam raised an eyebrow at me before grabbing his wallet and sunglasses off the dresser. "Suit yourself. You ready?"

"Yep." I jingled the keys in my hand. We clomped down the staircase and out the front door to my red Taurus parked in the street.

I'd driven about a block when he looked over and asked, "So why'd you want to know about Eileen?"

A nervous spasm shot through my insides. I scrambled to come up with an answer that would deflect any suspicion. "Uh, just wondering how polite I have to be tonight. If Randal's wife and Eileen are there, I'll try to keep my uncouth behaviors to a minimum."

He chuckled. "Not much you can't do or say in front of Eileen. Trust me."

You oaf! "Good to know," I said, continuing to drive.

It was the night before the opening game of the season. I had met Sam Judge five weeks earlier, at the start of spring training. That was when the Lincoln Giants had paired us together as roommates. The Giants were an independent minor league baseball team in the Central States League. Since we players earned little more than a pittance, team officials tried to find foster families to house the players during the season. Sam and I drew Dr. Hornsby, a widower and retired history professor who lived in an older neighborhood south of downtown.

1

Even though Sam and I had shared an upstairs room at Hornsby's place for over a month, we weren't what I would call friends. He didn't talk much and there was the not so small issue of *her*. Beyond that, the possibility of getting cut had hovered over me throughout spring training. For the final spot in the rotation, it came down to me and a wiry 19-year-old left-hander named Richie.

The last week before the season began, I made two shaky starts. Richie was even shakier. So he left and I stayed. With my stomach churning for most of April and May, I spent little time bonding with my roommate. Sure, we got along okay. After practices, we'd knock down a few beers with some of the other players. And I respected Sam's talent. He had pitched for the Giants the previous season and his status as the number one starter was a foregone conclusion before camp opened. But I didn't know the real Sam Judge at this point. And I never could have predicted the insanity that would befall him in the coming season.

My Taurus rolled to a stop about a block down the street from JK's, an eating and drinking establishment in Lincoln's Haymarket District that served free beer to Giants players. Over the course of spring training, the team had divided itself into different cliques for off-field activities. The group I usually hung out with included Sam, Randal Van Dyke (RF), Kenny Haldeman (2B), Bruce "Weed" Gleason (middle relief), and Dallas "Fender" Bender (closer). They were all present and accounted for, plus Randal's wife Cathy, on this occasion—an informal celebration of the start of the 1994 season. Claiming a long table near the bar, we ordered three pitchers of Lowenbrau and three large plates of Buffalo wings.

After about a half hour of drinking and devouring, I spotted a woman approaching. She stopped near our table and eyed us with a smirk. Her sun-blond hair was tied back in a ponytail and she wore a powder blue shirt and jeans that tightly hugged her hips and thighs. My palms dampened as I admired her curvy figure.

"What a motley crew," she said. "This place has really gone downhill."

"Tell me about it," said Kenny, sitting to the right of Sam. "They'll let anybody in here nowadays." The shortest guy at the table, Kenny had ruddy hair that emerged from his head like the bristles of a shoe brush. A cubic zirconia stud adorned his left earlobe.

"Where are your manners," Sam said, shoving his smaller teammate off his seat. "Yield your chair to the lady."

"Okay, okay." Kenny bowed to the woman and extended his hand in a sweeping gesture toward his chair. "My lady."

"Thank you, Mr. Haldeman." She slid into the chair and planted a kiss on Sam's cheek.

"Hey, girlie." He half-smiled and placed an arm across her shoulders. She was Eileen Palmer, starting first baseman for the University of Nebraska softball team. Her arms and legs were thicker than those of the average college girl, but this size came mostly from toned muscle. She'd led her team in home runs and RBI the previous season. Sam had spotted her last October when he attended one of the Husker softball games. Impressed by her power, he made a point to get her number after the game. Part of me despised him for that. It didn't matter that I was living in another city and didn't know either of them at the time.

"Hey Eileen," Fender said in a Texas drawl, "where are your teammates? We can't celebrate proper without some fillies. My lap's gettin' cold here." A toothy grin appeared under his black Stetson.

"They were coming out with me," she replied, "until I told them you'd be here. Then they all remembered they had to wash their hair. Weird, huh?" Her blue eyes sparkled.

"Yeah," Weed said, "Fender's the number one cause of dirty hair among women aged sixteen to thirty-four." Tall and skinny like Randal, Weed had an angular face, a protruding Adam's apple, and long stringy hair the color of straw. His eyelids remained perpetually half-closed.

After Weed and Fender finished a jesting exchange of profanity-laced putdowns, Eileen slid an empty glass down the table to me. "Hey Brian, pour me one, huh?"

"Brian?" Randal asked. "Who's that?"

"That *is* my name," I said.

"No it isn't," Kenny snapped. "You're Boo. What's the matter with you? You forget your own name?"

I shook my head and looked over at a table of thirty-something yuppies.

"But he seems to think he's a Brian." Eileen gestured at me. "Why do you guys call him Boo?"

"Oh come on, don't you see it," Kenny exclaimed, flinging a hand in my direction. "Look at him, the high forehead, mussed blond hair, those creepy eyes. He's Boo Radley from *To Kill a Mockingbird*."

"Spittin' image," Fender added. The Boo thing had started the first week of training camp. I'm not sure who said it first—Kenny seemed the most likely culprit. In any event, almost all the players were calling me Boo by week two. Sam was the exception.

Eileen smiled at me. "I guess you're Boo then."

About an hour later, our gathering broke up. We had a midnight curfew and did not want to get busted before the first game of the season. On the sidewalk outside JK's, Sam turned to walk toward my car down the street. "Hey!" Eileen pushed his shoulder from behind. "Aren't you forgetting something?"

"Sorry," he mumbled, turning to wrap his arms around her. She lifted her head and pressed her lips to his. After a fleeting connection, he pulled away. "I'll call you tomorrow, girlie."

"It's *tomorrow night* you're supposed to keep people from getting to first base, not tonight," she said with a wink.

"Easy now," he replied.

"You know this big tough guy can't handle PDAs," Kenny quipped while peeking over Sam's shoulder from behind. Sam turned to swat at him, but the second baseman darted away like a gnat. They all laughed. I did not.

The ballpark hummed with excitement the following night. Packed stands and unbounded spring optimism fueled a festive atmosphere at Sherman Field. After the national anthem, Sam Judge took the mound for his warm-up tosses. The fabric of his crisp white uniform stretched to contain the muscles within. Nonetheless, it was not his height or brawny physique that caught the eye at first glance. It was his hair. Dark locks cascaded in waves from his purple cap and did not stop until they touched the purple 15 on the back of his jersey. Though he had no musical talents to speak of, Sam's hair would've been well-placed on the head of a heavy metal guitarist.

The opening salvo of the Giants 1994 season was a fastball that caught the inside corner. Lincoln fans yelled and clapped with approval. From my vantage point in the third base dugout (a brick structure with a metal roof that was completely above ground), I leaned against the front rail and observed the man on the hill. Sam's motion was smooth and natural, like he was born to do nothing else but hurl a baseball over a plate 60 feet, six inches away. I studied his torsional delivery for pitch after pitch, trying to pick up any details that could help me when I was on the mound. And then, seemingly way too soon, the inning was over.

Upon reaching the dugout, Sam received high fives and clipped accolades for striking out the side. He made his way to the far end of the bench where I stood.

"Not bad," I said, as we slapped hands.

"Yeah." He sat on the bench and pulled off his glove.

"Gonna let your fielders do anything tonight?"

"Nah." A faint grin appeared between his moustache and goatee. "They need to save their energy for when you're on the hill." He wrapped a towel around his pitching arm.

"Thanks." I sat next to him and tore open a bag of sunflower seeds.

"Yep." He held out a palm, which I filled. As he shoved the pile into his mouth, a few seeds tumbled down the front of his jersey. Out on the field, the Giants hitters managed a single, but nothing else in their half of the first.

In the top of the second inning, I paced to the end of the dugout nearest home plate—the domain of Giants manager Don Angley. A pear-shaped man with a band of close-cropped white hair beneath his cap, he leaned against the brick wall at the dugout entrance. Next to him stood his coach, Tony Littel, who, like me, was a newcomer to the Giants this year.

"Look at that," Angley said. "Did you see the break on that hook?"

"Sharp," Tony replied. "Like he's dropping the ball in a bucket."

The cleanup hitter for the Bismarck Hawks stalked back to his dugout. Fans clapped as Giants infielders tossed the ball around the horn.

5

"That slider's working too." Angley ejected a stream of tobacco juice from his mouth.

"The change is about the only thing we haven't seen yet," Tony said, running his thumb and index finger in opposite directions over his thick dark moustache. He did not have to wait long to see the changeup he'd just mentioned. Sam used the pitch to induce a routine groundout from the next batter in the Bismarck lineup.

"That boy just might be a pitcher after all," Angley muttered. He watched as Sam used two sliders to get ahead of the next hitter, who then popped up a high heater to end the inning.

I returned to the far end of the dugout, where Sam again sat next to me. "Skip and Tony are talking about you," I said.

"Mmmph." He held out his hand for more sunflower seeds.

"They said you suck at pitching."

"Uh-huh."

"They also said you smell funny."

He crunched the seeds between his teeth and spat out a succession of shells. Moments later Randal doubled home Matt Thompson to give the Giants the lead. At the end of the inning, Sam tossed aside his towel and stood.

"Try to keep that stench under control," I said. Without looking, he flicked back his arm, smacking me in the face with his glove. "Ow! Damn it, Judge!"

Sam walked a batter to start the third inning, before retiring the side with a strikeout and two weak groundouts. He breezed through the fourth and the fifth too. At that point, I moved away from the end of the dugout where he dwelled between innings. All the other Giants vacated that area as well. So Sam sat alone on the bench. It had to be this way. Ballplayers always kept their distance from a teammate who was throwing a no-hitter.

When Sam went out to pitch the sixth, Angley and Tony resumed their conversation. "How did this guy not get drafted?" the young coach asked.

"Two reasons," Angley replied, his eyes glued on our pitcher. "One, he's got a temper. Got into a few scrapes in college. On and off the field. Made the papers. Teams got wary." The skipper released another shot of brown juice into the saturated dirt below. "Nobody wants a hothead."

"The other reason?" Tony asked.

"He wasn't really a pitcher. Just a big strong kid who tried to blow everybody away with hard stuff. And he could get away with it most of the time against college hitters. Too many walks though. Scouts could tell he was just a thrower. And that's what he was here for most of last season." Angley clapped and shouted an encouragement after Sam racked up another strikeout to start the sixth.

"Looks like you got him turned around. He's got all four pitches working."

"Yeah." Angley chuckled. "Gives me hope I didn't waste the entire off-season trying to teach him how to pitch. The biggest challenge was to get him to quit winging it in as hard as he could. Finally got him to drop the fastball down to 93, so he knows where the damn thing is going."

"It worked," Tony said. "His control is dead-on tonight."

"Yep."

"He still needs to lose the hair."

"Don't get me started on that," Angley grumbled.

The next batter sent a routine fly ball to centerfield for the second out. Bismarck's leadoff hitter then grounded out to end the top of the sixth. In the bottom of the inning, our first baseman, Vince Stenzel, doubled off the right field wall to drive in another run. Lincoln led 2-0 heading to the seventh.

The fans stood and clapped as Sam took the mound. Everybody in the ballpark knew what he had going. Bismarck's first batter in the inning struck out waving at three pitches: a slider, a fastball, and a curve.

"That boy didn't have a chance," Angley said, turning to us players on the bench. "Guessed wrong on all three pitches."

The next batter worked the count full. As Sam went into his windup for the payoff pitch, a loud blast cut through the night. The sound came from a train engine on the railroad tracks that ran about 100 feet behind the left field wall. Sam's pitch soared way high. Our catcher, Sergio "Sarge" Miranda, jumped up from his crouch to barely keep the ball from sailing to the backstop. Sam stomped off the mound and made an obscene gesture at the train rattling by.

"Come on, Sammy. Shake it off," someone on our bench yelled. Similar exhortations followed from other players and fans.

"Should I go out and say something to him?" Tony asked Angley.

"Nah. Let's see if he can handle it himself. He's got to learn to control his emotions."

Sam toed the rubber and glared in at Sarge to get the sign. Pitching from the stretch, he delivered a slider that caught the inside corner of the plate. He followed with high heat and a changeup to put the count at 1-2. Sam then conjured a curve ball that dropped so sharply, it looked like it rolled off a table. Another strikeout. The next Bismarck batter hit an easy one hopper to the shortstop to end the inning.

Lincoln plated three runs in the bottom of the seventh. With the game seemingly well in hand, I directed my attention to Abe, the Giants mascot. Abe was actually a guy on stilts wearing a dark overcoat, a stovepipe hat, and a mask that was supposed to look like Abraham Lincoln. The designer of the mask, however, must have been drunk on the job or completely ignorant of the appearance of our sixteenth president. Either way, the face he designed looked more like Richard Nixon. A wrathful Nixon.

The sound of crying children rang out as the stilted mascot staggered back and forth in front of the stands.

Giants booster Myrtle Schultz found a more effective way to fire up the crowd. Marching up and down the aisle before the front row of fans she bellowed "FEE FI FO FUM" at a volume unreachable by most humans. An obese woman who likely descended from a line of town criers, Myrtle then stomped one of her trunk-like legs four times on the wooden planks below.

It did not take long for this chant to catch on with the crowd. Soon all three thousand spectators were chanting and stomping their feet: "FEE FI FO FUM!" Thump. Thump. Thump. Thump. "FEE FI FO FUM!" Thump. Thump. Thump. Thump.

The ominous noise thundered through the ballpark.

Sam needed only ten pitches to retire the side in the eighth. The Giants half of the inning did not last much longer. When Sam marched to the mound for the ninth, a no-hitter was only three outs away. He fidgeted with the rosin bag before and after his warm-up pitches. He toed the rubber, but then stepped away to pace behind the mound. Fans yelled and cheered. Finally, he was ready. The first pitch, a slider, missed low. The next pitch was a fastball that

8

the batter tried to bunt down the first base line. But he got too much air under it. Sam stepped to his left and snagged the ball just before it hit the ground. One out.

The next batter was the Hawks leadoff man. Trying to go to the opposite field, he blooped Sam's first offering into shallow right. Randal took a step back, realized his mistake, and charged in. It was too late. He gloved the ball on one hop. A collective groan filled the stadium. Though Randal almost certainly would have caught the ball had he read it correctly, the official scorer had to call it a hit. Sam pounded his glove and kicked at the dirt beneath his feet. He then walked the next batter on a 3-2 pitch. Another walk followed to load the bases. Angley scooted out of the dugout, his thin legs chugging away beneath an expansive belly. Sarge joined them on the mound. Sam hung his head through the entire conversation. He finally nodded and the skipper returned to the dugout. Tony meanwhile signaled down the left field line for Fender to start warming up.

"Well?" Tony asked.

"I don't know," Angley said. "Just have to wait and see."

Baseball is undoubtedly a game of skill. Sometimes though, it doesn't hurt to be lucky. Sam hung a breaking ball to the next hitter, a lefty who smoked it down the line. I'm not sure if Vince at first base saw the line drive or not, but either way it came to an abrupt stop in his glove. He then stepped on the bag to double off the runner moving toward second.

The crowd gave Sam a standing ovation. Giants infielders gathered around him, but he broke away and headed toward Randal trotting in from right field. "Uh oh," Tony said. My body tensed in fear of what would happen next. Randal was almost as tall as Sam, but looked like a toothpick compared to the burly pitcher.

When Randal reached the infield dirt, he stopped and eyed his approaching teammate. The two men stood face to face as seconds ticked away. Sam then clapped the lanky right fielder's shoulder. One of them must have cracked a joke because they both wore smiles on their way back to the dugout. Those of us watching breathed a sigh of relief.

A group of children brandishing baseballs, programs, and caps surrounded Sam as he headed for the clubhouse, a rectangular wooden structure with peeling white paint about thirty feet behind the Giants dugout. He bantered with the youngsters and signed every item they pressed under his chin. I was already in my street clothes by the time he entered the locker room.

"You write slow," I said. "There are only eight letters in your full name for Pete's sake."

"Interview," he replied. "A reporter from the paper caught me just outside the door."

"Did you tell him I taught you everything you know?"

He chuckled. "Yeah, right." He peeled off his jersey to reveal a hairy chest and a ripped torso that would have made a pro wrestler envious. "You better not leave without me," he said, squeezing through our crowded clubhouse toward his locker. "Skip's gonna make me ice the arm for at least twenty minutes."

After a late supper at Village Inn, we headed home. Professor Hornsby was asleep when Sam and I crept into his dark house. We tried to be quiet, but the wood stairs creaked under our weight like snapping tree branches. We froze midway up the staircase, not moving until we heard snores resume from the downstairs bedroom. Fortunately, the professor was a sound sleeper.

Sam and I shared a fairly sizeable bedroom on the second floor of Hornsby's old Victorian home. Dropping onto my mattress, I stared up at the ceiling and listened to the rustling leaves of the oak tree outside the open window. The springs in the bed across the room squeaked and whined as Sam rotated his body trying to get comfortable. I guessed that he would not be asleep any time soon.

"Nice curveball tonight," I said.

"Yeah. It felt good." His deep voice spoke just above a whisper. "The whole game."

"Fastball, slider, and change weren't bad either."

He grunted. "I gotta admit, the old man knows a little something about pitching."

I flipped my pillow over to the cool side. "Bet you're glad you stayed in Lincoln over the off-season."

"Hated it at the time," he said. "Pushed a mop around that school until 3:00 every day and then had Angley on my case the rest of the afternoon. Felt like an idiot pitching to him with snow on the ground."

"I think it paid off."

"Maybe."

"And you got to spend time with Eileen by staying in Lincoln."

"Yeah." He was quiet for a while and then sat up in his bed. "You know, Brian, tonight I felt it for the first time."

"You gonna propose?"

"Not Eileen. I'm talkin' about the show. Man, those Bismarck chumps couldn't do nothin' against me. I owned 'em. Every one of 'em. And the hitters in this league are about at the AA level, right?"

"I heard something to that effect."

"I'm finally thinking it's going to happen. Tonight, I could taste it."

"Taste it?"

"The majors. For the first time, I really believe I'm gonna make it to the bigs."

I rolled onto my side, propping up my head with an elbow. "I bet you're not the only one who thinks that now."

He swung his legs off the bed and stood. "That would show 'em all. The teachers and coaches who got in my face 'cause they didn't like my attitude. The judge who railroaded me into juvy."

"You got sent to juvy?"

"Yeah, for three weeks when I was sixteen. These two punks saw me talking to this girl one of 'em liked, so they jumped me after school. I knocked their teeth out. All the other kids watching were their friends. Said I started it."

"That sucks."

"Yeah. People have always been trying to pin stuff on me. Even my old man never gives me a break. Just ask him what he considers his greatest disappointment in life." Sam thrust a thumb into his chest.

"Man." I didn't know what else to say.

"I admit I've done some dumb things in my life." His eyes moved to something on the wall above me. "But I don't go looking for trouble. It's just, some people know how to push my buttons and I can't let it go. Like those stupid fights in college." He slammed his fist into his hand. "That's why nobody drafted me."

"Forget about the past," I said. "This season is your chance. You'll show everybody you've got what it takes."

"Yeah … Man, I wish I could pitch again tomorrow."

"That'd be fine with me. You can pitch Saturday too. Just let me have the hill Sunday afternoon. I lost a lot of sweat trying to get that last spot in the Giants rotation."

He paced around the room causing the floorboards to groan beneath his feet. "Hey, I ain't gonna be gettin' to sleep for a while. You want to play some cards?"

I knew I wouldn't be getting to sleep soon either, especially if he kept clumping back and forth. "Fine." I turned on a desk lamp and grabbed a deck. We both sat on the floor with our backs against our beds and our legs stretched out before us. "What do you want to play?"

"I don't care," he said. "Just deal."

As I flipped the cards to him, a distant look formed in his eyes. Like he was watching himself pitch at Yankee Stadium … Wrigley Field … Fenway Park … Busch Stadium …

Chapter 2

"Well, if it isn't Mr. Radley," Kenny said in a fake southern accent. He plopped into the vinyl seat next to mine. "It is a glorious morning, I do declare." A pillow and two *Penthouse* magazines rested in his lap.

My body throbbed from the pain of being awake. "There is nothing glorious about anything at six a.m. Ever."

"Au contraire, lazy boy. This is going to be a wonderful day. In just eight short hours we will be out of this hick state and enjoying the majestic mountains of Colorado." A goofy grin spread across his face.

"Eight hours … urgh." I leaned my head against the window. The bus hissed and rolled forward, crunching the gravel of the Sherman Field parking lot beneath its wheels. At the front of the long vehicle sat Angley and Tony. In the row behind them were Jerry Hershberger, our trainer, and Chip Sandquist, the play-by-play man for the Giants radio broadcasts. Twenty-four ballplayers in various states of consciousness occupied the rest of the bus. The lucky ones stretched out across two seats, their heads propped against pillows. The unlucky ones had a wise guy chattering away next to them.

"Don't be so grumpy," Kenny said. "This is a great opportunity for us to visit. Get to know each other better. Share our feelings."

I thought about pushing him into the aisle. "Pass."

"Come on, Booberry. We have to do something to pass the time riding through this dreadful state."

"Read your magazines." I glanced at the picture on one of the covers.

"I'm not in the mood yet."

"Watch the movie," I gestured toward the television screen at the front of the bus. Tony had shoved a tape into the VCR player. The opening scenes of *Soul Man* appeared.

"Eh, I've seen it," Kenny said with a dismissive wave. "That's Ponyboy, you know. He's not really black."

"Yeah, I figured that one out myself."

As the bus accelerated onto Interstate 80 heading west, Tony made his way down the aisle distributing our meal money. Each player received five dollars per meal—a total of $105 for the seven-day road trip. There would not be too many steak dinners in our immediate future. After pocketing the cash, I let my eyelids fall.

"Are you going back to sleep?" Kenny asked, jabbing an elbow into my arm. "Fine. I'll let you sleep for two hours while I check out Rae Dawn Chong's sweet heinie. Then we are going to talk, mister. I want to get to know the real Boo."

"Great." I shifted my body into a position that I hoped would not produce a neck cramp hours later. "Then maybe we can braid each other's hair."

"That's the spirit!"

I dreamed that a real-life version of Bart Simpson had joined the Giants. This was probably a consequence of sitting next to an urchin with short spiky hair. As Bart skateboarded around the base paths at Sherman, a shrill racket ripped me into consciousness. "Ar Ar-Ar Ar-Arrrrr! I'm the Red Rooster!" Kenny stood in the aisle with his head tilted back. "I don't mean to be fowl, but it's time for breakfast! Wake up everybody! Ar Ar-Ar Ar-Arrrrr!" He then started strutting, his head bobbing forward with each step.

"You're gonna be the dead rooster if you don't shut up," groused a voice from the rear of the bus. Groans and two-word expletives directed at our second baseman filled the air. The bus meanwhile rolled down an exit ramp toward the town of Kearney. Zombies slowly came to life as the driver pulled into the parking lot of a roadside diner.

After breakfast the Giants shuffled back to their long metallic carriage. Our seating arrangements, unfortunately, remained the same. I grabbed the baseball I'd left lying in my seat. "Hey, didn't you go to college in this one-horse town?" Kenny asked as the bus maneuvered out of the parking lot.

"Yep. University of Nebraska-Kearney." I held the ball as if preparing to throw a fastball.

"Pitch there?"

"Yep."

"Any good?"

"Five and four, junior year. Seven and two, senior year. ERA under four both seasons."

"Really?" He rubbed his sandpaper patch of chin hair. "Get drafted?"

"Expos took me in the forty-second round in ninety-one. Pitched for their rookie team that summer and then their A team in Burlington the following year. A month into the ninety-three season, I thought I was ready to move up to AA. They thought I was ready for a career outside of baseball." I sighed. "Cut me loose last June."

"So how'd you end up with the Giants?" He flipped open one of his magazines.

"My high school coach knows the team vice president. Got me a tryout."

"Connections, baby." Kenny grinned. "Where'd you go to high school?"

"North Platte."

"Another Nebraska cultural hotspot."

"It has the largest rail yard in the world."

"Ooooohh! How do you deal with all the tourists?"

"We'll pass right by there in about an hour."

"Super." He switched on his Walkman and pulled the headphones over his ears.

After examining my slider grip from several different angles, I set the baseball down and grabbed the newspaper I'd tucked beside my seat. The front page of the sports section featured an article about the Nebraska softball team's victory in the NCAA regional the previous night. Eileen had two hits and three RBI. Though the accompanying photo showed the Husker pitcher, visions of the first baseman filled my head. This daydream continued until, appropriately enough, a bullhorn snore from behind me delivered a cold dose of reality. Shifting my body, I turned to see Sam sprawled across the two seats. His hair splayed against the window; his feet extended into the aisle. A line of drool trickled into his goatee. A familiar bitterness darkened my mood. *You slob. If she were mine, I'd be writing her a letter. You're probably dreaming of some other girl.*

A light bulb clicked on. Sam and another girl. We'd be spending seven nights on the road. It could happen. Then the 240-pound boulder blocking my dreams would roll away. As *Wayne's World* played on the TV screen at the front of the bus, I gazed out at the passing fields contemplating my plot.

Hours later, Kenny roused me from a nap. "We just crossed the border," he said, his boyish face aglow. "It's about time we got out of that godforsaken state."

"You mean Nebraska? The state you now call home."

"Never! Colorado will always be my home. I'm just serving time in Nebraska. Gonna have a big year and get back on track for the bigs. Then the Brewers can kiss my hairy—"

"How long were you in their system?" I interrupted.

"Two years. Bastards cut me last February. Too late to sign with another big league team. So here I am with the indie Giants." He raised his arms into a stretch, revealing a Calvin tattoo on his left bicep. A tiger named Hobbes, of course, occupied the right bicep. "Probably my last chance," he mumbled, looking away.

"Your folks coming down from Denver to watch the game tonight?"

"Mom and her boyfriend are. Dad's in California."

"Oh. Forgot they were divorced."

"Got a sister and some college buddies coming to the game too. So we'd better win. Good thing we got the big guy going tonight." He gestured at the seats behind us.

"Yeah. Lucky you." I turned to gaze out the window again.

The bus stopped in front of our motel in Colorado Springs a little after 2:00 p.m. Card games ended, books slammed shut, and Sony Walkmans clicked off. Escaping the confinement and stench of our rolling sardine tin, I drew a large breath of fresh mountain air into my grateful lungs. After we retrieved our luggage from the storage compartment, the Giants filed into the motel to get checked in. We then had two hours to eat and hang out before heading to the ballpark.

As in Lincoln, Sam and I shared a room. He would be on the mound for the first game of this road trip. Lincoln had won three of four from Bismarck to open the season. I started game four of that series, the only contest we lost. My parents and older brother Mark drove in to see me pitch, adding to my embarrassment at the outcome. I'd like to think it was nerves from my first start as a Giant that affected my performance. But it was more likely the many sliders I left hovering over the center of the plate. The Hawks put up six runs in my four and two-thirds innings of work. Fortunately, Eileen was out of town with her team and did not see the game.

Our hosts, the Colorado Springs Pikemen, had ripped the cover off the ball in their first series of the season. That didn't matter to Sam. After his opening day one-hitter, he figured he could shut down any team in the league. His confidence spread to our teammates, who buzzed with enthusiasm on the ride from the motel to the stadium.

After going down one-two-three in the top of the first, the Giants took the field. Crowds always responded the first time they beheld Sam and his rock star hair atop the mound. Some oohed, some (mostly women) whistled, some (mostly men) cracked jokes, and some sat transfixed. Most important was the reaction of the Pikemen, and they looked unsettled watching him warm up. Sam sent them down in order with two strikeouts.

The first inning foreshadowed events to come on this cool, breezy Colorado evening. Zero after zero filled the stadium scoreboard, which stood in relief against a distant mountain range. In the bottom of the sixth, Giants third baseman Matt Thompson threw a ball away, allowing a Pikeman to reach second. A bunt and a sacrifice fly brought him home to give Colorado Springs a 1-0 lead. Steam poured from Sam's ears, but he kept it together and struck out the next hitter to end the inning.

In the top of the seventh, Vince Stenzel, our first baseman, pulled a hanging curve over the right field wall to tie the game. Sam, however, still seethed in the dugout. In the bottom of the inning, he issued a couple of one-out walks. A sharp single brought in a run to give Colorado Springs the lead again. Sam had given up his first earned run of the season. The glare on his face intensified.

Channeling his emotions, he struck out the next two batters to prevent any further damage.

In the ninth, Giants centerfielder Willie Small singled and stole second. One out later, designated hitter Brad McGill drove him in to tie the game. Our dugout sprang to life in celebration. Sam shut down the Pikemen in the bottom of the inning, so after nine the score was knotted at two apiece. After the Giants did not score in the top of the 10th, Angley brought in Weed to pitch. Upon learning that he was done for the evening, Sam flung his glove against the dugout wall and stomped away to the clubhouse. I understood his frustration, but the skipper had no choice. Sam had already thrown 114 pitches and it would've been insane to risk blowing out his arm in the second week of the season.

Weed got through the 10th without incident, but the Pikemen knocked home a run in the 11th to win the game. Sam didn't say a word as we ate a late supper at Denny's. His ominous silence and the letdown from our defeat kept the other players subdued as well. Back at the motel, I unlocked the door and flipped on the light in our room. After dropping my wallet and keys on the nightstand, I dropped myself onto one of the beds. "Wanna watch some TV?" I asked.

He grunted. Not sure what that meant, I reached for the remote. "You had a great line tonight," I said. "Nine innings, one earned run, twelve strikeouts. I'd love to put that down for my next start."

His steel-melting glare lightened somewhat. "Yeah."

I flipped through the channels to find ESPN, which showed highlights from the Yankees-Blue Jays game. A sudden crash then shook the building. My body launched from the mattress and my head jerked toward the noise. Sam stood across the room pulling his fist out of the wall. Cracks radiated from the cantaloupe-sized hole he had created. Wincing, he used his left hand to cradle his bloody right hand—his pitching hand. "Dammit! Hit a stud."

I stared at him in disbelief. Moments later, someone pounded on our door. "What the hell is going on in there?" Kenny called from the other side.

Sam opened the door. "Go get Jerry," he commanded. "I hurt my hand." Standing frozen in a white tank top and heart-print boxers, Kenny dropped his jaw and then sprinted away. Rubbing his injured hand, Sam walked over to the hole to inspect the damage. "There goes my first paycheck." He looked over at me. "Now you know why I can't afford a car."

Angley called a team meeting the next morning. With no boardroom at the motel, we had to gather in the bus for privacy. Our manager bowed his bald capless head. Grimfaced Tony stood at his side. After a minute of torturous silence, Angley directed a fiery glare at us. "I am too damn old for this," he barked. "I thought I had a team of ballplayers, not a bunch of brainless imbeciles." Sam was not the only subject of his ire. Weed and Fender had stayed out past curfew and brought women back to their room—a double transgression. Another Giant, twenty-year-old reserve outfielder Danny McQuinn, had racked up a drunk and disorderly charge and spent the night in jail.

"You think this is some kind of joyride? Summer camp?" The skipper's wrinkled face turned from pink to red as he jabbed a finger at us. "You are *professional* baseball players. Only a select few get paid to play this game. It's a privilege you won't fully appreciate 'til you don't get to wear a uniform anymore." An icy quiet hung in the air. "You WILL respect this game." He stomped off the bus.

Tony remained, his eyes roaming from player to player. "Two years ago the Braves cut me," he said. "I'd played six seasons in the minors and I just wasn't good enough." He clenched his face in defiance. "I can live with that. I can live with that because I gave it my all … But I could never live with myself if I had the talent, but threw my chance away because of some adolescent stupidity." He somehow seemed to stare at all of us at the same time. "Never again, guys. Never … again." Then he was gone.

I glanced over at Sam in the seat next to me. Bandages wrapped his right hand. Anxiety wrapped his face.

That evening the chastened Giants won 5-2 behind seven strong innings from lefthander Clyde Eisenberg. Unfortunately, the next night did not go so well. In the rubber game, Colorado Springs jumped out early against Giants starter Burke LaVelle and held on for an 8-7 victory. The following morning was a Friday. The players tramped out to the bus as the sun rose from the plains of the Midwest. Nobody said much as we jostled into our seats. Even Kenny kept his trap shut for once. Losing two out of three to the

Pikemen was bad. Incurring the wrath of the coaches was worse. The prospect of playing the rest of the season without our best pitcher was nearly unbearable.

Actually, one of the Giants wasn't completely heartbroken about Sam's situation. I'm not proud to admit it, but I wondered how his injury might affect his relationship with Eileen. *Maybe the Giants will cut him and he'll go back home to Des Moines. Then they'd have to break up.* As the bus headed north out of Colorado Springs, I watched Sam sitting across the aisle from me. His left hand petted its wounded counterpart. The corners of his mouth sagged and his distant eyes contemplated an uncertain future—a future that had seemed so bright only a week earlier. A spear of guilt impaled my abdomen and I suddenly hated myself for hoping he'd get released.

Our bus entered Cheyenne, Wyoming, around noon. After checking into the motel and eating lunch, the players lounged around their rooms. I read a few dozen pages from my tattered paperback copy of *Ball Four*, while Sam lay on the bed watching *Oprah* and playing solitaire. On the ride to the ballpark later that afternoon, my stomach executed a series of backflips. I would be making my second start of the season. The flipping sensation remained as Tony reviewed with me the scouting report on our opponents, and as I warmed up in the bullpen. Between pitches, I noticed a blond girl with a ponytail in the stands. She reminded me of Eileen, who I thought might be listening to the game back in Lincoln. If not, maybe she would read about my start in the paper. Electricity coursed through my limbs. *Tonight, I dominate.*

After taking the mound in the bottom of the first, I surveyed the crowd. The stands were about two-thirds full. Many fans wore orange, the color of our opponents, the Cheyenne Mules. Their leadoff batter, a short guy with long dreadlocks, stepped to the plate from the left side. Sarge gave me the sign: the traditional one finger for a fastball. I nodded and started my windup. Pushing off the rubber with my pivot foot, I fired a bullet toward the plate. Sarge did not have to move his glove. The four-seamer sliced over the outside corner at the knees. Strike one. I always felt a charge of energy when a pitch did exactly what I told it to do.

At Sarge's prompting, I fed the Mules a mixed diet of fastballs, sliders, and changeups. Those were my three best pitches.

Occasionally, on an 0-2 or 1-2 count, Sarge called for a curve or a split-fingered fastball. I was rarely accurate with either, but sometimes they looked good enough to induce a swing before the ball skidded into the dirt in front of the plate. Cheyenne went down in the first with a groundout and two fly outs. Optimism bubbled within as I slipped my arm into a jacket and found a spot on the bench.

The Giants scored two runs in the top of the second. Cheyenne managed a leadoff single but nothing else in the bottom of the frame. In the home half of the third inning, their first hitter reached base after our shortstop, former major leaguer Eduardo Salazar, misplayed a one-hopper. I kept the following batters off balance by working both sides of the plate, changing speeds, and mixing my three main pitches. The inning ended when a Mule swung through a changeup for strike three. The baseball on this night was my servant, obeying my every command as it flew from my fingers. At times like this I was glad to be a pitcher so I didn't have to try to hit that little white sphere dipping and darting about.

In the bottom of the fourth, the Cheyenne boys decided to show me that hitting a baseball really wasn't all that hard. The first guy ripped a slider down the left field line for a double. The next guy hammered a fastball over my head for a single. The third Mule laced a changeup off the wall in right center for a double. I then got too careful and walked a guy. We finally got an out when the next batter popped a high fly to center. But then another hit followed, and then another. Angley stopped by the mound for a chat. I told him I wanted to clean up my mess, so he left me in. The next batter lined out to third. The guy after him hit a deep fly to right that Randal caught with his back to the wall. When the carnage ended, Cheyenne led 4-2.

Though the Mules put some good swings on my pitches in the fifth, their drives ended up in my teammates' gloves. Lincoln then narrowed the deficit to 4-3 in the top of the sixth. In the bottom of the frame, I struck out the first batter. But then a wooden barrage commenced. Fastball—crack! Slider—crack! Another fastball—CRACK!!! Angley was halfway to the mound when that last hit finally landed near a large oil drum about fifty feet beyond the left field wall. "Alright kid," he said, patting my shoulder. "Get 'em next time."

My head down, I trudged off the field as the Cheyenne fans mocked my performance with a chorus of sardonic cheers. Seven runs, all earned, in five and one-third innings. I passed through the silent dugout and headed for the locker room, where Jerry waited to wrap an arm that was already ice cold.

After the game, Weed, Fender, Randal, Kenny, Sam, and I visited a cowboy bar not far from our motel. We emptied pitcher after pitcher of cheap beer. In honor of my stellar night on the mound, the boys ordered a shot of vodka for me. I downed it in one gulp. We talked about getting a few more shots, but our meager meal money allotment precluded additional orders of the hard stuff. My head nonetheless numbed fuzzy after I helped finish off another pitcher. Fender returned to the table; I didn't realize he had left. He leaned over my shoulder, his breath thick with alcohol.

"Hey Boo … ya need somethin' good to happen tonight. Well yer buddy Fender took care of ya. Gotcha a date." He gestured to the bar. "Check her out." Through the smoky haze, I saw curly blond hair and an interested face. The accompanying wardrobe featured a low cut red blouse, tight denim shorts, and brown cowboy boots. A smile invited me over before meeting the lip of a beer glass.

"I appreciate that, Fender. But I'll pass."

"The hell you will. You know how hard I had to work to land you that little filly? Told her ya just got called up to the majors and yer gonna be makin' two million a year." He belched. "Oh yeah, yer name is Sam Judge."

"Better take advantage of this, Boo," Weed added. "It's not easy finding girls dumb enough to mistake you for a good pitcher."

"Yeah," Kenny said. "Cheyenne scored plenty off you tonight. You need to score one off Cheyenne."

After more prodding from the crew, I sauntered over to the bar. Her body was nice enough, but her face bore a thick coat of paint that looked better from a distance. It took only a few generic lines to confirm that she was willing to hook up with a soon-to-be star big leaguer. But even through my inebriation, all I saw was a woman who wasn't Eileen.

"You want to get out of here?" she asked.

"I wish I could. Curfew is in fifteen minutes."

"That ain't stopping your friend and my friend." She gestured at Fender escorting a thin brunette toward the exit. He had apparently forgotten about the lecture Angley delivered to us a few days ago.

"Well he doesn't have a big league contract waiting for him. I could lose *mucho dinero* if I get busted now."

Her expression dropped as she turned and gulped a swig of beer. "So you're just going to leave me here at this bar all alone?"

Opportunity knocked. "I wouldn't do that. See, I've got a buddy who would love to meet you." I pointed to our table. "See the big guy with the long hair?"

She glanced over there. "Yeah." Her cherry red lips parted into a smile.

"His name is Sam. And he knows how to treat a lady. Plus, he's almost as good a pitcher as me." This attempted treachery made my skin crawl.

"Sam, huh? What's his last name?"

"Judge."

"Sam Judge." She shook her head and scowled. "Your friend told me that was *your* name. Just what kind of game you guys playin' with me?"

Crap! "Uh … well …"

Before I could push out an explanation, a gush of beer doused my face. Profane insults assaulted my ears as I rubbed the stinging liquid from my eyes. When I could see again, she was gone. I slunk back to the table, drenched in alcohol and shame.

Kenny smirked at me. "Dude. A circus freak could've scored with that chick. What gives?"

"She wasn't my type."

"She's everybody's type," Weed said. "Remind me not to take you along next time we go hunting for tail."

Back at the motel, I crawled into bed and buried my head in a pillow. Sam picked up the phone and dialed. I knew who would be answering on the other end.

"Hey, girlie." My stomach considered ejecting all that I'd ingested earlier in the evening. "Yeah, good news," he said. "Jerry looked at it tonight. It's okay. I'm clear to pitch tomorrow … No, there's no pain … I know. I'm never going to do anything that stupid again."

23

I was so caught up in my own misery, I'd forgotten about Sam's hand. The news brought mixed feelings.

"We lost, eight to four," Sam said. I cringed upon hearing him mention the game. "Yeah, a rough start for our boy. But I'll get 'em back tomorrow. Those Cheyenne punks are going to pay for what they did to Brian." He paused to listen. "Hey Brian, Eileen says to forget about tonight. You're gonna rock next time."

"Thanks," I muttered, wishing I could completely erase this evening from my memory.

True to his word, Sam tore through the Cheyenne lineup with a vengeance. He tossed a three-hit shutout with thirteen strikeouts. Lincoln won again the following night to take two of three from the Mules. The players were upbeat as they piled onto the bus for the trip back to Lincoln. I was the exception. Not in the mood for seven hours of Kenny, I claimed a seat next to Vince, the big country boy who played first base.

"Hey Brian," he said, a bright grin extending from one round cheek to the other.

"Somebody other than Sam actually remembers my real name," I grumbled. "Might as well call me, Boo. Everybody else does."

His look fell serious. "What do you prefer?"

"Boo's fine … doesn't really matter though."

"Why do you say that?"

I flipped the baseball in my hand into a changeup grip. "The team is six and four. I've made two starts. Lost 'em both. So I'm single-handedly responsible for half of our defeats this season."

He ran his fingers over the white-blond fuzz atop his head. "Don't think like that, Brian. You were pitching good last time out. Just had a couple bad innings, that's all. Could've happened to anybody."

"I'm a mediocre backend starter for an indie team. Ballplayers don't get much more expendable than me. Last year I got cut in June, just four weeks into the season. This year I might not even last that long." My brother's admonishments about wasting my time chasing a silly pipedream echoed through my head.

"Naw. We're just getting started. You'll get plenty more chances to show the team what you can do."

24

I shook my head. "One more crappy start from me, the Giants are going to bring in someone else just like that." I snapped my fingers. "A fireballer right out of high school who might catch a scout's eye. The Giants make good money selling our contracts to major league teams at the end of the season. They can't waste time on guys not getting the job done."

"You'll pull through this." He shifted his body to face me. "Tell ya what. Starting tomorrow, you and me will show up an hour before practice to do some work. You pitch to me and I'll tell ya what I see from the batter's box."

My eyes dropped to my knees. The team's best power hitter was offering to add an hour to his practice time each day to help me, the team's worst pitcher. "Thanks Vince. We'll see."

"I'm serious. All of us on this team are in the same boat. We've all been cut or ignored at some point. We Giants got to stick together."

"Yeah? That's cool of you to do this for me."

"No problem."

"So who would cut a guy who hits four-hundred-and-fifty-foot home runs?"

He glanced up at *The Highlander*, now playing on the bus's television screen. "Cubs. They drafted me in ninety-one after my sophomore year at Northeast Missouri State. Played rookie ball after that. Then A-ball. Made the AA team in Orlando in ninety-three. Then I tore up my knee the first road trip of the season. Didn't play again that year. Last winter, got a letter cutting me loose."

"Really? With your power, they didn't give you a chance to come back?"

"Nope." A pained smile cracked his face. "Scouts like speed and I don't exactly burn it up on the base paths, you know."

"They'll realize their mistake by the end of the season." I knocked an elbow into his ribs. "Guaranteed."

I watched the movie. He opened a book. A while later, he looked over at me. "Hey Brian, you a believer?"

I had my doubts, but I didn't want to dampen his enthusiasm about helping me. "Yeah, I'll get it turned around on the mound."

"Nah, I'm talkin' about God. Do you believe in Christ?"

I noticed that the book in his lap was a Bible. "Oh. Yeah, sure."

"Do you go to church?"

"No." For some reason, I felt bad about telling him that. "Used to as a kid. Confirmed Methodist. Haven't gone to church much since moving to Lincoln."

"I'm thinking about starting a team Bible study," he said, his blue eyes beaming. "We'd meet once a week or something. Would you be up for that?"

I wasn't overly thrilled at the idea, but after his offer to help me I didn't want to turn him down. "Sure, man. I'll check it out."

"Do you think the guys you hang out with might come?"

Do the words "never in a million years" mean anything to you? "I don't know, Vince. I guess you could ask."

He closed his Bible and leaned forward toward Kenny and Weed in the row in front of us. "Hey guys. I'm thinking about starting a Bible study. Interested?"

Though I couldn't see the expression on his face, I imagined a dozen smart-aleck comments fighting to escape from Kenny's mouth. "I'm going to say no, Vince," he said. My jaw dropped when nothing else followed. Kenny may have been engrossed in the movie or he may not have wanted to offend a guy six inches taller and seventy pounds heavier than him. Either way, that's all he said.

"How about you, Bruce?"

Weed stopped chomping the Doritos he'd been eating. "Actually Stenzel, I'm active in another faith. So I won't be able to join you either."

"Really?" Vince asked. "What faith is that?"

"I'm an Aamestologist." Weed's voice almost sounded sincere. "We worship the one true god, Willie Aames."

"Willie Aames?" Vince sat back and scrunched his large round face. "Buddy on *Charles in Charge*?"

Weed turned around to face us. "The Buddy character is just one of the many ways he tries to reach lost souls with the true gospel of Aames."

"Aamestology isn't a real religion," Vince said, as if trying to reassure himself.

"Oh, but it is." Weed's voice danced with enthusiasm. "Just like Christianity, we have apostles. But where you have twelve apostles, we only need eight. For as the exalted one has proclaimed, 'Eight is enough.'"

"Got a lot of people in this religion?" I asked.

"You bet. We have thousands of members. We're very active in community service. For example, we have the Adam Rich prison ministry. And then we've got the Dick Van Patten hair-loss counseling program. There's also—"

"Okay," I interrupted. "I think we get the point." I turned to Vince. "Looks like he's out." Weed rolled his irises into the back of his head and his face slowly disappeared below the seatback in front of us.

"Yeah, I guess so." Vince furrowed his brow.

"I'll join your study," Randal said from across the aisle. "Sounds cool."

"Great," Vince said, recovering from his confusing conversation with Weed. "That's great, Randal." He turned to me. "How about Sam? Think he'd be interested?"

I stifled a scoff. I wanted to spare Vince another rejection, yet thought it best he hear it directly from Sam's mouth. "Maybe. One way to find out."

Vince looked over the back of his seat. "Hey Sam … Sam."

My roommate awakened with a snort. "Huh?"

"I'm starting a Bible study. You want to join us?"

A long silence followed. I hoped that Sam would be polite. Finally a deep voice replied, "Sure, Vince."

Chapter 3

Ants swarmed inside my stomach as I removed my cap and brushed the sweat rivulets from my face. The crowd at Sherman Field murmured. The game was tied and there were Bandits from St. Joseph on all three bases. The guy on third had drilled a fastball over the heart of the plate into center. The runner on second had slapped a lazy slider into right. The guy on first had walked. My pitches were starting to disobey me. Like unruly children, they darted off to wherever they pleased. For six innings they had minded like little angels. Now in the seventh, they challenged my authority like rebellious teenagers.

I toed the rubber and watched as Sarge flashed through the signs. He wanted a changeup. Not a bad call with the bases loaded, two outs, and the dangerous Bobby Kalkwarf at the plate. In his last at-bat, he had roped a double into the left field corner. With the bases juiced, he'd again be ready to tear into one. The ants established new colonies in my liver and spleen. My eyes caught a glimpse of Grant Wright and Kevin Mendenhall sitting in the stands behind home plate. Both were prominent Lincoln businessmen and forty-something ex-wannabe ballplayers. More importantly, they were the Giants president and vice president. All through the game, I'd been able to block out their scrutinizing presence. Now, their stares fixed on me like a spotlight—hot and bright. Two days earlier, when the team returned to Lincoln on Memorial Day, they'd lowered the axe on Danny McQuinn for his drunk and disorderly arrest in Colorado Springs. I was 0-2 with the highest ERA on the staff. Though nobody said anything, it seemed certain that if I lost tonight I'd be the next to go. I could already hear my brother's "I told you so" speech.

I started the windup—my right leg drove off the rubber, my left leg planted, my hips rotated, and my arm whipped the ball toward the plate. The past two days, I'd worked with Vince before practice. He had noticed that I'd been telegraphing my changeup with a slower motion. Eliminating that fatal delivery flaw had made a huge difference. Through six and two-thirds innings, the Bandits had collected only six hits and two runs. But that meant nothing if I couldn't get one more out.

The burly Kalkwarf unloaded a mighty swing. A booming crack followed. My body flinched as the ball soared down the left field line, spawning the terrifying possibility of a grand slam. Happily, the drive veered left, missing the foul pole and eventually striking a vehicle about 500 feet away in the parking lot. The fans enjoyed the echoing sound of denting metal.

Sarge tossed a new ball to me. I looked for the sign. He wanted a fastball, up and out of the strike zone. He figured Kalkwarf would be anxious to take another rip against a tiring pitcher. Behind me, my fielders readied themselves for action. Some chattered. Kenny's words from second rang the loudest. "Come on, Boo, no hitter here, shoot to him, now …"

My four-seamer sailed straight and true toward Sarge's raised glove. The ball crossed the plate at eye level. The batter hacked away, fouling it straight back to the screen.

While waiting for another baseball, I again glimpsed the stands. My nerves flared. But it wasn't Wright and Mendenhall—the men who controlled my baseball future—who caused the reaction. It was *her*. I'd first noticed Eileen sitting behind the home dugout when I walked off the field after the first inning. A purple scrunchy held her blond hair back in a ponytail. A tight pink T-shirt did little to conceal her lovely curves. Whenever I glanced up at her after pitching an inning, she flashed a bright smile at me. Now she wore an anxious look. It's almost as if she were trying to say …

FOCUS, YOU MORON!!

The baseball section of my brain jerked my attention back to the matter at hand. Namely, a bull of a hitter capable of launching the ball into the next county and driving the final nail into the coffin of my pitching career. Sarge flashed the signs. He wanted a slider, low and away, beyond the batter's reach. A typical call for an 0-2 pitch. I just had to make sure I didn't bounce it to the backstop. The pitch

29

sailed about a foot outside. Kalkwarf didn't flinch. Sarge then called for a fastball up and in. I gave it to him. Ball two.

The ants started chewing my organs. With the score tied and the bases loaded, I couldn't walk this guy. Sarge jogged to the mound. Since he didn't speak much English and I didn't speak much Spanish, our conversations were usually short. This was no exception. "Slider," he said in a Puerto Rican accent. "Low, outside, pretty." He wanted the same pitch I'd thrown at 0-2, but closer to the plate so the batter might swing at it.

As my fingers formed a slider grip on the ball inside my glove, thunder rumbled through the ballpark. "FEE FI FO FUM!" Thump. Thump. Thump. Thump. The pounding of two thousand feet sent lightning shooting up my spine. From a full windup, I slung the ball toward the outside edge of the plate. It looked good, like it might catch the corner for a strike. Kalkwarf stepped and swung, his heavy wooden club rushing toward its target. But the white orb dipped and curved outside, as if it had eyes and could steer away from impending danger.

The bat swished by, hitting nothing but oxygen molecules. The ball nestled safely in Sarge's mitt. Kalkwarf staggered trying to keep his balance. The umpire punched the air. The crowd roared. The ants disintegrated.

High fives greeted me from all directions as I neared the dugout. I sat next to Sam at the end of the bench and exhaled. "Good," he said, chewing sunflower seeds. "I didn't want to have to break in a new roommate."

Offering no response, I just breathed and looked out at the field. Angley came down and shook my hand. "Helluva job, Carter. That was some real pitching tonight. Bullpen will take it from here." A proud grin accompanied his nod.

Minutes later the crowd roared again as Lincoln scored a run to take a 3-2 lead. Great news, to be sure. But as I depressurized, the events on the field seemed to be happening in a far off place.

Weed came in to pitch the eighth. He had a smooth easy motion that glided into a side-armed delivery. When he was on, his bobbing junkballs gave batters fits. The first Bandit grounded out to short. The next guy walked. Then a fly out and a single put two on with two out. The crowd tensed, but Weed looked as relaxed as ever. A sharp groundout to second ended the inning.

After the Giants went down in order in the bottom of the eighth, Fender ambled toward the mound to pitch the ninth. Though not all that tall, he was sinewy and, appropriately enough, somewhat bowlegged. Fender's fastball could hit 90 mph with late movement. Complementing his heat with an effective changeup, he beat out Weed for the closer position during spring training. That didn't prevent the two relievers from becoming best friends by the start of the season.

Fender tended to get wild on occasion. Tonight, he wasn't. Two strikeouts and a tap back to the mound ended the game. My teammates and I congregated on the field for handshakes and high fives. "Hey, you got your first win," Randal said, knocking the bill of my cap down against my face.

"We got us a new ace," Kenny quipped while cutting a jig on the mound.

I approached Weed and Fender, who were scanning the stands for some young ladies they had spotted during the game. "Thanks for saving it for me, guys. I needed the W."

"That's our job, dude," Weed replied, his straw hair hanging lank below his cap.

"Yeah, Boo," Fender said with a toothy smirk, "we had no choice. You getting a lead ain't gonna happen much. We had to make sure ya got at least one win this year."

After clearing out of the dugout, we met a crowd of autograph-seeking children on the cement walkway under the stands. That was normal. The unusual part was that most of them were waiting for me. "Have fun," Sam said, continuing on toward the clubhouse.

As I repeatedly scribbled my name, Wright and Mendenhall passed by. "Congratulations Brian," the team vice president said. "Well done tonight." Both men wore restrained smiles that suggested I was still one bad start away from a pink slip.

On my way to the shower, several teammates snapped me with their towels. A reward for my first win as a Giant. After dressing, I walked with Sam to the parking lot. Eileen leaned against the side of my car creating a vision of what I wanted my life to be. She sprang forward as we neared. I could feel her arms pulling me in, her body pressing into mine. But of course her arms wrapped around Sam. Always around Sam.

31

The next day the St. Joseph Bandits departed and the Pierre Cavaliers came to town. Before the game, I helped Randal with his stretches. "Working with Vince this week has helped, huh," he said, lying on his back in the outfield grass. "Is that an everyday thing?"

"I dunno. We came out here early Tuesday and Wednesday. Skipped today since I just pitched last night." I lifted one of his legs and pushed it back over his head.

"That's cool of him to help you out." He grimaced as his knee neared his face. "He's all right, you know."

"Yeah ... you really interested in that Bible study?"

"Sure. You mean you're not?" His bushy eyebrows rose until they disappeared under the wave of chestnut hair that covered his forehead.

"I could take it or leave it." I looked around to see who was nearby. The only players within twenty feet were Sarge, Eduardo, and Manny Gomez, a reserve infielder. Discussing something in Spanish, they paid little attention to us.

"Gotta get right with the Lord, my friend," Randal said. "And with your so-called fastball topping out at eighty-three, you need all the help you can get."

"Funny."

"Vince is thinking Monday morning for our first study. Says he's got six or seven guys interested. Gonna be there?"

"Yeah, I'll be there." I felt like I owed Vince.

"Wish it could've been today. Sam could use some time in the Good Book before tonight."

"Why do you say that?" I lowered Randal's long leg to the ground and hoisted up the other one. "He doesn't get nervous before starts."

"But he's facing the Cavaliers tonight. That means Harvey Jorgenson."

"Who's that?"

He squinted at me. His long thin face sometimes reminded me of a greyhound. "You don't know? Geez, Boo, you're his roommate."

"I wasn't here last year, Grandpa." The guys sometimes called Randal that because he was twenty-eight and in his third year with the Giants. Our 35-year-old shortstop Eduardo was the only player on the team older than Randal.

"Thought you might have heard. Harvey was Sam's teammate at Iowa State and with the Giants last season. Harv played shortstop for us." He motioned for me to lower his leg. "They were roommates. Sam never mentioned him?"

"No."

He sat up. "Guess I'll start from the beginning then. See, Sam had this girl in college. They're all serious, you know. She moves out to Lincoln last summer when he does. Joined at the hip, those two."

My brain replayed his last statement to make sure I understood correctly. "Wait a minute. Sam had a girlfriend last season, before Eileen?"

"Yep." Randal stood. "He loved that gal. Her name was Felicity."

"And . . ."

"And Felicity and Harvey started fooling around. Sam had no idea. Blinded by love. Even sold his car to get her a big rock."

"Did you know about Harvey and this girl?"

"Some of us suspected something, but nobody dared say anything. Know what I mean?"

I nodded. We both looked over at the bullpen, where Sam was getting ready to start his warm-up tosses with backup catcher Charlie Christianson.

"Sam was gonna propose at the end of the season. After the final game he had to sign a bunch of autographs, so he was the last one out of the shower. He finally gets to his locker and there's an envelope there from Harvey. The note says that he and Felicity are in love and are going to get married."

"I bet Sam flipped out."

"That's putting it mildly. I'm standing by the concession stand when he grabs the keys out of my hand and peels out in my pickup. Races around Lincoln looking for Harvey. Of course, he and Felicity had already skipped town. It's a good thing too. If Sam had gotten his hands on Harv, that boy would be dead and our star pitcher would be in prison."

"Ouch."

"Sam ends up back here later that night. Tears apart the clubhouse and then flushes the engagement ring down one of the toilets." Randal shook his head. "That thing cost about three grand."

"Wow." *And now Sam's got another roommate who wants to steal his girlfriend.* My eyes dropped to the ground.

"Giants traded Harvey in the off-season. So tonight will be the first time Sam sees his old buddy since all that went down."

"Oh, brother," I sighed. "You're right. We should've had a Bible study this morning. I assume the skipper knows the situation."

"Oh, yeah." Randal gestured to the bullpen. As if on cue, Angley tottered over to Sam. The old man put a hand on his pitcher's shoulder. It reminded me of a father imparting wisdom upon a son. Sam's body stiffened as he looked away. After a minute or so, he nodded and seemed to relax somewhat.

Before the game it looked like a typical night at the ballpark. Bat boys lugged equipment to the dugout and put our helmets and bats in place. Managers met with umpires at home plate. Players and fans stood for the national anthem. Sam started pitching. The first batter grounded out. The second guy struck out. And then Harvey Jorgenson stepped to the plate. I wasn't sure how many people knew their backstory, but it must have been quite a few because the stands and both benches fell unusually quiet. Harvey positioned his tall, lean athletic body into a closed batting stance. I held my breath as Sam started his windup. A fastball blazed in for a strike. A second fastball brought the same result. The big guy then unleashed a curveball that sent Harvey bailing out of the box before breaking across the plate for strike three. Inning over.

Sam didn't say a word in the dugout. He just sat at the end of the bench and glared at the Pierre shortstop. He issued a walk in the second, but nothing else as the Cavaliers fell before him. Lincoln took a 1-0 lead in the third. With Sam's no-hitter still intact, Harvey came up in the fourth inning. He bunted the first pitch down the third base line. Matt Thompson charged in and barehanded the ball, but Harvey just beat his throw to first. Pierre had its first hit of the game. Visibly agitated, Sam lost his focus. A walk and a single brought Harvey home to tie the game at one. Another hit put the Cavaliers ahead.

Pierre still led 2-1 when Harvey batted in the sixth. Sam hesitated a little longer than usual after getting the sign. He then fired a cannon ball that slammed into Harvey's back just above the numbers. A loud thwack rang through the ballpark as the batter collapsed in a cloud of dirt. Sam approached the plate. "Get up," he barked. Cavaliers poured onto the field. Three of them sprinted toward Sam, but pulled up when he dropped his glove and faced them with raised fists. The entire rosters of both teams crowded onto the infield. Some minor shoving and major shouting ensued, though nobody threw any punches. Sam tried to get at Harvey, but Vince, Matt, and Tony directed him away from the fray.

After the dust had settled, the home plate umpire ejected Sam. A pinch runner replaced Harvey, who sat on the Pierre bench icing his back. Reed Perry, a big Mormon lefty, came in to pitch for the Giants. He held down the Cavs, allowing Lincoln to tie it in the seventh and take the lead in the eighth. Fender pitched a scoreless ninth to pick up his fourth save of the season.

Sam, Weed, Fender, Randal, Kenny, and I gathered at JK's following the game. On mounted television screens, *Baseball Tonight* commentators discussed the possibility of a strike ending the major league season. "That'll never happen," Randal said. "With all the money they're making, they'd have to be complete idiots to stop playing." Fender and Weed offered contrary opinions. As the discussion picked up, a group of Pierre players swaggered through the front doors and claimed a couple of tables not far from ours. I counted nine Cavaliers. Harvey was not one of them.

The loud comments commenced almost immediately. The largest Cavalier, a bald guy with tattoos on both beefy arms, bellowed, "What kind of man lets his hair grow long like a chick? Ought to have some rules in this league."

"Yeah, but this is Lincoln," another guy said. "All they got here are steers and queers. Guess which one they had pitching tonight." His friends laughed.

Sitting with his back to their tables, Sam finished his beer, stood, and turned around. The room quieted. "You got a problem with me?" he asked.

"Yeah we do," the bald man answered, rising to his feet. "Your beanball knocked our shortstop out of the game. We got a *big* problem with that."

"It slipped."

"The hell it did. You threw at his back on purpose."

"No, it slipped. I was aiming for his head."

The other Cavaliers shot to their feet, their chairs clattering backwards across the floor. The guys at our table followed suit. "You think you're funny, Crystal Gayle?" The bald man stepped toward Sam. They were about the same height.

"No." Sam shook his head. "That wasn't funny. But *this* is." He smashed his fist into the bald man's jaw. Two other Cavaliers leaped on Sam. The rest of them charged at us. My brain didn't completely believe that what was happening was actually happening. It got caught up in a hurry when a guy rushed at me like a linebacker. I crouched and wrapped my arms around his waist as his momentum carried us down under a table. Pitchers and glasses tipped over, showering us in beer. Pressing the heel of my palm into his neck, I pushed him away and scrambled to my feet. Bodies moved through the room in a dance of frenzied chaos. Fender broke a bottle over someone's head. A big guy picked up Kenny and was sliding him down the bar like a shuffleboard disk. I started heading in that direction when my feet slipped out from under me. My hands barely had enough time to prevent my face from slamming into the wood floor. The man who had tripped me pounced on my back, his weight flattening my lungs. As I struggled to breathe, something clicked in my ear and a blade glinted in the corner of my eye.

"I'm gonna carve my initials in your face," he hissed. His rank breath punished my nostrils. The knife inched closer to my cheek. My heart thudded and a cold tingly sensation ran down all four limbs.

An instant later the weight lifted from my back. Rolling over, I saw my wide-eyed adversary rising above me as if being sucked up by a vacuum in the ceiling. Instead it was Sam who had hoisted the man above his head into a military press. Growling like a beast, my roommate tossed the Cavalier over the bar; a shattering of glasses and bottles accompanied the impact.

Sam moved on to another adversary, a quick interaction that similarly ended with a crash. Using a chair to pull myself up, I surveyed the establishment. It looked like a bomb had gone off, leaving behind shards of glass, overturned tables and chairs, and pools of blood and beer. Eight Cavaliers lay strewn about like broken action figures. One more groaned from behind the bar. Sam stood in the middle of the room looking for more targets to annihilate. But there were none. The enemy had been vanquished. Weed and Randal pulled Kenny off the bar. Fender rubbed his left arm.

Sam knelt on one knee over the bald guy, who lay flat on his back with red ooze streaming from his nose. "You tell Harvey his old roommate says hello, alright?" Sam then headed for the front door, the five of us trailing behind. Wary patrons peeked out from under tables and other makeshift barricades as we exited the building.

Friday night the Giants beat the beat-up Cavaliers 11 to 5. Saturday afternoon we won again, 5-2. That evening Randal and Cathy invited us over to their house for grilled burgers. Since Sam rode with Eileen, who had remained in town for summer classes at the university, I drove alone to the Van Dyke residence in Lincoln's Witherbee neighborhood. My stomach sank when I reached the back patio. Everyone had showed up with a date. I knew Eileen and Cathy would be there, but I didn't expect to see the tall blond twins with Weed and Fender, or the short Asian girl with Kenny. It took about five seconds for someone to notice that I was the only one who had arrived alone.

"Now, Boo, you didn't have to come stag," Kenny said. "You could've brought that special guy of yours. The Army may have a 'don't ask, don't tell' policy, but we Giants accept all lifestyle choices. It's time to proudly don that pink feather boa and come out of the closet, my friend."

My reply took the form of a middle finger.

Eileen came over and slid her arm around the small of my back, pulling me into a side hug. "I'll be your date, Boo. It's not like Sam will talk to me tonight." My knees wobbled at her touch and the scent of her perfume. I felt like screaming, "*You're killing me here, woman.*"

"There's nothing more to say," Sam groused from a lawn chair.

"Ooh, what's Sam keeping from you?" Weed asked.

"Like you don't know," she said, returning to her boyfriend's lap. My eyes lingered on her tight-jeaned derriere as she walked away. "I go out of town to visit my folks for a couple days and the first thing you boys do is get into trouble. So who's going to tell me what actually happened after the game Thursday night?"

"Not much to tell," Fender said. "About a dozen of them Pierre boys came into JK's looking for trouble. And we gave it to 'em. Stomped 'em but good." He smacked his fist into his hand.

"Really?" Eileen asked skeptically.

"Well, I think there were nine of them," Randal said, shrouded in a plume of steam rising from the charcoal grill.

"And Sam did most of the stomping," Weed added.

"Oh come on," Kenny said. "You nailed that black guy's fist with your face."

"Shut up, twerp," Weed shot back. "About all you did was let a dude use you as a dishrag to wipe off the bar."

"I was just keeping him busy until the big guy came over." Kenny gestured at Sam.

"Sam did bust some heads that night," Randal said, closing the round black grill lid. "That boyfriend of yours is a one-man wrecking crew."

Eileen shook her head. "Fighting like school kids."

"Boys will be boys," Cathy said. She had just exited the back door of the house, a small two-bedroom ranch that needed a new coat of paint. Her and Randal's three-year-old daughter Haleigh and their dog Freddy bounced past her into the yard.

"So how much trouble are you guys in?" Eileen asked. "I bet the skipper blew his stack."

"He doesn't know," Sam replied.

"What?"

"Nobody called the police," Kenny said. "Nobody told the skip."

"What about the other guys? Didn't they press charges?"

"There was nine of them against six of us," Fender said. "And they got their tails kicked. Plus one of 'em pulled a switchblade. They ain't tellin' nobody nothin' about what went down."

"What about JK? Didn't his place get busted up?"

"Yeah. About four thousand dollars' worth," Kenny said. "He was amazingly cool about it though. No cops. No reporters. No coaches. But we have to cover the damages. He put the six of us on a payment plan. We'll be donating ten percent of our checks to him the rest of this season."

"And no more free beer at his place," Weed said. "That's what hurts the most."

"At least you all got a check at the end of May," Eileen said. "This big dummy donated his entire first month's salary to the Motel 6 in Colorado Springs." She pecked Sam's cheek.

"Yeah, they got all twelve cents," he said. "And I was gettin' so damn rich pitching here in Lincoln."

"We're all gettin' rich brother," Kenny said. The guys then toasted their crappy minor league salaries. Needing a break from the image of Eileen in Sam's lap, I walked over to Haleigh, who was playing catch with Freddy.

"Is he a good fielder?" I asked.

Her ash brown pigtails bounced as she spun her head to look up at me. She wore a purple Barney T-shirt that reached her knees. Dirt smudged her bare feet.

"Yes … watch." She threw a red rubber ball to the dog, which caught it in its mouth on one bounce. "Give it back, Fuzzy," Haleigh said.

"That's what she calls him," said Cathy, who'd joined us in the yard. Her hair, the same color as her daughter's, hung down her back in a long ponytail. "She didn't like saying Freddy when she was a baby. So now our dog has two names, depending on who's calling him."

"I see." Freddy bounded around the girl before dropping the ball and batting it with his nose across the ground to her. "Wow," I said. "He knows tricks?"

"Oh yeah, lots of them. He's a smart dog."

I watched the canine catch another of Haleigh's tosses. The dog's face and floppy ears were black, as were the many spots that mottled the light gray fur on his body. "What's his breed?" I asked.

"Oh who knows," Cathy said with a laugh. "Looks to me like he's part blue tick hound, part lab, part whatever. Got him from the pound a couple years ago." She turned to Randal on the patio. "Why don't you show your friends the new trick you taught Freddy?"

Randal wiped his hands on his apron and marched out to the center of the yard. "You stand over here, Haleigh. Remember, toss the ball really high." He then snapped his fingers at Freddy and pointed to a spot behind him near the fence. The dog trotted over there as Randal crouched like a football lineman. He raised his left arm. "Okay sweetie, now."

When he dropped his arm, Haleigh tossed the ball underhanded straight above his head. Freddy sprang forward, bounded onto Randal's back and leaped high into the air where his jaws snatched the ball. The dog landed in the grass and paraded around with his prize, his thin tail waving back and forth.

Everybody oohed and clapped. "That mutt fields better than Kenny," Fender exclaimed.

"Shut up, redneck," Kenny said. "At least I'm not named after the place where I was conceived."

A while later the burgers were ready. Freddy visited each of the guests as we ate. Though Randal told him not to beg, he sat back on his haunches with his front paws folded in front of his chest until somebody threw him a morsel. After supper, Haleigh brought out her favorite picture books. Eileen sat on the back stoop reading to her while the boys passed the night talking about past victories and future possibilities.

The next morning I stood on Professor Hornsby's front porch watching the people pass by on their way to church. I glanced up through the trees to check the sky. Grey and white clouds covered the expanse above.

"Don't worry," a voice said. "I just checked the radio. No rain today." The professor stood behind his screen door, his eyes peering at me from above the spectacles resting on his nose.

"That's good," I replied, though disappointed at the news.

"Ready to eat?"

"Yeah, you bet."

Sam and I sat at the round oak table in the kitchen. Hornsby scraped steaming food from a skillet onto our plates. "Breakfast burritos," he announced. "Learned to make them some years ago when my wife and I vacationed in New Mexico."

"Looks great," I said. "They're huge. Thanks for making breakfast for us today."

"Happy to," Hornsby said, joining us at the table. "You boys have won four in a row now. That'll be five after Brian completes the sweep against Pierre today. But if the Giants start losing, look out. Then you two just get bread and water." A grin stretched across his wide face.

"Guess you'd better win today," Sam said to me. "I'd hate to miss out on grub like this."

I nodded while swallowing a sip of orange juice. The three of us dug into our food. A stack of toast and a bowl of strawberries complimented the main course. About halfway through my burrito, I broke the silence. "Professor, I was checking out the books in your study. Did you write something about baseball?"

"Indeed I did." Toast crumbs dropped from his white beard to roll down his ample belly like a miniature avalanche. "Two baseball books so far. One of them describes the game's transformation in the 1920s. The second one discusses baseball's impact during the Great Depression. This fall, I'll finish a new book about baseball during World War II."

"I didn't know college professors could write about sports," Sam said. "Did you teach about baseball in your classes?"

"I taught a sports history class for ten years before I retired."

"Cool," I said. "Did you major in that when you were in college?"

"Oh, no." He chuckled. "I studied American social history. Wrote my dissertation on civility and manners in the Victorian Era. That later became my first book."

Sam and I looked at each other. "Civility and manners," I said. "There are a few guys on our team who should read that one."

"I'm not sure those guys can read," Sam said. "Maybe they could look at the pictures." We chuckled.

"So how did you go from manners to baseball?" I asked the professor.

"Oh, I grew up with baseball. Played Legion Ball as a teenager, then spent a year in the minors after high school. Third base. Hit .303 that season."

"Wow. Then what happened?"

He touched his mouth with a napkin. "Pearl Harbor happened. World War II. Went to North Africa and Italy. When I came back two years later with shrapnel in my leg, I figured there was no point trying to play again. Went to college on the GI Bill. And then I was back to just being a fan of baseball."

"Who was your team?" I asked.

"Red Sox. An unfortunate byproduct of growing up in New Hampshire. Listened to them on the radio every day in the summer.

41

In September, I ran home from school to catch the end of the games."

"Was that when Ted Williams played?"

"Oh yes. Williams, Doerr, Pesky, Foxx. And after the war, the Sox had a guy named Don Angley pitching for them."

"No way," Sam exclaimed through a full mouth. "Skip pitched in the majors?"

"Indeed he did. He was with Boston for three seasons."

"We'll have to give him crap about only lasting three years," I said, grinning at Sam.

Hornsby's expression dropped. He looked down at his plate and sighed. "Maybe it would be best not to do that. Don had some tough breaks as a pitcher. He doesn't talk too much about those days anymore."

My face heated with embarrassment as we ate in silence. The professor then asked about our team's promotional appearance at Gateway Mall that afternoon. Six Giants had to show up and sign autographs for two hours. Sam and I were two of the lucky ones this time.

After lunch, I returned to Hornsby's study and sat in a padded armchair flipping through his baseball books. Finely crafted oak and maple furniture filled the room. On the wall above a massive rolltop desk hung several framed pictures. I walked over for a closer look. One was a portrait of Hornsby and his family. His three children looked to be in their late teens or early twenties at the time. Their clothes indicated that the photo was likely taken in the 1970s. My eyes next moved to a picture of a baseball team. It was the 1949 Boston Red Sox. I recognized only two faces, Ted Williams and a guy in the front row who resembled the skipper. My brain struggled to process the reality that our bald and portly manager was once a young man, an athlete even.

What happened, Skip? What happened to end your career?

A grandfather clock across the room chimed. It was about time for Sam and me to take off for the mall. My thoughts drifted to the game a few hours away. *How is it going to go this time? Is tonight my last start as a professional ballplayer?* I glanced at young Angley again. *Then what will I do?*

Chapter 4

"Alright guys, this is a good stopping point." Vince closed his Bible and scanned the other five men in the Giants clubhouse. Clockwise from Vince were Sam, Randal, me, Bobby Evans and Brad McGill. Freddy lay on the floor at Randal's feet. "I was thinkin' we'd close with prayer requests," Vince said. "Anybody got anything?" I examined my shoes. Nobody said a word.

"Or praises," Vince added. "This is a time when we can share stuff that God is doing our lives. Things we're thankful for."

The ensuing quiet kept my eyes fixed on my shoelaces. Randal finally spoke up. "Hey, I'm thankful that Boo here is going to be around a while longer." He backhanded my arm as the other guys chuckled.

"Amen," Vince said, grinning at me. "You pitched another great game last night."

"But we lost," I said.

"*You* were great though. Seven strong innings. Three runs, only two of 'em earned. You gave us a chance to win." His smile widened.

"Well, you've really helped me get things turned around. Thanks."

"Happy to do it," Vince said. "We're gonna keep it up too. Brian Carter started the season with the Giants and he's gonna finish the season with the Giants."

"Yeah. Thanks, man." My words came out as a mumble.

"Anybody else?"

"Alright, I got something," Sam said. A grimace then materialized on his face, as if he regretted speaking.

Vince nodded at him.

43

"You all know about that fight I got into last week. That was just stupid. So was hitting that motel wall . . ." He glanced at the lockers. "With all the work Skip did with me in the off-season, I'm feelin' real good now on the mound. Like I got a real shot at the majors." He looked at Vince. "Would you pray that I don't do anything dumb like that again? That I keep myself outta trouble."

"Sure, Sam," Vince said. "We'll pray for you. We're all brothers here, you know." He beamed at us. "We back each other up on and off the field."

The image of Sam saving my hide at JK's last week popped into my head. Thoughts of Eileen followed. *Gotta let her go. I can't keep plotting to break them up anymore. From now on this season, I'm going to focus on baseball.*

"All right, guys," Vince said. "I'll close in prayer." As he prayed aloud, I uttered a silent supplication of my own, asking for the strength to get over Eileen.

Seconds after Vince's amen, Weed clattered into the clubhouse. "Look at this," he said. "It's the God Squad."

"You're welcome to join us," Vince offered. "Anytime."

"Nah. You know I got my own beliefs." Weed pointed inside his locker to a poster of Willie Aames holding a surfboard.

"Your homosexual crush on Tommy Bradford doesn't count," Randal said.

"Blasphemer," Weed exclaimed, jabbing his finger at Randal. "My faith is just as important to me as yours is to you. Do we Aamestologists not hold Sunday morning services? Do we not have study groups, just like yours?"

"Uh no," Randal said. "I don't think you do."

"Well, you're wrong. The people of my faith often get together to discuss deep theological issues. Just last week, we tackled the question of 'If Willie Aames is the one true god, then why does he allow Charles to be in charge?'"

"You've smoked one joint too many," Sam said, shoving his shoulder as he passed by.

"Maybe you should study how to quit blowing ballgames," Brad said. "Think Willie could help you figure that one out."

Weed glowered at our designated hitter before firing back a profane reply. He then added, "How about if you learn how to use a glove someday, lardass?"

Brad winked as he exited the clubhouse. The normally laid-back Weed shot a few more expletives at the closing door. His recent mound woes had left him with a short wick. The previous night he came in to pitch the eighth inning of a game I'd left tied at three. By the time he trudged off the mound, the Cavaliers led 6-3, which ended up being the final score.

After dressing for practice, we headed out to the ball field. While most of us stretched and bantered, Randal took Freddy to home plate to teach him how to run the bases. The guys were impressed with how quickly the dog learned to run all the way around the diamond, touching each base along the way.

"Freddy ought to be our mascot," Bobby said.

"Anything would be better than that stilted monstrosity we got now," Brad added.

Angley and Tony showed up. "Get that mutt outta here before he defecates all over my field," the skipper commanded.

Randal led Freddy off the diamond and tied him to a fencepost near the clubhouse. The dog's subsequent whines carried all the way to the outfield. "Aw come on, Skip," Brad said. "The pooch just wants somebody to play with him."

But no amount of protesting from us, or Freddy, could convince Angley to change his mind. "We're here for *baseball*," he groused. "The sooner you numbskulls learn that, the better."

After practice, Sam and I ate at the Rock 'n Roll Runza downtown. As waitresses roller-skated to and fro in their poodle skirts, Sam and I discussed how much it would cost to buy a 50s-style jukebox like the one standing near our table. When we'd finished eating, I drove Sam to Buck Beltzer Field on the University of Nebraska campus, where he had volunteered to help teach at a youth baseball clinic. After that, he would be walking to JK's to rebuild the shelves behind the bar that were destroyed in the fight.

Since the Giants would be starting an eight-day road trip the next morning, I went home early that night. With Professor Hornsby out with former colleagues, I had the house to myself. I settled into a comfortable chair and flipped on the TV for some *Monday Night Raw*.

45

While Gorilla Monsoon and Randy Savage previewed Bret Hart's upcoming title defense against Diesel, I reflected on my day. It felt good to get the Eileen issue resolved. No more pining. No more longing. No more scheming. I accepted that she and Sam were a couple. Sam was my friend and Eileen was his girlfriend. End of story. Now I could devote my full concentration to pitching for the Giants.

The phone rang. It was, of course, Eileen.

"Hey Boo. What's up?"

"Uh, nothing." My heart thudded. "Just watching some wrest— um, some television. Flipping, you know."

"Cool. Sounds fun."

"Sam's not here. He's at the baseball clinic on campus."

"I know."

"You do?" The thudding in my chest accelerated.

"Yeah. I'm, uh …" She sighed. "I'm wondering if you would want to hang out. I'm bored."

I paused to keep from choking on the gasp of air rushing into my throat. "Hang out?"

"Yeah. Maybe we could meet at The Watering Hole. Get a beer or something."

There were several good reasons why I should have declined. But what I said was, "Okay. Sounds good."

Leaping into action, I shaved away my stubble, patted on some cologne, and donned the one stylish shirt I owned. My eyes paused on Sam's ISU cap lying on his bed. *What am I doing? This is insanely stupid.* I thought about calling Eileen and telling her I had to cancel. But images of her and me alone at her apartment flashed into view. Bursting out the front door, I nearly tripped down the steps of Hornsby's front porch.

Eileen was already at a table when I arrived at the bar. She wore no ponytail, allowing her hair to fall in beautiful blond waves down to her shoulders. My hands trembled as I slid into the chair across from her.

"Hey Boo. Thanks for coming out." Her smile enslaved me.

"Yeah, sure." My eyes roamed her face. Even the hoop earrings dangling from her lobes wielded power over me. I banished all thoughts of Sam from my head.

"I ordered a pitcher of Miller Light. Is that okay?"

"Yep." My brain danced at the reality that I was really alone here with her.

She looked around the room. "This place isn't as lively when college is out."

"That's true." Not wanting to lose her attention, I quickly threw out, "Hey, did you catch the season finale of *Frasier*? Didn't you say you liked that show?"

"Yeah, I do like that show. But I missed a few episodes once baseball season started. The last *Frasier* I saw was in April sometime when I was babysitting Haleigh." She snickered. "That kid is such a riot."

"Yeah. She and the dog could put on a show."

"*That* would be hilarious." After another snicker, her expression fell serious. "Hey Boo. You know Sam pretty well, right?"

"Um. Sort of." My hopes rose. *Is she going to ask me the best way to break up with him?*

"Well, you guys have been roommates for two months now."

"Yeah."

Her gaze lowered as she contemplated her next statement. I prepared to play it cool if she suddenly expressed her feelings for me. After an exhale, she locked her eyes with mine. "This isn't easy," she said. "It's just …"

Here it comes.

"I really like Sam, and … I think he could be the one. But I wonder if he feels the same way about me."

The flood of ice water took only a second to fully douse my body. But my subsequent shocked silence apparently lasted a bit longer. Impatience marked her face. "Well?"

"He likes you, Eileen."

"Yes, but does he *like* me?"

I wanted to crawl away. "Yes. Sam *likes* you."

Our pitcher of beer arrived. I felt like ordering a bottle of Vodka. Eileen filled our glasses. "See … I'm not sure where I stand with him. Sometimes he can be really sweet. Especially when we're alone. But other times he gets quiet and he'll treat me like I'm just one of the guys."

"You know Sam. He's a man of few words."

"Yeah, but … I don't know. I mean, Sam never told me anything about almost getting engaged last year. And we've been together for seven months now."

"He never told me either. That's not a great memory for him."

"But he got so upset when he saw Harvey. It's like he's still hung up on that other girl."

A swig of beer slid down my throat. "I don't think he's still hung up on Felicity. He never mentions her. Last week happened because a guy he thought was his friend betrayed him."

The tension remained on Eileen's face as she sipped her beer. "I shouldn't ask you this, but … when you guys are out on the road does Sam talk to the girls? You know, the ones who hang out after the games to hit on the ballplayers?"

I recalled with shame the vixen I tried to send his way in Cheyenne. "No, he doesn't do that."

"I shouldn't have asked. That was bad." She grabbed my arm. "Please don't tell Sam, okay?"

"Don't worry about it."

"It's just, I haven't let myself feel this way about a guy in a long time. I had a serious relationship in high school that ended badly. Someone I loved really hurt me. So I didn't date much my first two years of college. Then I met Sam. I think we really have something."

"Yeah. You guys make a great couple." I tried to sound convincing.

Her face brightened. "You think so?"

I nodded. "If you and Sam have kids someday, just imagine what great ballplayers they'll be."

She smiled. "Little superstar pitchers."

"And hitters. I've seen what you can do at the plate. What'd you hit this year, .367 with nine homers?" I had her softball stats memorized.

"Wow. You know my numbers better than I do. Wish we would've made it to the World Series."

"Next year. With your power, nobody will stop the Huskers."

Her expression dimmed. "At least I've got one thing over the skinny girls, huh?"

"Skinny girls?"

"Well, yeah. I'm not exactly a candidate for the *Sports Illustrated* swimsuit edition."

Under different circumstances I would've said, "*Eileen, you are a goddess. Your hotness cannot be captured with mere words. I never knew true beauty until I saw you.*" Instead what sputtered from my lips was, "Eileen, you're not that …"

"Fat?" Her mouth fell open in shock. "Gee thanks, Boo." She chugged the rest of her beer and glared at something across the room.

"No! I wasn't going to say that. You're not fat at all. You look great."

"Sure." She nodded, still looking away.

My face burned hot. I'm not sure if I'd ever experienced a worse feeling. I wanted to deliver a lengthy monologue celebrating the endless wonders of her gorgeousness. But her heart was with Sam, so any effort to dig myself out of this hole would have to include him. "Eileen, you have nothing to worry about. Sam is crazy about you. He doesn't want anybody else."

"Really?" She sounded like a little girl.

"Absolutely." I wasn't actually sure about the depth of Sam's feelings for Eileen, but I couldn't stand to see her upset at something I had said. So the exaggerations continued. "He talks about you all the time when we're on the road."

"Really?" A spark returned to her eyes. "What does he say? No, wait. Don't tell me. That's between you and him." She fiddled with a coaster.

Eileen and I talked for a while longer. About Sam, mostly. For me, the conversation was something like hearing fingernails scrape across a chalkboard.

Around 9:00, she decided to go. After we exited the bar, she said, "Hey, maybe it's best if we don't tell Sam about this. Us meeting. I mean, we didn't do anything wrong, it's just—"

"No problem," I said in total agreement.

"Thanks." She smiled. "Boo, you're a good friend."

Of course I am.

The next morning the Giants piled onto the bus for a four-hour trip to Topeka, Kansas. Sam sprawled across the two seats behind me, already asleep before we exited Lincoln city limits. He had gotten home late from working at JK's the previous night, long after I'd gone to bed. Based on our brief conversations in the morning, he didn't seem to have any idea about my secret meeting with his girlfriend.

The bus ride went relatively fast, thanks in large part to Tribond, a game in which players are asked, "What do these three have in common?" For example: a car, a tree, and an elephant. They all have trunks. Randal and I were partners. We didn't lose a game. That's because our opponents, Weed and Fender, kept distracting each other by making up their own questions. For example: their three favorite parts of the female anatomy, three bodily functions that make a funny noise, three words that can't be spoken on television, and so on. I didn't mind their antics because we each bet one dollar per game. After Randal and I won our fifth straight game (and five dollars apiece), Weed and Fender left to join the poker game at the back of the bus.

That evening, Sam took the hill for our first game against the Topeka Titans. On this occasion they were more like the Titanic. And Sam was the iceberg. He had flirted with a no-hitter a couple times earlier in the season. This time he got it. Only three Titans reached base all night—two walks and an error. But the home team tallied no runs and no hits. Zero.

The beer flowed freely after the game. Skip even pushed our curfew back to 1:00 a.m. I'd never seen Sam smile so much. One thing I noticed amid the levity, however, was that he never called Eileen to tell her about his big accomplishment. I hoped she missed the radio broadcast of the game, though that seemed unlikely. She'd even considered driving to Topeka to watch Sam pitch. My mind started conjuring explanations for why he didn't call. After what I had said about Sam's feelings for her, I felt an obligation. I wanted Eileen to keep thinking that he was crazy about her, though that was probably an exaggeration. I was the one who was actually crazy about her, but that had to remain unspoken. Love stinks.

Before our next game the following evening, Kenny got his hands on the official statistics issued by the Central States League. Several of us huddled around him in the dugout scanning the pages to find our names. "Damn, Kenny," Fender said, "you're hittin' .232 with no home runs and three RBIs. That's pitiful. If you were a horse, we'd have to put ya down."

"I bet Sam's girl can hit the ball farther than you," Weed added.

"I know she could," Fender said. "Remember when she beat him in arm wrestling?"

"Shut up!" Kenny's face reddened. "Let's check *your* stats Weed. Look at that. The ERA's over 5.00 now. That kinda sucks. And Fender, you've been getting lucky."

"Hey, hey, what's my average?" Randal asked, sticking his head into the scrum.

Kenny ran his finger down the list. "Let's see, .288 for Van Dyke. Two dingers and eight ribbies."

"Who's got the best average on the team?" somebody asked.

"Looks like Willie Small at .333," Kenny said. "Then you got Jamario at .320."

"That's right," Willie said, slapping hands with Jamario. "The brothers leadin' the way, showing you white boys how it's done."

"What about home runs?" Randal asked. "Is Vince leading the league?"

"Vince Stenzel has seven taters. That is …" Kenny flipped to another page. "One behind Kalkwarf in St. Joseph."

"Hey, what's Michael Jordan's average?" Matt asked. "I bet I'm hitting better than him."

Kenny rolled his eyes. "He plays for Birmingham, nimrod. They're not in our league, so he's not on here."

When he flipped back to the Giants page, I scanned the pitchers' names for Brian Carter. In four starts, I had one win, two losses, 15 strikeouts and a 6.38 ERA. The stats were a cold reminder that just one more bad outing could end my days in a Lincoln uniform. I then looked at Sam's line. Over five starts, he had a 3-0 record, three complete games, 55 strikeouts, and a microscopic 0.44 ERA. My eyes remained glued on that last number, which defied reality.

A hand reached into the huddle and snatched the papers from Kenny's grasp. Several guys yelled "Hey!" as we turned to see who had grabbed the stat sheets. It was Tony and his dark bushy mustache. Angley stood beside him, arms crossed. Neither looked pleased.

"Of all the things you numbskulls do to waste time," the skipper said, "this has got to be the dumbest. These numbers don't mean nothin'. Especially this early in the season." He shook his finger at us. "The only numbers you should care anything about are the team's record. And I don't even want you thinking about that too much. You boys just get yourselves ready to play the next game. You'll have plenty of time to worry about your statistics once the season's over." Both coaches turned and stalked toward the bullpen.

"Dang," Fender said. "What's got him so riled up?"

"I don't know," Randal replied. "We're eleven and five. He acts like we're five and eleven."

Angley had good reason to be concerned about his team. The Giants dropped the next two games to the Titans. Too much no-hitter celebrating likely caused the first defeat. The sluggishness of getaway day contributed to the second loss. On our last day in a given city, we players had to check out of our rooms in the morning and pile all our stuff and ourselves into three rooms (that's all the team would pay for since we wouldn't be staying the night). So from lunch until we left for the ballpark later that afternoon, there were two dozen guys packed into three motel rooms. Time inched by under such conditions. Hence, the sluggishness.

From Topeka we traveled to St. Joseph, Missouri, for a three-game series against the Bandits. It was my turn to start that Friday evening, but the game was rained out. So we played a doubleheader the next day. In the afternoon game, my pitches resisted going where I intended them to go. The Bandits put runners on base in each of the six innings I pitched. Fortunately, three double plays and two base running blunders limited them to only four runs. Lincoln's bats exploded for ten runs, giving me my second win of the year.

Sam dominated in the nightcap, tossing eight innings with 12 strikeouts and only two earned runs. Lincoln swept the doubleheader.

After losing the series finale to St. Joseph on Sunday, we traveled to Columbia for a two-game series against the Patriots. The Tuesday night game would have been my spot in the rotation, but the doubleheader had left me with only two days rest since my previous start. So Reed Perry took the hill that night for the Giants. He did not pitch well. Though part of me felt bad for him, another part of me viewed his struggles as helpful to my job security.

On Wednesday morning, the bus carted us back to Lincoln. Aside from the excitement of Sam's no-hitter, it had been a typical road trip: eight days of motels, bus rides, fast food, and, of course, pranks. Kenny came up with the best one when he used eye black to draw a Hitler moustache on a dozing Fender. Diners at an IHOP in Columbia reacted with a combination of amusement, disbelief, and revulsion when the "cowboy Führer" sauntered in. He didn't figure out why people were staring at him until he visited the restroom after we had finished eating.

It was good to be back home. And it was great that we didn't have a game that day. Unfortunately, the Giants president had scheduled a promotional appearance at a used car dealership. Twelve of us, myself included, had to show up at Ralph's Motors on North 27th Street at 2:00 that afternoon. Though the long hours in the bus wore heavily on us, we showed up at the dealership like good soldiers.

A large banner proclaiming "MEET THE LINCOLN GIANTS" fluttered above the cars in the lot. Signs in the showroom window promised, "Grand Slam Deals," "Home Run Financing," and "Giant Savings."

"Welcome!" Ralph bellowed. His lack of height called attention to the sparse comb-over plastered across his shiny head. "Thanks for coming. I've got you boys set up over there." He gestured at a long table in the lot near the showroom window. "Just take your seats and greet the customers when they come by. Sign whatever stuff they got for you. There are some team posters we'll be giving away too." He pointed to a stack at the end of the table. "If you could sign those ahead of time, that'd be fantastic."

As the twelve of us approached the table, Ralph sidled up to Sam. "This must be the no-hitter man, right here. Ha-ha. Alright, I'm thinking we'll start the demonstration in about an hour." He flashed a pointy grin.

"Demonstration?" Sam's brow furrowed in confusion.

"Yeah. Didn't Mister Wright or Mister Mendenhall tell you about that?"

"No."

"Oh, well they agreed to this." Ralph nodded at a clearing in the middle of his lot. "I'm gonna have you throw some pitches for the customers. You know, show 'em the Sam Judge fastball. One of these other guys here is a catcher, right? See, I rented a radar gun and we'll be bringing customers over from time to time. Whatever speed you throw on your next pitch is the discount in dollars they get on their car purchase. Great, huh?" He slapped Sam's back. "You don't throw 500 miles per hour, do ya? Ha-ha."

"How many pitches do you expect me to throw?" Sam asked.

"Oh, not many. Fifty. A hundred. Enough to keep 'em interested. Let's face it, you boys ain't the Husker football team. Lotta people don't know who you are. We need to give 'em a show."

The fuse was lit. I could tell from Sam's expression that he was trying to decide whether to throw Ralph through the giant glass window of his showroom or out into the traffic of 27th Street. Randal made the same observation. We quickly steered the big pitcher over to the table. "Forget about him," I said. "Let's just sign some stuff and then we'll figure some way to get you out of this."

Sam grumbled something unintelligible. We took our seats. The player on the end grabbed a poster, signed it, and passed it to the next guy.

"This sucks," said Kenny, sitting to my left.

"Yep." I watched a salesman across the lot extolling the virtues of a maroon Chevy to a middle-aged couple.

"The things we do to play professional baseball."

"Keepin' the dream alive." I scribbled my name on a poster and slid it over to Randal, who sat to my right.

"I hear there's gonna be a scout coming to watch Sam pitch tomorrow night," Kenny said.

"So I heard. Marlins, right?"

"Yes sir. The big guy might be on his way."

"Yep." I glanced at the line of autograph seekers forming in front of Sam, who sat to the right of Randal. He and Vince were the only Giants to attract any attention thus far.

"Guess I should get a couple hits while that scout's watching," Kenny said. "Might be my big chance to get out of Husker hicksville."

"Better put one over the fence to make sure he notices you."

"Yeah." He waved at a couple of young women browsing the cars. They ignored him. "I'll need to face a crappy pitcher to pull that off. Any chance you could get traded to Council Bluffs before tomorrow?"

I was about to offer a reply of the profane variety when a towheaded boy appeared before us. He held a Giants cap in his hand. "Who are you?" he asked Kenny.

"Kenny Haldeman, second base."

"Okay. I've heard of you." The boy handed his cap to Kenny, who signed it and gave it back. "Thanks."

"What's your name?" Kenny asked.

"Billy."

"Do you play ball?"

The boy nodded. "Yeah."

"What position?"

"Second base."

"Right on, brother!" Kenny gave him a high five.

"Who are you?" the boy asked me.

"Brian Carter, starting pitcher."

"Okay. I've heard of you." Billy handed me his cap.

"You can call him Boo," Kenny said.

The boy scrunched his face. "Really?"

I shot a glare at Kenny. "Yeah, some of the guys like to call me Boo."

"Why?"

"Because when I pitch, the hitters don't stand a ghost of a chance."

The boy's blank stare suggested that he did not share my amusement at that statement.

"Eat your Wheaties, kid," Kenny said. "Then someday you can be a big bad second baseman like me."

"Nah, I don't like playing second base," he said. "I want to pitch like Sam Judge." He pointed at his hero and then moved down the table.

The next hour crawled by. Kenny helped pass the time by making up fake dialogue for the salesmen and customers in the lot. Around 3:00, Ralph appeared. "Alright Sam, you about ready for your demo?"

Saying nothing, he pushed back his chair and stood.

"Great. I'll meet you over there." Ralph started for the clearing. "I've got the bullhorn charged up."

Randal, Kenny, and I gathered around Sam. "You're not really gonna do this, are you?" I asked.

"Wright and Mendenhall call the shots," he grumbled.

"Yeah, but you're pitching tomorrow. You could blow your arm out. Think Skip knows about this?"

"I don't know," Sam said. "But I've already gotten in enough trouble this season. If I cross the front office, I could get cut. I can't afford that with my reputation."

"Well, don't throw very hard," Randal said. "I'll go grab a couple gloves from my truck."

A blue Pontiac then barreled into the lot and skidded to a stop a few yards from our table. Angley rolled out and slammed his door. Ralph approached with hand extended. "You must be the manager. Pleased to meet you. I'm Ralph."

Skip blew past him as if he weren't there. "Show's over," he barked at us. "Get in your cars and go home."

"Excuse me," Ralph said, scooting to catch up with him. "I've got a deal with your boss. Sam Judge is going to pitch a baseball demo."

"The hell he is!" Angley got in Ralph's face like he was arguing with an umpire. "These boys are going home."

"Grant Wright signed off on this. I have a contract."

"I don't care what anybody signed. I'm the manager and I ain't allowing my players to do some jackass demo at a car lot."

"Shall we call Grant?" the dealer asked with defiance. "He agreed that Sam Judge would stage a pitching exhibition at Ralph's Motors."

"So I found out about fifteen minutes ago." Angley's face reddened. "It's the damn dumbest thing I ever heard of."

"This is a breach of agreement. I'll call my lawyer."

Skip turned to us. "You heard me. Get outta here."

We started walking. Ralph was about to object when Angley muted him with a withering scowl. Sam and I got in my car and drove away from Ralph's Motors.

Neither of us said anything for about a mile. Then Sam spoke. "Yeah, I kinda like Skip."

"Me, too."

Chapter 5

We sat around the table in silence, our eyes fixed on the mounted television screens above. Nearly everyone else in JK's did the same, allowing news commentary to replace the usual din of patron chatter. Even the waitresses stopped their rounds to keep up with the breaking story.

"Unbelievable," Randal said when a commercial finally broke our trance. "I used to watch him on TV when I was a kid. I remember the game when he set the single-season rushing record back in seventy-three."

"I loved him in *The Naked Gun* movies," Kenny said. "He was hilarious. And now he's a murderer? Say it ain't so, Juice."

"Too weird," Weed added. "Just can't trust anybody, no matter how nice they seem."

Our eyes again trained on CNN's continuing replays of a white Ford Bronco being tailed by a dozen police cars. The images of the slow-speed chase through Los Angeles defied the limits of believability. After absorbing more commentary about the double homicide in southern California, we returned our attention to Lincoln, Nebraska.

"Man, Clyde got hog-tied tonight," Fender lamented. "Good thing you tossed a helluva game yesterday, Big Shooter," he said to Sam. "That was downright purty."

Sam grunted, before swallowing a gulp of Samuel Adams.

Eileen leaned into Sam. "Oh, he was just showing off for the scout."

"How many strikeouts you get?" Weed asked.

Sam shrugged his shoulders. "Eleven," I said. "Three hits, three walks, and only one earned run. Fourth complete game in seven starts."

"Not too shabby," Fender said. "Ole Hoss just keeps knocking 'em down."

"You never did tell us what that scout said to you after the game," Kenny said.

Sam's forehead wrinkled. "Eh, he didn't say much. Something about throwing a good game. Nice mix of pitches. If I keep it up, I might be hearing from the Marlins down the road."

"Yeah, them and about twenty other teams," Kenny quipped. "He say anything else?"

"Uh, said I topped out at ninety-four on his gun. He liked that."

"Did you tell him you can hit a hundred if you want?"

A smiled cracked through Sam's facial hair. "Nah. Throwing that hard just causes problems. Can't control it. At ninety-four, I can put the ball where I want."

"Did the guy talk money?" Weed asked while grabbing a handful of nuts from a bowl.

Sam shook his head. "He didn't say much else to me. Wanted to talk to Skip though."

"Wonder what they discussed." Weed's rising eyebrows disappeared behind a shock of straw-colored hair.

"Yeah, I wonder," Fender said, adjusting his black cowboy hat so he could better observe a young lady at the bar. "Hey, speakin' of Skip. What's the deal with him? Couple of the boys in the locker room were whispering that he's gonna get the axe."

An uncomfortable quiet blanketed the table. Finally Kenny piped up. "This is what I heard from Tony. Wright and Mendenhall were royally pissed after Skip pulled us off the car lot. And the old man's even madder at them for not telling him about Sam's pitching demo. So the three of them had it out in Wright's office." Kenny downed a swig of beer.

"And?" Eileen asked.

"Well, what Tony said is that Mendenhall wants Skip gone now. But he can't fire him with the team doing so well."

"And Skip's got a lot of support in this town," Randal added. "He's been here since the seventies. Players come and go, but Don Angley is the one constant for the Lincoln Giants."

"So you guys have to keep winning or the skipper loses his job?" Eileen's brow furrowed with concern. "That sucks. I like him."

"We all do," Randal said.

Storms brewed in Sam's eyes. "They'd better not fire Skip," he uttered in a low voice.

Sam's ominous tone left everyone silent for a while. Most of us directed our gaze back to the televisions.

"Hey Randal, how's the hammy?" Kenny asked after a couple minutes had passed.

The corner of Randal's mouth twitched. "I'll be alright."

"Dude, I about filled my drawers when you rounded second and kept on going," Weed said with a grin. "I've never seen you move like that."

"He just wanted to impress the scout," Kenny said.

Suppressing a grimace, Randal rubbed the leg that he'd injured a night earlier.

"Well, he did make it to third," Eileen said. "And that got the crowd fired up."

"We're gonna have to start calling you Van Dyke the Trike," Fender joked.

We bantered for a while about Randal's mad dash triple and then moved on to other topics. Around midnight we paid the bill. On our way out, Kenny gestured at the wall behind the bar. "Hey Sam, those new shelves look nice. I had no idea you were such a skilled carpenter."

Sam looked over at his handiwork and nodded.

"So how long until you toss someone over the bar and knock them down again?"

"Keep yappin' and you'll find out."

Saturday night we played the rubber game against Council Bluffs. Our bats came alive to support Burke LaVelle's seven strong innings and Lincoln prevailed 8-4. Sunday afternoon I took the mound at Sherman Field against St. Cloud. My command was pretty good but the defense behind me was pretty bad. Four errors led to four unearned runs in my six-and-a-third innings. Though my ERA improved, my record fell to 2-3. The next day Sam tossed his fourth shutout of the season. The Giants claimed a share of first place in the division with a record of 17 and 11.

Tuesday was an off day. After a Bible study that afternoon, we moseyed onto the field for practice. Hearing the call of nature, I went back in the clubhouse. Randal, standing at his locker, flinched at the sound of the door opening. Something fell from his hand and bounced a couple times on the concrete floor.

"Damn it!" He reached down and snatched the object.

"There goes your Gold Glove," I said. Then I saw what he'd dropped—a syringe. He quickly shoved it into his gym bag.

Drug use among players was a fact of life for the Giants and pretty much every other professional baseball team. Some of the guys wolfed down greenies like M&Ms. Weed and Fender did it all the time, openly. Kenny showed more discretion, but he too snuck an upper every so often. Sam and Vince, on the other hand, never took anything to enhance their performance. Oddly enough, they were respectively the best pitcher and best hitter on the team. I tried amphetamines when I pitched for Burlington a year earlier. They didn't seem to help me all that much and I felt guilty for doing it. I hadn't taken any pills since arriving in Lincoln, though I drank a can of Jolt Cola before every start.

A couple of my teammates took steroids. Matt Thompson and Willie Small made only a modest attempt to conceal their juicing. I suspected that they were not the only two, but never would have guessed that Randal was among their ranks.

I looked away, wishing I'd never walked back into the clubhouse. "I'm just going to the can."

"Hey." His interjection stopped me just before I reached the bathroom entrance. "This isn't what you think."

I turned. He stood before me with a pleading face. "Don't worry about it," I said.

"It's the hamstring, man. I can't afford to miss any more time."

I nodded.

"This is just to help me heal." He glared at his gym bag. "I'm not a juicer."

"I get it." My words sounded terser than I intended.

"Do you?"

"Randal, it's fine. Half the guys on this team are taking something. None of what they do or what you do is any of my business." Try as I might, I couldn't filter the disappointment from my voice.

He slumped onto a stool in front of his locker. "At my age, I don't have much of a chance anymore. I know that. But if I have any shot at all, it's got to happen this year. None of the big league teams are ever going to look at me again if I stay in Lincoln another season."

I stepped closer. "It could still happen for you. You're hittin' good this year ... and you're not that old."

"I'm pushing thirty. Not too many rookies at my age." A bitter chuckled escaped. "I make less than seven grand a year playing for the Giants. And I got a wife and kid."

"You make some money at the lumberyard in the off-season. And Cathy has a good job at the bank."

"We still don't bring in that much." He hung his head. "I know she'd like to quit her job and have another baby. She's been real supportive. Letting me chase this stupid dream of playing baseball."

I grabbed a stool and sat next to him.

"You probably think I'm a hypocrite now," he said, "especially since we're in this Bible study."

"No, Randal. I understand."

His eyes drifted to the far wall. "We were just reading about David and how he didn't take shortcuts. Could've killed Saul and became king. But he didn't. He trusted God. And here I am taking 'roids like Jose Canseco."

I put a hand on his shoulder. "No. It's not the same. You're just taking them to heal."

He nodded slowly. "Yeah, that's the only reason. One week. Two, tops. Then I'm done with them for good."

"Right." The clock on the wall ticked away the seconds. Finally, I stood. "I still gotta piss."

"Hey, Boo." He looked up at me. "I'd rather that Vince and none of the other guys find out about this. Alright?"

"No problem."

The next day the Giants endured a ten-hour bus ride to Bismarck, North Dakota. We lost Wednesday and won Thursday. I started Friday night—a good outing. My slider had a nice cut and the fastball nipped the corners. I pitched into the seventh and gave up only two runs. The win evened my record at 3-3 and lowered my ERA to 5.14. I felt better about my job security, though Wright and Mendenhall continually made clear their intention to dump any Giants they deemed unproductive. The axe had just fallen on a reserve infielder named Tucker earlier in the week.

After the game Friday night we boarded the bus for Pierre, South Dakota, for a two-game set against the Cavaliers. We'd be facing the boys we tangled with at JK's on their home turf. Sam was slated to pitch the first game. A sizeable crowd filled the stands on that cool June evening. Between innings, the ballpark speakers regaled us with Top-40 hits and PA announcements inviting fans to compete for prizes by tossing a ball into a barrel or by outracing the Cavalier mascot. There was also plenty of trash talk from our opponents, especially their big bald first baseman.

While on the mound, Sam usually didn't let anything distract him. But this was Pierre, and he surrendered two runs in the first. One of the key hits was a single drilled up the middle by Harvey Jorgenson. After the inning, Sam threw his glove against the back wall of the dugout. Deciding to give him some space, I sat next to Randal, who had the night off because of his hamstring.

"Is Harvey getting to him?" I whispered.

Randal shook his head. "That's not it," he said, his good leg in perpetual vibration.

"Then what is it?"

"Felicity's in the stands. Sitting right behind home plate."

"Oh, no."

"Yep. It's the first time he's seen her since she dumped him at the end of last season. And now she's another man's wife."

When Sam took the mound in the second, I watched his eyes. They kept roving above Sarge and fixing on someone in the crowd—the woman he'd once planned to share his life with. The Cavaliers scored a run in the second and added another tally in the fourth. Lincoln's bats also heated up. When Sam headed out for the bottom of the fifth, the game was tied at four apiece. With one out, Harvey sent a booming drive over the left field wall. I half expected Sam to bull rush his old friend during his home run trot. That didn't happen, but I could tell that Sam fumed inside. He walked the next two batters, but escaped further damage when Kenny and Eduardo turned a pretty double play.

Angley had seen enough. Between innings, he told Sam that he was done for the night. My roommate sat like a statue for about a minute and then stomped away to the clubhouse. He'd given up five runs in five innings, his first bad outing of the season.

In the top of the seventh, Vince ripped a double into the right field corner to drive in two runs and put Lincoln ahead 6-5. That meant Sam would not figure in the decision, keeping his record at six wins and zero losses. Unfortunately, Fender gave up a three-run homer in the ninth and Lincoln fell 9-7. The guy who hit the game winner was the same guy who'd held a knife to my face at JK's. As the Cavaliers celebrated at home plate, several of their players made taunting gestures toward our dugout.

A lack of hot water in the dilapidated shack that passed for a visitors' clubhouse kept the Giants' shower time to a minimum. Afterwards, Tony informed us that we would be heading to Country Kitchen to eat supper as a team, and then straight to the motel. He and Angley had apparently heard enough banter on the field to know that some sort of post-game incident had occurred when the Cavaliers were in Lincoln. They didn't want to risk any new trouble in Pierre.

After supper, Sam and I watched SportsCenter in our room for a while before lights out. His tossing and turning kept me awake. Around 12:30 he slipped out of his bed and started getting dressed. When he grabbed the doorknob, I spoke.

"You going somewhere?"

"Yeah. Just goin' for a walk. Go back to sleep."

"Oh … okay." I didn't know if I should offer to go with him or not.

"I won't be long. Go to sleep, Brian."

The door eased shut behind him. A parade of red flags shot up in my head. I scooted over to the window and peeked through the curtains. He headed west on the sidewalk in front of the motel. With no time to debate, I threw on my jeans and a T-shirt and set out after him.

I remained about a block behind so he wouldn't spot me. A mile down the highway, he reached a cluster of taverns. He disappeared into the first establishment, a bar called Azag's. About two-dozen cars populated the parking lot. Not sure what to do, I loitered among the vehicles. I tried to sneak a peek through the window, but it was too dark inside to see any faces. No smashing or crashing sounds ensued, giving me hope that this evening might pass without incident.

Eventually, I found myself leaning against a lamppost at the edge of the parking lot. My tired brain tried to assess what I was doing there. I felt silly, but didn't want to leave Sam alone in that bar. Especially since there could have been a gang of Cavaliers inside looking for revenge. Or, even if no players were in there, a drunken fan might issue an unflattering comment about the opposing pitcher's long hair. After about fifteen minutes, I summoned the initiative to find out what, if anything, was going on.

It was dim and quiet inside Azag's. Nothing unusual seemed to be happening among the late-night tavern denizens. Nobody at the tables looked familiar. My eyes then scanned the bar. There he was, sitting with his back to me, talking to a girl. Not wanting to get spotted, I slunk back toward the doors. Before making my exit, all I'd noticed about Sam's new friend was raven hair and an ample chest.

I retreated to the lamppost, my mind processing the image I'd just seen. Not long ago, I very much wanted something like this to happen. Now that it was reality, the sight made me uncomfortable. While my stomach continued to churn, Sam and the girl emerged from the front doors. She leaned into him as they snaked through the lot. When they reached her Fiat, she handed him the keys. They each got in and he drove off down the highway. My eyes watched in shock as the shrinking taillights moved away. I returned to the motel and crawled into bed.

Sleep came sporadically that night. I recalled how Eileen's eyes lit up when she told me about her feelings for Sam. *How can he do this to her?* Then I thought about how this evening could be a long-awaited opening. How Sam's apparent indiscretion could be the first step leading to Eileen and me getting together. I'd wanted that for so long, yet feelings of unease roiled my gut.

The piercing beeps of my watch alarm jolted me from a dream. Light crept into the room past the edges of the drapes. Sam's bed lay unoccupied and unmade, just as he'd left it hours earlier. A visit from Angley or Tony would have been a disaster. While in the shower, I debated what to do. *Go look for Sam? Where would I start?*

When I walked out of the bathroom, these questions were answered. Sam slouched in a chair next to the window. Deep in thought, he barely noticed my entrance.

"You look like hell."

He glanced up at me and then down at the floor again. "Yeah."

Not knowing what else to say, I got dressed.

"Met a girl at a bar last night." His gaze remained on the carpet. "Went to her place."

"Oh yeah?"

"Yep." He looked at me. His eyes, normally orbs of power and strength, now appeared uncertain and hesitant.

"So uh … she just dropped you off?"

He shook his head. "I walked. Got up around four and took off. She lives with a dude. He works the night shift somewhere. Probably just gettin' home about now."

"You took off at four?" I checked the clock on the nightstand. "Then where've you been the past four hours?"

"Walking. Just walking around in the dark." His eyes floated to a distant place. Maybe somewhere 24 hours ago, before any of this had happened. Though neither of us said her name, Eileen's presence filled the room.

That afternoon the Cavaliers hammered Eisenberg, and the Giants bats had no reply. Randal struck out three times and made two errors. The 9-0 defeat dropped Lincoln two games behind Pierre in the standings. It was a long bus ride back to Nebraska that night. Angley started to lecture us about our crappiness, but got too fed up to continue. He bowed his head mid-sentence and returned to his seat at the front of the bus. The incident underscored the precariousness of his job situation.

Somewhere in South Dakota, our driver made a wrong turn in the dark and headed down the wrong highway. The delay added another hour to our trip. We didn't reach Lincoln until 2:00 a.m. All of us were happy that no game was scheduled for that Monday.

Six players, including Sam and me, met at Sherman Field in the afternoon for a Bible study. Learning about David's faith during adverse circumstances encouraged me, but the troubled faces of Randal and Sam cast a gloomy shadow over the room. At the end of the study, Sam asked for prayer about an issue he did not reveal to the group. Randal did the same.

That evening Sam went out with Eileen. I drove to Wilderness Park. As I hiked through the trees, a voice kept reminding me of the opportunity that had fallen into my lap. All it would take was one phone call to Eileen. I could even disguise my voice to keep it anonymous. Once she heard the news, she'd have to ask Sam about it. And there was no way his guilt-addled mind could forge a convincing denial. Their relationship would end. And then she could be mine.

Trees, bushes, and nature were everywhere around me. So too were images of Sam. I saw him sitting across from me, playing cards and dreaming about the majors. Then he was out on the mound, mowing down opposing hitters. Then he was pulling a guy off me in a bar fight. Then his face appeared, clouded by shame after an evening of regret. But through the cloud I saw a friend. A friend who'd endured some tough breaks in the past. A friend who'd never do to me what I plotted doing to him. Finally, a resolution came. I would not tell Eileen. Not tonight. Not ever.

Later that evening, Sam and I watched *Baseball Tonight* at Hornsby's. The commentators discussed the possibility of Ken Griffey Jr. or Matt Williams breaking Roger Maris's single-season home run record. Then they moved on to Tony Gwynn's chances of hitting .400. A discussion about the labor dispute between the owners and players followed. Afterwards, we turned to CNN to learn the latest developments in the O.J. story.

We went to bed around midnight. I could tell by the lack of snores that Sam wasn't falling asleep. I didn't want to imagine the tortured thoughts careening through his head. Not knowing what to say, I lay in silence.

"Hey, Brian."

His words surprised me. "Huh?"

"I need you to take me somewhere."

"Now?"

"Yes . . . please."

"Okay." I slid my legs over the edge of the bed and sat up. "Where do you want to go?"

He stared out the window. "Eileen's. I gotta tell her."

For some reason, I wanted to yell, "*No! You can't! You'll crush her!*" Saying nothing, I got dressed.

We crept out of the house as quietly as possible. Neither of us spoke as I drove to Eileen's. With no traffic on the roads, it didn't take long to reach her apartment complex east of campus. Without a word, Sam got out and walked to the building. His stride lacked its usual confidence. I shut off the engine and rolled down the window. My nerves tightened in fear of what was about to happen. It almost felt like I was the one going in to confess.

I closed my eyes and leaned my head back. Images of what could be happening inside Eileen's apartment played over and over. None of these imagined scenarios were pleasant. Sometime in the passing minutes, I fell asleep.

The shutting of my car's passenger door jolted me awake. I looked over at Sam. He just sat there, staring straight ahead without expression. I checked my watch. It had been over an hour. I started the engine.

After driving a few blocks, I couldn't take it anymore. "What happened?"

"It wasn't good."

"You guys still together?"

He let out a long exhale. "Yeah, we are."

"Really?"

"Yeah."

"She pissed?"

"Nope."

"Really? I figured she'd be really …"

"I didn't tell her, Brian. Couldn't do it. Not after what happened to her in high school."

Eileen's face hovered before me as I continued driving.

Chapter 6

Tuesday afternoon before practice the team gathered in the clubhouse to meet with a visitor from out of town. Angley didn't tell us beforehand who the guy was or why he wanted to see us.

"Alright gentlemen," the man said at the end of our hour-long meeting. "That concludes our business." He placed a stack of papers into his briefcase and snapped the lid shut.

Players bobbed around like excited little kids. Clutched in our hands were packs of baseball cards and checks that the man had given us. My pulse quickened as I stared at the line, "Pay to the order of: Brian Carter." Sure the amount was small, but the hope it represented was priceless.

"Most minor leaguers don't cash those," the man said. With gray streaks running through his dark hair, he looked about fortyish. "Some guys frame 'em or put 'em in scrapbooks and save 'em as mementos." His name was Lawrence and he was a representative of the Topps baseball card company. The contracts we'd just signed gave Topps the right to use our images on their baseball cards when we made it to the majors. Our signatures netted us each five dollars and two packs of cards. Topps would pay us additional money based on future card sales, *if* we made it to the big leagues. Never mind that most of us had little chance of reaching that level. Nothing could dampen the excitement of our dreams that afternoon.

Lawrence weaved his way through the players toward the clubhouse exit. "Good luck, gentlemen. That could be you one day." He nodded at a couple guys already thumbing through the cards pulled from their recently opened packs.

"Yeah!" Fender exclaimed, looking like a little kid on Christmas morning. "Got a Nolan Ryan!"

"So Topps really thinks we got a shot at the majors?" Weed asked Lawrence.

"You never know. You gentlemen are all professional ballplayers. With the right breaks you could someday be wearing a different Giants uniform, one with 'San Francisco' on the front."

"I wish," Weed said. "I'm surprised Topps has even heard of the Lincoln Giants, let alone wanting us to sign contracts."

"Of course we've heard of you," Lawrence said. "We have files on every professional baseball team. All leagues, all levels. The only people who know more about you guys are the big league scouts … and gamblers."

"Yeah right," Kenny chortled. "I'm sure Vegas has a daily line on us."

Lawrence raised a brow. "Maybe not Vegas, but Kansas City does."

"Kansas City?"

"Oh, yeah. There's a big syndicate there. They got an operation in Omaha too."

Kenny scoffed. "You're telling me there's an actual gambling syndicate in this hick state?"

"Yes sir. They're known as the Reapers. They pretty much control sports betting in the Midwest. I learned about them a couple years ago from an ex-ballplayer in KC."

"And these Reapers," Kenny said with a smirk, "they take bets on our games? The games these knuckleheads play?" He gestured at his teammates, most of them still entranced with their cards and checks.

Lawrence nodded. "There isn't much gamblers won't bet on. If there's a competition, no matter the sport, no matter the level, you can be sure somebody has money riding on the outcome." He chuckled. "Minor league baseball, high school basketball, your little sister's Pee Wee soccer games. If teams are playing, somebody's betting."

Kenny shook his head. "Amazing."

Not long after Lawrence left, the players stashed their checks and cards into their bags and filed onto the field for practice. Randal dawdled at his locker. He kept flipping through his cards, gazing at the guys who had made it: Van Slyke, Lemke, Cone, McRae, Greenwell. A lifelong hope held right there in his hands. He looked up at me with a melancholy smile and guilty eyes. Though the odds were stacked against him, he still believed a syringe could inject life into a dying dream. I grabbed my glove and exited the clubhouse.

We opened a three-game series against Cheyenne that evening. Our starter, Burke LaVelle, pitched well for four innings but lost his command in the fifth and Lincoln fell 6-5. I took the hill the following night. The good news was I didn't issue any walks. The bad news was my pitches got ripped all over the park. Angley pulled me in the fourth with Lincoln behind 5-1. Our bullpen didn't fare much better. The four-game losing streak dropped the Giants into third place, three games out of first.

During batting practice Thursday afternoon, the pitchers like usual trudged to the outfield. It was our job to shag fly balls—one of the more unglamorous tasks of a minor league pitcher. Sam and I took up posts in right field, somewhat off by ourselves. We faded back to the warning track when Vince, a lefty pull hitter, stepped to the plate. His first swing sent a line drive in our direction. Sam took two steps to his left and snagged the missile with a one-handed catch. He then tossed the ball to Reed Perry in shallow right field.

"Nice catch," I said. He grunted.

Vince ripped another line drive that Sam fielded on one hop. The third hit came my way, a little to the right. I lunged at the ball, but it whizzed past, smacking into the Lee Booksellers sign painted on the outfield wall. A couple pitches later, Vince started launching balls over the fence. Sam and I looked up in admiration at the rockets sailing overhead. After our first baseman finished his barrage, Jamario Rhoades stepped into the batting cage. He batted from the right side, so Sam and I would not be getting as much traffic in our neighborhood.

"Think I could hit 'em as far as Vince?" Sam asked, his eyes fixed on the new hitter.

"Maybe." I watched Jamario drive a pitch into left field. "Go in and take some cuts."

"You know Skip won't allow that." He snorted. "It sucks playing in a DH league. I know I can still rip some dingers. You should've seen some of the shots I hit in high school." He glanced over at me with a half-smile.

"Yeah?"

"Man, my senior year I hit one that flew all the way over the four-lane street that runs behind the left field fence. The ball nailed the front door of a house on the other side of the road. Probably went close to 500 feet."

"Impressive. But you know it's your arm that's going to get you to The Show."

"Yeah." He watched Jamario loft a ball to the warning track in left center.

"Can't blame Angley for banning you from the cage. How'd that look if our star pitcher pulled a muscle taking batting practice? The Giants are expecting to sell your contract for big bucks at the end of this season."

"A couple swings wouldn't hurt," he mumbled. "Then maybe I could pinch hit sometime."

"Forget that, man. Pitchers in this league don't bat. Period. When you're in the National League someday, then you can pick up a stick." I stepped in toward a pop-up, but it was too shallow to warrant further attention. Turning back to Sam, I said, "With his shaky job situation, Skip can't risk you batting. He's got enough trouble—" Remembering that this was a sensitive subject with Sam, I cut myself off.

A minute passed. "Heard anything more?" he finally asked.

"Skip?"

"Yeah."

"Just the usual. Guys talkin'. Nobody knows anything for sure."

"Dropping four in a row ain't good," he said grimly. "I bet those two clowns are waiting for just one more loss to drop the axe. I'm surprised they haven't done it already."

"We've still got a winning record," I said. "And you'll end our losing streak tonight. We'll get it turned around. Then Wright and Mendenhall can't touch Skip." I tried to sound upbeat, but inside I too was worried that Angley would soon find a pink slip on his desk. My own contribution to the team's recent failures added to this disquiet.

"They better not fire him," Sam growled. "I'm outta here if they do." His face hardened in defiance.

Looking to change the subject, I asked, "Is Eileen coming to the game tonight?"

"Yeah." He squinted at the batting cage.

"Cool. So you haven't uh …"

"I haven't told her," he said with a tone that discouraged further inquiries about his girlfriend. We stood there saying nothing as Sarge, the new batter, peppered line drives into left field. "Hey." Sam knocked his fist into his glove. "Can I ask you something?"

In my experience, those words usually mean the asker wants to know something I don't want to reveal. "You wouldn't have to," I replied.

"Thing is," he said, unfazed by my response, "I've never seen you with a girl. Nobody has. What gives?"

The hairs on the back of my neck bristled. "Nothing gives. I just haven't had time for a girlfriend."

"No time for the ladies? Come on, man. Even Kenny scores sometimes. And you've never mentioned any girls from your past either."

Though my eyes remained on the batter, I sensed him looking at me.

"It's okay with me if you don't like girls," he continued. "It's just, I'm your roommate. I'd like to know if you're uh … you know."

"I'm not gay," I snapped. "Okay?"

"Did you have a girl in college? Or high school?"

This was pissing me off. Truth is, I had never been all that smooth with the opposite sex. Sure, I'd liked plenty of girls. And some of them seemed to like me. But the few dates I'd gone on never amounted to much. I'm not sure why. A lack of confidence on my part. A lack of social skills. Maybe both. Dates made me nervous. Sometimes my lack of success with women really annoyed me. Other times, I told myself that I was just waiting for the right girl. And now, I'd finally found her here in Lincoln. Too bad she was already spoken for. But I knew something that could change that.

"Of course I did." My voice sounded defensive, I'm sure. "This is a new town for me. I just haven't found anybody here. And with my spot in the rotation so shaky, I need to keep focused on baseball. One more bad start and I could get cut. You wouldn't know what that's like." *Yeah, good answer. Turn this back on him.*

"Alright, man." He faced the infield again. "I was just wondering."

"Well, now you can stop."

Neither of us said much the rest of batting practice.

A large crowd came out to watch Sam pitch that night. Sherman Field averaged around 2,500 spectators for his starts, more than twice the number that showed up when anybody else pitched for us. While loitering near the stands before the game, I heard a few fans speculating that Sam's poor outing in Pierre might carry over to tonight. These concerns quickly evaporated when he needed only six pitches to send the Mules down in order in the first. It was the first act of a masterful complete game performance. Cheyenne managed only five hits, two walks, and one earned run. Our losing streak was history.

Sam's victory lit a fire under the Giants. We dominated Colorado Springs Friday night and then again on Saturday night. That gave us a three-game winning streak heading into my start on Sunday afternoon. More pressure. I did not want to be the guy who extinguished the flames of our resurgence. Though butterflies played racquetball in my stomach before the game, I kept it together on the hill. My pitches obeyed my commands. The fastball hummed over the plate with some extra zip and late movement. I struck out seven batters over eight innings, while allowing only six hits and two runs. My best outing as a Giant.

The next day was July 4th. Wright and Mendenhall made it no secret that they wanted a big crowd. A home game on Independence Day was a golden opportunity for the team to sell tickets, merchandise, food, and beer. The baseball planets fortuitously fell into alignment that day: blue skies, temps in the mid-80s, a four-game winning streak, and, most importantly, Sam on the mound. Not an empty seat could be found at Sherman Field that afternoon.

I had never seen such a lively atmosphere at a baseball game. The crowd buzzed and hooted as Sam threw his warm-up tosses. This commotion amplified into a roar after his first pitch slammed into Sarge's mitt with an earsplitting crack. Though declining in volume between pitches, the cheering didn't stop. When a knee-bending breaking ball finished off the third batter, the fans exploded. Sam pumped his fist in the air and stomped off the field amid a rousing ovation.

After Lincoln tallied a run in the bottom of the first, Sam reclaimed the mound to pick up where he'd left off. The Colorado Springs batters looked helpless against the towering presence they faced. Sam commanded all four of his pitches with razor sharp precision. He didn't give up a hit until the fourth, when a Pikeman blooped a single into shallow right field. A subsequent strikeout ended the threat and preserved Lincoln's lead.

The intervals between innings brought a flurry of activity. Bon Jovi, Styx, and Poison blared from the stadium speakers as attendants tossed hot dogs into the stands. A T-shirt cannon followed with a barrage of purple cotton. Fans participated in races (burlap sack, three-legged, and wheelbarrow) to win batting helmets, caps, and other souvenirs. The stilted Lincoln mascot pranced around in front of the dugouts. The crowd *oohed* in anticipation whenever it looked like he was about to fall. He never did, much to everyone's disappointment.

The highlight of the extra-baseball activities came after the sixth inning. Wright and Mendenhall, wanting to dazzle the holiday crowd, hired a human cannonball to perform. The guy wore a red, white, and blue polyester body uniform with matching helmet. Two assistants wheeled his cannon onto the infield, between the mound and home plate. Two others set up a net in left field. The man waved to the fans before lowering himself down the barrel. An assistant lit the fuse. The crowd hushed as the wick slowly burned away.

BOOM! The human projectile shot from the barrel amid a cloud of white smoke. His body straight with arms flat at his sides, he flew higher and higher. The people murmured in wonderment. Upon his descent he started a slow midair rotation, as if planning to land in the net on his back. But there was a problem; someone had miscalculated. The man sailed over the net. Way over the net. Now flying inverted, his feet up and his head down, he smacked back first into the left field wall with a loud *thunk*. The crowd gasped as the upside down man seemed to defy gravity by remaining plastered to the wall, right in the middle of the Lincoln Chiropractic Center sign. An instant later, his legs flipped forward and his body plopped prone onto the warning track. Sousa's "Stars and Stripes

Forever" burst from the ballpark sound system, inspiring the crowd to cheer. Most fans were apparently unaware that what had just happened wasn't supposed to happen.

The man's assistants raced out to him. Both teams' trainers followed. Remarkably, the human cannonball was on his feet in a matter of minutes. He even walked off the field under his own power. Several players, myself included, went out to shake his hand. Judging by the daze in his eyes, I didn't think he would remember any of this the next morning.

When the game resumed, Sam continued his dominance. The visitors flailed in desperation at pitches they had little chance to hit. When the last Pikeman struck out in the ninth, Sam had completed a two-hit shutout with 17 Ks. The victory moved Lincoln into a tie for first place in the Western Division.

Moments after the game, the sports anchor from KLKN television interviewed Sam for that night's news broadcast. Meanwhile a hundred young fans camped in front of the clubhouse, hoping for an autograph from their conquering hero. Undaunted by their numbers, Sam signed for each one of them. He even seemed to be having fun, cracking jokes and sometimes asking the kids a riddle. Since I was his ride, I didn't get to leave until Sam left. We were still at the ballpark nearly two hours after the game had ended. All of our teammates, as well as Eileen, had long ago taken off. We would be meeting them later for supper at Brewsky's and then driving to Holmes Lake to watch the fireworks show. The wait didn't really bother me. It was fun to observe firsthand the hoopla surrounding around a guy who might someday star in the major leagues.

When Sam was dressed and ready to go, we exited the clubhouse to what I thought would be an empty concourse. But there was one more autograph seeker waiting for Sam. And this one wasn't a kid. More like college age, I guessed. She sat atop a picnic table near the concessions building. Flowing auburn-red hair danced upon her shoulders. Her white shorts were tight. The blue halter-top tighter. And they each revealed an ample amount of skin. Gorgeous dark eyes glanced at me before fixing on my roommate.

"Hi Sam," she said, stepping down from the table. "Would you sign my ball?" The corners of her lips curved upward. A dimple and a sprinkling of freckles added to her allure.

"Uh, sure," he said. With a tentative motion, he plucked the baseball from her hand. His voiced wavered into a stutter when he asked who to make it out to.

"Danika." Her voice lilted with a rich melodious quality.

I looked away so she wouldn't catch me staring at her striking physique. It didn't matter though. Her gaze remained on Sam, and after he'd signed the ball, his eyes locked on her.

"Thanks," she said, eying the autograph. "Great game today."

"Thank you." He sounded like a little boy.

"Maybe I'll see you around." She flashed a smile that could shake foundations, and then turned and walked away. Sam and I watched the entire show as she passed through the front gate and glided to her car in the parking lot. The motion of her stride was like music—a rock anthem with a smoking chorus that burned into memory. Neither of us moved nor spoke for at least a minute.

"So that was Danika," I said, still enjoying the perfume aroma that lingered in the air.

"Yeah ... Danika."

There was no game the next day. With no practice or promotional appearances either, it was a true day off. In the morning Sam and I lifted weights at the Y. That afternoon I drove him to the university for his youth baseball clinic. I passed the hours meandering around downtown. That evening we attended an unofficial team function. The host family that Matt Thompson and Brad McGill lived with, the Dufresnes, had just departed on a vacation trip to Florida. So Matt and Brad decided to throw a party. Located in an affluent new development on the south side of town, the house was not quite a McMansion, but it was big and had many rooms. And everything inside—furniture, artwork, lamps, carpeting, appliances—was top of the line. It seemed a certainty to me that the Dufresnes did not agree to any parties being held in their immaculate castle.

By 10:00 p.m., the revelry raged with full force. Rap music from massive speakers rattled the windows. Beer flowed freely from the keg set up in the kitchen. Food options included daVinci's pizza, an assortment of Frito-Lay chips, and anything that could be found in the Dufresnes' cupboards and refrigerator. Joining the Giants players at this event were about two-dozen college students.

Most of them females invited by Matt and Brad during a recent visit to the University of Nebraska campus.

Wandering out the sliding glass doors to the back patio, I saw Weed and Fender sitting in a hot tub with three girls who looked about high school age. After declining Weed's offer to join them in the water, I went upstairs to check out the sizeable deck. There I found Sam, Eileen, Randal, Cathy, and Kenny sitting in deck chairs and enjoying the evening breeze. I claimed the last empty chair as their discussion about the Giants' pennant chances continued.

"We're the team to beat in the West," Kenny proclaimed with a wave of his nearly empty beer cup. "Pierre can't hang with us. The division is ours."

"Season's not even half over, Haldeman," Randal said.

"Baseball is a game of momentum," Kenny lectured. "And we've cornered the market on that. Shoot, the only thing that can stop us now is if the big guy signs with the Yankees." He finished off his last swig of beer. "But those guys are going on strike soon, so we've got nothing to worry about."

Randal scoffed. "Momentum changes overnight in this game. There's a lot of baseball left to be played."

"Think you'll get an offer from one of the big league teams before the end of the season?" Cathy asked Sam.

Staring off into the night, he did not respond.

"Hey dummy." Eileen backhanded his chest. "She asked you a question."

He swiveled his head. "Huh? Who did?"

Eileen pointed at Cathy. Before she could repeat her question Kenny jumped in. "She asked if you and Eileen had picked a church for your wedding this fall."

Sam's eyes widened into a dumbfounded expression. "Huh?" The shocked look on his face made the rest of us laugh.

"Oh leave Sammy alone," Cathy said. "He's got a lot on his mind lately."

Sam's eyes shot over to her, but he offered no comment.

"Sorry, big man," Kenny said. "I'm just messin' with ya. Cathy asked if you thought you'd get a big league contract before the end of the season."

"Oh … I dunno. Teams will probably wait to see how things go the rest of this summer."

"Have you heard from any more scouts?" Cathy asked.

"No."

"That'll change," Kenny said. "They're all gonna be coming here to check out the Judge. Word is gettin' out on you, my man." He grinned at Sam.

We bantered for a while longer about Sam's major league prospects, before the conversation subsided and all we heard was music from inside and splashing from the hot tub below. Noticing Eileen's empty cup, I offered to get her a refill. Seeing her and Sam together still made me uncomfortable, so I'd been looking for an opportunity to go back in the house.

As I walked down the hallway, I noticed Turk Mitterwald, a reserve infielder, at the far end with his back to me. A couple steps later, I realized that he was urinating on a houseplant standing in a corner. A crash then emanated from the dining room downstairs. The shattering noise sounded to me like the glass in the hutch or one of the Dufresnes' oriental vases. It turned out to be the latter. I decided to survey the rest of the house to see how much Matt and Brad owed their hosts thus far. A beer stain on the living room carpet and a busted lampshade in the den were the only other mishaps I observed. Out back the bubbling hot tub was now empty. A college-age kid loitering nearby told me that Weed and Fender and their new friends had decided to check out the basement.

After stopping at the keg for Eileen's refill, I returned to the deck. She flashed a bright smile when I handed her the plastic cup of beer. "Thanks Boo. You are so sweet."

"No problem."

The group had been discussing their picks for best movie of the year. Randal and Cathy voted for *The Lion King*, which they had just seen with Haleigh. Eileen stated her case for *Speed*, the Keanu Reeves-Sandra Bullock thriller. When it was his turn, Kenny stood and waxed rhapsodic about the merits of *Ace Ventura: Pet Detective*. He then turned around, bent over, and grabbed his butt. "Can I ass you a question?" he said, flapping his cheeks back and forth. It took only a few seconds before his Jim Carrey tribute had all of us cracking up.

Actually, all of us but one. Without expression, Sam stared out at the Dufresnes' dark backyard. He was sitting there among us, but he was miles away. I didn't know exactly where, but I had a good idea who he was with.

Chapter 7

Wednesday morning we had to be at Sherman Field by 6:45 a.m. Fifteen minutes later the Giants bus rolled away for an eight-hour trip to St. Cloud, Minnesota. Sam and I had left the Dufresnes' house the night before around 1:00, so we weren't in too bad of shape. Matt and Brad, on the other hand, looked like the twin brothers of the Crypt Keeper. Their party had raged on until about 4:00, so I heard. They each lay sprawled across two seats, their heads buried in large pillows. Weed, Fender, and a couple other guys assumed similar poses. Angley and Tony did not look pleased at the condition of their players, but they said nothing.

My zombie teammates must have gotten some decent rest traveling through Iowa and Minnesota, because the Giants prevailed that night to push our winning streak to six. A three-run homer from Sarge, who had skipped the party, proved to be the decisive blow. Thursday night, however, the streak came to an end when reliever George Lazzeri gave up a grand slam in the eighth to St. Cloud's cleanup hitter.

Friday night was my turn to start. It was a sweltering, humid night at the ballpark. My pitching, however, was more temperate. The Trappers had little trouble getting on base, but I avoided disaster thanks to three double plays. Angley pulled me after five innings with Lincoln ahead 6-4. We pulled away in the later innings. The victory upped my record to five wins and four losses, the first time I'd been over .500 all season. The next evening, Reed Perry confounded the St. Cloud hitters with his big sweeping curveball and Lincoln won again, taking three of four from our hosts.

After Saturday's game, the team boarded the bus for an all-night trip down I-35 and I-80 to Council Bluffs. There, we opened a two-game series against the Black Squirrels. Sam got the start that afternoon. A bit sluggish from all the travel hours, he allowed the home team to make solid contact with several of his pitches. But after surrendering three runs early, he regained his focus to deliver eight strong innings. Our bats stayed hot and Lincoln triumphed 8 to 3.

Since we were only sixty miles from home, Wright and Mendenhall did not want to pay for a motel in Council Bluffs. The players would ride the bus to Lincoln that night and then return to Council Bluffs the next day. Sam was the exception. His folks had driven in from Des Moines for his start, and he planned to have dinner with them afterwards. Then he would ride back to Lincoln with Eileen, who had also attended the game. Sounded like a nice plan. The surprise came when Sam asked me to join them. I didn't want to be a fifth wheel, but he really seemed to want me there.

Eileen looked surprised when both Sam and I approached her green Camry in the parking lot. She didn't ask why I was there and I didn't tell. Truth is, I didn't actually know why I was joining Sam and her for dinner with his parents.

"So this is the first time your folks have seen you pitch this year?" I asked from the backseat.

"Yeah." He paused. "My old man works third shift at a tire plant. Fifty, sixty hours a week. Not much chance to drive out to Lincoln for a ballgame."

"It's nice you got the start today. This is our only Sunday game in Iowa all season."

"Yeah."

Eileen glanced over at him with traces of apprehension in her eyes. Her hair, sans ponytail, gleamed radiant. Lipstick and mascara enhanced an already gorgeous face. Delightful perfume wafted back to dance inside my nostrils. For an instant I wondered if Sam knew about my longing and had invited me along just to torture me.

Mr. and Mrs. Judge waited for us on a bench near the entrance to Applebee's. I trailed behind Sam and Eileen as we approached. "These are my parents, Marshall and Annie," Sam said to his girlfriend. "This is Eileen," he said to his parents with nonchalance.

It then struck me that this was the first time she had met Sam's folks.

After they exchanged pleasantries, it was my turn. "And here's Brian, my roommate," Sam announced. His parents seemed surprised by my presence. I was getting used to that reaction.

"Pleased to meet you, Mr. and Mrs. Judge."

"Oh Brian, please call us Marshall and Annie," Mrs. Judge said with a pleasant smile. A thin woman, she wore gold-framed glasses that complemented her green skirt. Her dark silvery hair hung down straight and long. Mr. Judge, though stout, stood nearly as tall as his son. His short, curly grey-black hair receded back from a large creased forehead. He wore a grizzled expression that barely changed when he greeted me with an authoritative handshake.

Nobody said much after we took our seats at a table in the restaurant. I sure wasn't going to be the one to get the conversation started. After we'd glanced at our menus for a while, Annie eyed her son, "You pitched well this afternoon."

"Thanks, Ma."

"What's your record now?"

"I dunno." Sam scrunched his brow. "Brian here is better with the numbers."

"Sam's got a 9-0 record after today," I said. "Leads the league in wins, strikeouts, and ERA." For some reason, a nervous chuckle escaped from my throat.

Annie smiled and glanced again at her menu. Sitting stiffly, Marshall appeared as if he'd just swallowed an entire lemon. Eileen looked like she might comment, but said nothing. Fortunately, a waitress came over to cut short the silence.

After we'd placed our orders, Annie asked Sam, "Your team is in first place, right?"

He nodded. "Yep." His gaze remained on the sports memorabilia adorning the wall behind his parents.

"The Giants are 28 and 18," I added. "One game ahead of Pierre."

Annie nodded with a Mona Lisa smile, while Marshall directed his hard stare at me. Regret for speaking when not spoken to heated my face. I was a ten-year-old kid again.

When the food arrived, I unwrapped my silverware and prepared to dive into the cheeseburger before me. Then I noticed

Marshall and Annie bowing their heads. Sam, following suit, sent an elbow into my ribs. My head went down as Mr. Judge started praying out loud, right there in the restaurant. I wondered what Kenny, Weed, and Fender would say about this scene. After the deep voice finished thanking God for our food, we started eating.

A few bites in, Annie began asking questions to learn a little more about her son's girlfriend. I was familiar with most of the details Eileen shared: her dad runs a grocery store in Nebraska City, her mom is the best cook in the world, her younger sister wants to play ball for the Huskers. What I did not know about was her love for horses, and that she used to have a pony back home named Sparky. Later in the conversation, Annie inquired about the Huskers softball season. "The team did well," Eileen said. "Made it to the NCAA regionals. I had an okay year, but nothing like what Sam is doing now with the Giants." She smiled.

"Let's hope this season ends better than his senior year at college," Marshall said with a grim demeanor.

"I did fine in college," Sam said.

"Yes, you were just great when we weren't bailing you out of jail."

"Marshall." Annie placed a hand on her husband's arm.

Sam dropped his fork onto his plate and glared at his father. A few seconds later, he shook his head and started eating again. The clanking of silverware produced the only sounds at our table during the uncomfortable minutes that followed.

Annie eventually broke the silence by asking Sam, "Have you found a church yet in Lincoln?"

"No, Ma. Haven't found one yet."

Mrs. Judge looked disappointed. Marshall grunted. "Of course not."

"We've been going to a Bible study," I said. "Me and Sam."

Both Judge parents shifted their eyes to me. "Really?" Annie asked.

"Yeah. Vince, our first baseman, leads it. There are six or seven of us who go. We meet about every week or two."

"What are you studying?" Mr. Judge asked.

"The life of David. Just got to the part where he becomes king."

Marshall's expression softened. "Well, how about that. It's good that young men study the life of King David. They need to learn that mistakes bring serious consequences. Right, Sam?"

"You bet," Sam said with some attitude.

When Mr. Judge's eyes fell on me, I nodded like a bobblehead doll, hoping he wouldn't ask me to recite anything from the Bible.

"David was a great man," Sam's father continued, "blessed with great abilities. It's important for such men to acknowledge God. Otherwise, they can get prideful, distracted, led astray." Marshall's eyes locked on Sam, who continued to focus on his food. "Without a firm grounding in the Word, ability and success are dangerous. Look no further than David to see that. Even great men of faith stumble when they stray from the Lord. And the consequences can be devastating." Mr. Judge raised his brows and glanced at my still nodding head. "That is why finding a church home is vital for young men out on their own."

"Do you attend church, Eileen?" Annie's soft voice provided a pleasant contrast to the hard timbre of her husband.

"Uh, yeah." She cleared her throat. "I've been going to a place called Lincoln Berean for about a year. I really like it."

"Great," Marshall said with a faint smile. "Maybe Sam will start accompanying you on Sunday mornings. A man shouldn't let his lady go to church all by herself."

I'll go with her! The stray quip echoed through my head.

"Oh, Sam's come with me once," Eileen said. "We'll get him out there again one of these days." Sam flicked back some stray locks and looked over at her.

The rest of our time together passed with Annie and Eileen doing most of the talking. Their topics included movies, books (both were fans of John Grisham), and the best places to shop in Lincoln. Sam said about eight words the whole time. When the check arrived, Marshall pulled out his wallet and gave the waitress several bills.

In the parking lot, I shook hands with both Mr. and Mrs. Judge and thanked them for dinner. Annie hugged Eileen. "It was wonderful to meet you," Annie said. "We hope to see you again after the season." She then turned to hug Sam. "Call us sometime, okay? We like to hear how you're doing."

"Alright, Ma."

Marshall nodded at Sam before turning toward his car.

Eileen steered her Camry out of the parking lot and we started our trek to Lincoln. "Your parents are nice," she said.

"Yeah," he replied. "At least the old man didn't mention my hair this time." He turned the radio dial to The Eagle rock station, and cranked up the volume.

The Giants fell in extra innings the next day to split the two-game set in Council Bluffs. We had Tuesday off and then opened a four-game series against the Columbia Patriots at Sherman Field. Burke tossed eight strong innings to propel the Giants to victory in the first contest. I pitched the following night. Though the visitors had little trouble getting on base against me, they failed to capitalize on most of their opportunities. Angley pulled me after I got in trouble again in the fifth, but the bullpen carried the Giants to another win.

Friday evening was Sam's turn to take the hill. At practice before the game, he seemed loose, cracking jokes and slapping backs. He even wrestled Matt Thompson and was about to get the pin when Tony showed up and chewed them out for horsing around.

Very few seats at the ballpark were unfilled that night. Sam threw the first pitch at 7:05 p.m. By 7:07 the side was retired. All three Columbia batters shook their heads in bewilderment trudging back to the dugout.

In the top of the second, Sam fell behind the Patriots cleanup hitter 3-0. The next fastball cut across the heart of the plate. Then a slider caught the outside corner to fill the count. The payoff pitch was a fiendish curve that seemed to defy the laws of physics while nipping the inside corner for strike three.

Angley, leaning against the wall at the dugout entrance, pumped his fist and turned to his coach with a big grin. "Did you see that?"

Tony stood nearby with his arms crossed and feet shoulder-width apart. "Glad I'm not trying to hit that stuff."

Angley sent a deluge of tobacco juice into the dirt below. "Damn right." His rare grin remained in place. "You know, pitching is just like real estate."

"How so?" Tony asked.

"It all comes down to the same three things. Location, location, location."

Sam went to work on the next batter. A groundout and a strikeout later, the Giants were on their way back to the dugout. Sam plopped onto the bench next to me and held out his hand. "You suck," I said, tipping my bag of sunflower seeds over his palm.

"Yeah, I just don't have it tonight." He shoved the pile into his mouth. A stray seed hung in his facial hair, before he brushed it away and grabbed a towel for his arm.

"Can't believe your useless hide hasn't been cut yet."

"I'll probably get the axe after the game."

"Hope so. I'd prefer a roommate who doesn't snore so much."

When the Giants finished batting in the second, Sam stood and flicked his glove back at my head. Having taken a face full of leather several times already this season, I ducked early so the Rawlings swooshed by without making contact. "You're finally getting smarter," he quipped, starting his jaunt to the mound.

I was about to yell something back when I noticed Kenny backing toward me. The greasy rip that erupted from his bony rear end nearly knocked my cap off. I rose to swat at him, but the rodent second baseman scurried onto the field where I couldn't follow.

"Haldeman, you jackass," I yelled, before moving down the bench, away from the toxic cloud he left in his wake.

By the fifth inning, the crowd at Sherman hummed with anticipation. Sam had yet to allow a hit. The prospect of seeing a no-hitter was exciting enough, but the potential here was even greater—Sam was working on a perfect game. Fifteen up and fifteen down thus far. He usually walked about two or three batters per start. Not this time. On this night his pitches painted the corners of the plate with Rembrandt-like precision.

Sam induced three quick outs in the sixth. Before he reached the dugout, we all cleared away from the spot where he sat. In the bottom of the inning, Vince drilled an opposite field home run with a man on to put Lincoln ahead 2-0.

The first two Patriot batters in the seventh struck out, looking silly in the process. Sam needed only seven more outs for perfection. But he fell behind the next hitter with three balls and a strike. Knowing that one more ball would end the perfect game,

Giants fans and players tensed. Sam fired in a fastball that the hitter popped high above foul territory down the third base line. Matt drifted over to our dugout but did not have a play. A sudden gunshot overhead sent me jumping nearly out of my uniform. It took me a second to realize that the sound came from the baseball landing on the dugout's corrugated metal roof. While my heart rattled like a paint shaker, Sam remained cool on the mound. With the count full, he conjured a changeup that the batter tapped into a weak ground out.

A routine fly ball and a strikeout produced two quick outs in the top of the eighth. Then the third batter, the Columbia DH, ripped a one-hop bullet toward the hole between first and second. Kenny sprang left into a dive. The ball slammed into the web of his glove, but then popped out and started to roll away. Like a crab, our second baseman scooted over, grabbed the ball, and flung it to first. Vince stretched toward him as far has his large frame would allow. From my vantage point in the dugout, the ball appeared to beat the runner by a hair. The umpire, however, stood motionless as the crowd hushed. An instant later, he punched the air. An explosion of cheers followed.

All color had left Kenny's face by the time he reached the dugout. Though everybody praised his incredible play, his hands continued to shake as he donned a batting helmet and stepped out to the on-deck circle. Nobody wanted to be responsible for ruining the perfect game.

Sam took the mound in the ninth amid a standing ovation. Myrtle Schultz then transformed the cheers into a menacing "FEE FI FO FUM" chant. As if facing an overpowering pitcher wasn't difficult enough, the Columbia hitters now had to deal with the yelling and stomping of three thousand boisterous fans.

A pop-up to Matt near third started the inning. A three-pitch strikeout followed. With one out left, Columbia sent up a lefty pinch hitter. He turned on Sam's first pitch, a changeup, and drove it into right field. But the batter had swung too soon, hitting the ball off the end of his bat. Though still hobbled by his hamstring injury, Randal needed to move only a couple steps to make the play. The ball disappearing into his glove brought an eruption from the crowd. Sam pumped his fist. Sarge ran to the mound and jumped into a bear hug. The rest of the Giants converged on the infield to mob our victorious pitcher.

The revelry continued for several minutes. As Sam made his way off the field, he pointed to someone in the stands. I looked up and saw Eileen, three rows behind our dugout, smiling and waving. My eyes then recognized someone else two rows back and a few seats over. Though I'd seen this woman only once, her face was unforgettable. Clapping along with everyone else, Danika's gaze remained fixed on the man of the hour.

Shouts of celebration filled the clubhouse. Even the Spanish-speaking players showered Sam with accolades. Well, I actually didn't know what they were saying, but they sounded positive to me. Angley and Tony stepped in and eventually quieted the din. I'd never seen such joy beaming from the old man's face.

"That was beautiful," he extolled. "In all my years of coaching, I've never seen a pitcher throw a perfect game." We all cheered. "Beautiful, just beautiful," our manager continued. "See what can happen when you numbskulls listen to me?" A grin wide enough to show both rows of teeth followed. After a few more words of praise, the coaches left. Jerry then appeared and wrapped Sam's arm in ice.

"Guess we're going to have to call you Mr. Perfect now," Kenny said, flexing his muscles like a WWF wrestler.

"And if you would have botched that grounder in the eighth," Weed said, "Sam would have powerbombed your head into home plate."

The jovial atmosphere continued for about twenty more minutes. After showering, the guys dressed and started filing out. Hearing that Angley wanted a word with him before he left, Sam went into the coach's office, a glorified supply closet just off the main locker room area. My ears had little trouble picking up the conversation that ensued behind the closed door.

"Judge, you've got talent," Angley began. "That's no secret. And tonight you showed what happens when talent combines with hard work and preparation. That game you just threw is a product of all the time you invested last winter and spring." He paused. "It's all coming together for you now."

"Thanks, Skip."

"You're on track to be pitching in the bigs. Maybe as early as next year. You're that good."

In the silence that followed, I pictured Sam nodding at our manager's words.

"Just keep your head on your shoulders," Angley continued. "Be smart. More and more people are taking notice of you. You've gotta avoid the distractions that have derailed you in the past. Watch your temper and keep your nose clean. Alright?"

"Yeah."

Another pause followed. "I'm proud of you, son."

"Thanks."

Sam emerged from Angley's office and we left to join the gang at JK's.

Saturday afternoon the Patriots exacted a measure of revenge by pummeling us 11 to 2. They feasted on Clyde's pitches, which had to seem fat after facing Sam's unhittable pills. More than a few Giants looked sluggish on the field, a product of too much celebrating the night before. And so we missed our chance at a four-game sweep. The no longer beaming Angley chewed our butts and gave us all ten laps around the ball field after the game. The discipline got our attention and Lincoln bounced back Sunday afternoon with a win over Topeka.

Practice Monday afternoon started off like normal, but near the end of our stretching exercises a couple visitors appeared in the stands. A young guy with feathered blond hair, a white polo shirt, and khaki pants sat a few rows behind home plate. An older gentleman in a tan suit claimed a spot in the top row on the first base side.

Like usual, the pitchers moseyed to the outfield for batting practice. When Sam and I took our posts in deep right field, I noticed a third stranger in the stands. This one wore sunglasses, a light blue shirt, and dark jeans. After watching for about a minute, he moved toward the visitors' dugout and passed through a gate onto the field. As he made his way down the right field line, the other two visitors hurriedly followed the same path.

With Eduardo Salazar shooting line drives from home plate, the man in the blue shirt crossed the foul line into right field. "Sam

Judge? I'm Carson Dixon." He extended a hand as he approached. "It is awesome to meet you."

Sam eyed the man and knocked his fist into his glove. "Well Carson, you might want to watch out for flying objects." He gestured toward home plate, where Eduardo had just hit a sharp grounder into right center. "The ball gets out here in a hurry."

"Ah, good point," Carson said, turning to face the infield. "I won't take up much of your time. Just wanted to introduce myself. Set up a time for us to talk about representation."

"Representation?"

"Absolutely. A man of your talents deserves an agent committed your success. And I can assure you that the Carson Dixon Sports Agency will ensure that you receive top dollar when you sign your name to that first big league contract."

Tony, having noticed the two other strangers hustling down the right field line, stopped pitching. "Hey," he yelled. "Get off the field." He then spotted Carson standing beside Sam. So too did Angley, now emerging from the Giants dugout. The old man's voice cut through the air, firing off profanities that I thought were unfamiliar to men of his generation. Even 300 feet away, I could see Skip's face glowing red as he scooted toward us. Tony headed our way too.

"Guess this is a bad time," Carson said. "Perhaps we can meet later on to discuss options. How about dinner tonight?"

"Got a game," Sam replied with an amused smirk.

"Sam! If I could just have a second," the fast-approaching guy in the polo shirt huffed. "I'm Jimmy Kirsch. I've called your team's office and left several messages. Did you get—"

"It's not polite to interrupt, Jim," Carson said. "Mr. Judge and I are having a conversation."

"Don't listen to either of them, Sam," the older man in the suit called out. He stopped about twenty feet away to bend over and catch his breath. "You need an agent with experience."

"Get the hell off my field," Angley roared. Moving in a quick waddle, he continued his barrage of curses as he passed from the infield dirt onto the right field grass. Sam, meanwhile, had three business cards thrust under his chin. He hadn't taken any of them before Tony arrived and started herding the agents away.

"I suggest you gentlemen leave before he gets here," the coach said, looking over his shoulder at Angley. The agents glanced at the onrushing ball of fury and hastened their retreat. Tony directed them back toward the visitors' dugout. Angley changed course and looked like he might intercept them until Sam moved over to block his path.

"It's all right, Skip. No harm done."

"Don't ever let me catch you parasites on my field again," Angley shouted as he tried to get past Sam. Tony escorted the three unwanted guests through the gate by the dugout.

The players were still buzzing about the agents after practice ended. A few of us crowded around Sam as he sat in the dugout tightening the laces of his glove. "Looks like Sammy's got some suitors," Fender said.

"Yep, he's hittin' the big time," Weed added. "Gonna remember our names next year?"

"I don't remember your names this year," Sam replied, still focusing on his glove.

"Very funny. So you gonna sign with one of those agents?"

Sam shook his head. "Nah. They seemed too desperate. I'll wait for Boras or Steinberg to call."

We all laughed. "Boys we're talkin' to a future millionaire here," Fender said. "You gonna invite us to your big mansion someday?"

"Hell no. I've seen what you animals do to a place."

"Speaking of that," Weed said. "Did Matt and Brad ever find a new host family?"

"Nope," I answered. "No takers yet. They're still staying at the Y."

"It's a shame the Dufresnes kicked them out," Weed said. "They sure had a nice hot tub."

That evening I pitched against Topeka. The first two innings breezed by, six up and six down. But then in the third the Titans started driving the ball. My heater seemed to lose some velocity, and I wasn't sure why. Though they had to do a lot of running, the guys behind me made some nice defensive plays to limit the scoring. Angley pulled me in the sixth with the game tied at three apiece. We ended up losing 7-4.

Skip wanted Sam to have four days rest before his next start, so he gave Reed Perry the ball Tuesday night. With few off days scheduled over the next six weeks, Angley planned to use Reed more as a starter, giving the team a five-man rotation. The big Mormon responded by allowing Topeka only five hits and one run over eight innings.

Sam started the final game of the series against the Titans. His stuff was okay, but not the dominating arsenal he'd unleashed in his previous start. Topeka scratched out seven hits and two runs in seven innings. Since Sam had thrown 110 pitches by that point, Angley sent Weed in to pitch the eighth. The score was tied at two, so Sam would not add to his league-leading win total. Lincoln nonetheless prevailed in the bottom of the ninth when Jamario laid down a perfect suicide squeeze to drive home the winning run. The victory gave Lincoln a 6-2 record on the home stand and a 34-21 mark for the year. But our lead over Pierre in the standings remained slim at one and a half games.

That last contest against the Titans had started early (6:05 p.m.) because the team would be heading out for a long road trip afterwards. With a game in Cheyenne the next evening, we would be riding all night on the bus. Departure was 11:00 p.m., so the players had just enough time to grab something from home if necessary. Since neither Sam nor I had finished packing, we both went back to Hornsby's.

As we threw our stuff into the open suitcases on our beds, the professor appeared in the doorway of our room. "I listened to the game," he said. "Nicely done."

Since I played no role in the victory, I said nothing. Sam after a pause said, "Thanks."

"The team is on quite a roll," Hornsby said with a cough. "Excuse me, boys." He grabbed a handkerchief from his shirt pocket and pressed it to his mouth for a couple more hacks.

When he'd finished, I pointed at Sam and said, "Yeah, this big oaf is finally carrying his weight. Got us into first place now. That even puts Angley in a good mood sometimes."

"Oh, I bet," Hornsby said. "It's been quite a while since his team has made the playoffs. In his twenty years here, he's never won a league championship. I know he'd love to get one before he retires."

"Really?" Sam said. "I figured Skip had won at least three or four titles with the Giants."

"Nope," Hornsby replied, hooking his thumbs into his suspenders. "Don did have some good teams back when Lincoln was still part of the San Francisco farm system. The Giants even played for the league championship twice, in seventy-eight and eighty-four, but they lost both times."

"Well, this year we'll get him that title," I said, snapping my worn grey suitcase shut.

Not responding to my statement, Hornsby stared at the wall behind me. "Yep, poor Don's sure had some tough breaks. It all started with that forty-nine season." He stroked his white beard and shook his head. "The man does persevere."

I started to ask for more elaboration, but another coughing fit hit the professor. He lurched away to the bathroom down the hall. Sam and I looked at each other. "You all right, Doc?" he asked.

"Yes, I'm fine," a labored voice replied. We heard the squeak of a sink handle turning followed by the sound of running water.

"What should we do?" I asked Sam. "We have to leave soon."

He pushed the lid down on his suitcase. "Go ahead and take off. But take my bag, will ya? I'll hang back for a while. Eileen's giving me a ride to the ballpark."

"Oh. Alright."

Hornsby reappeared in our doorway. "Sorry about my abrupt departure boys. Just had one of my spells."

"Anything we can get for you?" I asked.

"Oh no. These spells come and they go. I'll be fine."

I said goodbye to the professor and took off. After parking my Taurus in the lot at Sherman Field, I stowed the suitcases in the luggage compartment and boarded the idling bus. Finding an empty window seat, I propped my pillow against the seatback and shut my eyes.

Not a minute later someone plopped into the seat next to mine. "Boooooo," an unwelcome voice sang. "Yay, we get to sit together for seven hours!" Kenny's yuks bored into my ear canals.

"Oh goody," I mumbled. "Hey, I think Weed and Fender are startin' up a poker game in back. You won't want to miss that."

A fist hit my arm. "Now Boo, you're not trying to get rid of me are you? We have much to discuss."

"No, I don't think we do."

"First we'll be talking about the recent title match between Hulk Hogan and Ric Flair. I personally think the Hulkster got lucky. The next time they meet, the Nature Boy will slap on the figure-four leglock and regain his belt. Your thoughts?"

"I think you're a moron."

"Hmpf. I guess *somebody* hasn't been keeping up with recent events in the world of wrestling. No matter, we can return to that later. First, though, we should review the topics we'll be discussing on our trip. We'll start with another installment of 'who's hotter.' Today's contestants are Sharon Stone and Michelle Pfeiffer. I brought pictures to consult during our debate. After that we'll discuss foods that taste good with ketchup *and* mustard, but not just one or the other. Then we can talk about …"

As Kenny continued rambling, my eyes slid open to gaze at the city rec softball field at Sawyer Snell Park across the street. Seconds later I noticed a car pull into view from the far side of the park. The driver stopped behind a cluster of trees a couple hundred feet away and killed the headlights. My first thought was that it might be Sam and Eileen wanting to say goodbye without an audience. But the vehicle, from what I could discern through the darkness, distance, and trees, didn't look like Eileen's Camry.

After a few minutes, someone got out of the car and remained behind the trees near the softball field. The headlights then flipped on and the car headed back to the far entrance of the park. Before it disappeared I got a decent view of its silhouette, which looked to me like a Pinto. Moments later, a figure emerged from the shadows and jogged across the street toward the bus. As this person neared, I recognized the stride as that of my roommate.

Chapter 8

The Giants dropped three out of four to Cheyenne. I started the Saturday afternoon game and lasted only four innings. Couldn't get any heat on my fastball again and the slider kept veering out of the strike zone. The loss evened my record at 5-5.

On Monday we traveled to Colorado Springs to start a four-game series against the Pikemen. Sam pitched the first game and had little trouble subduing our last-place opponents. The home team rediscovered their bats against Clyde the next night and we fell 11 to 4. Then we lost game three in ten innings. Before the series finale on Thursday, I received a summons for something I had successfully avoided all season. I didn't want to do it, but escape was unavoidable. Chip Sandquist, the voice of the Giants, wanted to interview me during his pregame show. *Crud.*

I took a seat next to Chip in the cramped broadcast booth. He was a pudgy man who always wore a light colored button-down shirt with sweat stains in the usual spots. I'd heard that up until a couple years ago he'd worn a toupee. Having abandoned the rug, his smooth pate now gleamed forth in all its shiny glory. After standing a microphone in front of me, he flipped a switch and turned a knob.

"Welcome Giants fans to the pregame show. Tonight we wrap up a four-game set against Colorado Springs. Lincoln will be looking to even the series after dropping two of the first three to the Pikemen. And toeing the rubber for your Giants will be right-hander Brian Carter, our guest tonight. Brian, thank you for joining us."

"Uh, sure. Thanks for having me." My armpits dampened, much like Chip's, as I imagined all the people who were now listening to my voice.

"Since this is your first year with the Giants, many fans might not know much about you. Where did you pitch in college?"

"UNK."

Chip frowned and rotated his hand in circle. "And that is the University of ..."

"Nebraska-Kearney." I already felt foolish.

"Are you a native Nebraskan?" He knew the answer.

"Yes. I was born in North Platte. Grew up there too."

Chip continued by asking about my family, my previous experience in the minors, and my impressions of Lincoln. He then switched gears. "Brian, baseball players are known for their superstitions and pregame rituals. Some of your teammates sure have some interesting ones, as we've learned on this show." He raised his brows and shook his head. "Is there anything special that you do before a start?"

Chip had warned me not to mention anything lurid or illegal. He'd already earned reprimands for allowing Fender to discuss his amorous conquests in the equipment shed, and for when Weed told our fans that a nice doobie helps him relax before a game. "Not really," I said. "I'll sometimes read a passage from *Ball Four* before a start, but that's about it." Fans didn't need to know about my Jolt Cola fix.

"A true classic," he said with a grin. "I love Bouton. So what has been the highlight of this season for you?"

"Well, that has to be my start against Colorado Springs on July third. It felt really good to shut them down and keep our winning streak going."

"That was truly a dominating performance." He nodded. "And that winning streak you mentioned propelled Lincoln into first place in the Western Division. But the team has hit a rocky patch on this current road trip, dropping five of its last seven to fall a game and a half behind Pierre. Meanwhile, Cheyenne is right on your heels for second place. Looks like this is shaping up to be quite a battle down the stretch. How do you assess the team's chances to make the playoffs?"

"I think we're looking good. We've got a lineup that can score runs. Good gloves in the field. And we've got the best pitcher in the league."

He reviewed a stats sheet. "You, of course, are referring to Sam Judge, who boasts a perfect 11-0 record so far. He needs only four more wins and 31 more strikeouts to set the club records for a single season. And there are still six weeks left to play."

"He's having quite a year."

"For our fans who don't know, Sam is your roommate, right?"

"Yeah, that's right."

The corners of his mouth curled into a Grinch-like expression. "So, are there any stories about Sam you'd like to share?"

My muscles tensed at the unexpected question. "Uh …" I scrambled to come up with something to break the silence. "Well, he snores really loud."

"He snores, huh," Chip said, rolling his eyes. "How about pranks? Does Sam ever hit you or the other guys with some zingers?"

"No. That would be more Kenny's style."

"Uh-huh. I bet our female fans would like to know about Sam's dating life. Does he have a girlfriend?"

Why did you have to go there? "Oh yes. Her name is Eileen Palmer. Great girl." I wondered if I should be talking about her on the air.

"Ahh, I see. So what can you tell us about Eileen? Are they serious?"

"Yeah, sure. Maybe. Been dating for eight months." Waves of nervousness crept up to my neck, compelling me to talk faster. "Always together, those two. She's a lot of fun to be around. Great sense of humor. You know she plays softball for Nebraska? Hit .367 last season. Nine home runs. Forty-three RBIs. And she's a junior so she'll be back next year." *Why won't my mouth stop running?* "Wish she played for the Giants, you know. We could use a hitter like that. She could bat third. Yes sir." A couple chuckles escaped from my burning face. "Wonder if the league would let us have a girl on the team. I think they'd have to, 'cause she's so good, you know. And—"

"Well, okay then," Chip interrupted. "I think we get it. Eileen's a good ballplayer. And it sounds like she and Sam make a good pair. Sorry ladies, Sam Judge is taken." He paused. "Well, we should probably let our guest get ready for his start tonight. Brian Carter, thank you for joining us."

"You're welcome, Chip. My pleasure."

Still shaken by the interview, I didn't think much about my impending start. That proved to be helpful. My pitches stayed low in the strike zone. The velocity on my fastball still wasn't great, but I could place it where I wanted. "Location, location, location," as Skip would say. I was still on the mound in the eighth—the first time that had happened since my July 3rd start. But we trailed 3-2 and the home team had a man on with a man out when Angley pulled me. Fortunately, Weed retired the side with no further damage and Matt knocked home two runs in the ninth to give the Giants the win.

The team boarded the bus for an all-night ride back to Lincoln. Since Kenny didn't sit next to me, I slept for pretty much the entire nine-hour trip. After arriving at Hornsby's, I grabbed the *Lincoln Star* to read about our game: *"Though he didn't figure in the decision, starter Brian Carter delivered a workmanlike performance, surrendering only seven hits and three runs in 7 1/3 innings."*

Sam headed straight up to our room, where he remained until lunch. He hadn't said much to me since leaving Colorado, and he seemed annoyed as we ate our sandwiches in Hornsby's kitchen. "Something bothering you?" I asked, after the professor went outside to water his flowers.

He looked up at me, his face hardening into a glare. "Yeah Brian, there is."

My stomach tightened. "What's up, man?"

"That radio show you did … you talk too much."

My fears were confirmed. "Sam, I'm sorry. I'm not used to being on the air. I didn't know what to say."

His eyes remained on me and then slid over to the window.

"I don't want to cause any trouble for you and Eileen. Is she pissed at me?"

After making me wait a few moments, he shook his head once and grunted.

"I'm sorry. Nobody listens to that stupid show, do they? Is anybody bothering you or her about what I said?"

"No Brian. Forget about it." He set his plate in the sink and went upstairs.

It took a while before I had the energy to move from the kitchen table. Finally, I skulked up to our room and asked if he was ready to go to Bible study. His face remained concealed behind the *Baseball Weekly* he was reading. "Nah, I'm not going." The paper didn't move.

Not asking why, I left.

Our study group was now meeting in the stands at the ballpark. The sprinklers watering the freshly cut grass sounded like salt shakers. The light wind was just strong enough to flip the pages of my Bible if I didn't hold them down. Only three of us attended this time. Brad had stopped coming about a month ago. Randal also did not show up. As with Sam, this was his first absence. When Vince asked about them, I said I didn't know why they weren't there. For Randal that was the truth. For Sam, I had an idea why he didn't come, but I kept it to myself. So it was just me, Vince, and Bobby Evans who learned about David moving the Ark of the Covenant to Jerusalem.

A little before 2:00 p.m., our teammates started filing into the ballpark for practice. When Vince, Bobby, and I entered the locker room, Fender asked why we had wasted such a beautiful afternoon on a Bible study. Vince tapped his leather NIV and replied, "This book changes lives. The message within is mighty and powerful. It can really move people."

Fender scrunched his forehead. "Mighty and powerful with the ability to move people. That sounds just like one of Kenny's farts."

Kenny of course responded with a juvenile comment, which then set off a ribald free-for-all. Angley, however, sobered everybody up in a hurry when he passed through the door and asked Clyde to step into his office. Though we weren't great friends, I thought Clyde Eisenberg was a decent guy. We'd both been starters all season, and a solidarity had formed among us guys in the rotation. Since he'd had some rough outings recently, I feared the worst for him.

Clyde was still in the manager's office when Tony started shooing us onto the field. A few minutes into our stretches, Angley appeared at the gate near the dugout. His expression revealed no clues about our teammate's fate. My concerns for Clyde immediately disappeared when Skip looked over at me and barked, "Carter!"

Stunned, I rose to my feet and plodded toward the gate. I felt like a dead man walking. As I passed through my teammates sitting in the grass below, my eyes caught Kenny's paling face. "Oh no," he said. "Not Boo."

A beefy arm then draped over my shoulders, taking me by surprise. Vince walked beside me. "I'm praying for you, buddy. I'll be praying the whole time you're in there."

"Thanks." His words helped, but didn't change the fact that I was likely heading to my own execution.

Angley didn't say anything as we passed through the clubhouse toward his office. Clyde sat at his locker with his back to me, shoving his stuff into a gym bag. My intestines knotted. One thought echoed through my head. *Now what am I going to do?*

"Have a seat," Angley said, pulling the door closed behind us. I dropped into a hard chair as he moved around his beat-up wooden desk and sat down. Pictures of past Giants teams hung askew on the walls of the tiny room. Papers, files, and notebooks, strewn and stacked, covered nearly every inch of his desktop. A stained coffee pot perched atop the file cabinet in the corner. The stench of tobacco and caffeine penetrated my sinuses.

With eyes lowered, Angley removed his cap and slid a hand over his stubbly bald head. A heavy sigh escaped. "Carter, management is making some changes. They decided to release Eisenberg and you."

A wave of tears built up behind my eyes. Determined not to embarrass myself, I tensed my face to keep them in.

"They found a couple of kids just outta high school to take your spots ... but one of them wouldn't sign. At the last minute, he got a deal from the Padres." Skip fixed a hard stare on me. "So you're staying, for now."

My ears heard the words, but my body remained clenched. "Okay," was what I first squeezed out. And then I followed with something that was supposed to stay in my head. "Why me instead of Clyde?"

Angley looked surprised at my question. That made two of us. "You and Eisenberg got about the same numbers this season," he said. "But he's twenty-six, a year older than you. And the new guy we signed is a lefty, just like him. We'd rather not have three southpaws in the rotation, so that's why he goes and you stay."

I nodded. The haggard expression on the old man's face matched how I felt. With an exasperated exhale, he dropped the palms of his hands onto his desk. "See, the suits have watched the team slide in the standings and they're gettin' nervous. They see a couple guys who've had some rough outings lately, and they want to get rid of 'em."

"Oh."

"Your last start was a good one, but we need better consistency. Think you can do that?"

"Yeah. Things felt better last night."

"Good. I thought so. You and Vince still working on your mechanics before practice?"

"Uh, we haven't done that as much lately." I didn't tell him that Vince had wanted to keep helping me, but I got tired of the extra practice time. "We'll start up again though."

"Might be a good idea. Me and Coach Littel got a lot of players to work with, so the more you boys can help each other out, the better."

"Right."

He nodded and looked away for a moment. "Carter, don't take this personal. The suits here don't understand how things work." He lowered his voice. "Neither of 'em lasted more than a month as pro ballplayers. They can't see that seasons have rhythms. We drop a game or two and they want to stick their fingers in the pie and start messing things up." He snorted with contempt. "This isn't about you, so much. Just go out and pitch the way I know you can. You'll be alright."

"Thanks, Skip. I'll get the job done."

"You better. I stuck my neck out for you." He flashed a quick grin. "And I'm too old to deal with putting that cowboy in my starting rotation."

I smiled as my eyes found a small black and white picture of Skip and Ted Williams on the wall behind him. It reminded me of Hornsby's words about Angley's past frustrations in baseball. A spark of determination ignited. "We'll get back on track. The team will start playing better."

"Good." His stare remained on me. "Say Carter, what's the deal with this 'Boo' thing?"

"Oh, uh, that's something the guys started calling me earlier in the season."

"Hmpf … that's strange, Carter."

"Yes sir. Very strange."

"Alright, let's get out there. You can skip shagging flies today. Head to the bullpen. I want to watch you throw a few."

That evening, Weed, Fender, Kenny, and I drove to the university's East Campus to get some ice cream at the Dairy Store and go bowling at the Student Union. With recent events still rattling my nerves, I was glad to go knock down some pins. I still wondered about Sam and if things were really okay between us. When I left Hornsby's, he was getting dressed and ready to go out. He didn't say where he was going and I didn't ask.

The next day was Saturday. The St. Joseph Bandits came to town. Sam dominated, tossing an efficient, complete game victory. Afterwards, I overheard him tell Randal that he and Eileen were going out right after the game. So I left the ballpark without him.

Sunday afternoon marked the debut of Ted Pottebaum, Clyde's replacement. A beanpole just out of high school, the new guy threw six strong innings, baffling hitters with his sinker. Lincoln prevailed 6-2 to sweep the two-game series against the Bandits.

Sam had been in a better mood before the game. He'd even joined some of the guys for their pregame ritual of flipping the ball to each other with trick motions. While watching Ted pitch during the game, he cracked some jokes about the kid's herky-jerky delivery. Things seemed to be getting back to normal.

Sam told me he didn't need a ride home, so I again left the ballpark without him. For supper, I ate tacos with Hornsby. Just as we finished the dishes, the phone rang. Eileen wanted me to come over to her apartment. Without thinking, I told her I was on my way. On the drive over, my head was like one of those ball-popper toys that children push around. I had figured that Eileen was out with Sam. Now, I didn't know what to think.

Eileen opened the door and squinted at me through puffy eyes. She wore no makeup and her scraggly hair was pulled back in an off-center ponytail. Without a word, she turned and sank into a papasan in the living room. I found a spot on the sofa.

Wearing red Husker sweatpants and an oversized Opus T-shirt, she raised her knees close to her chest. "So, you've probably heard."

"No, I haven't heard anything."

"Really?" Her distressed eyes studied me. "I figured he would've been overjoyed to tell everybody his big news."

"Sam? He didn't say much about anything today."

She scoffed. "Well … he broke up with me last night."

"Eileen, I'm sorry." Despite all my past longings, I didn't want to see her miserable like this.

"He had me drive him to Valentino's so I wouldn't make a scene." She grabbed a Kleenex and dabbed her eyes. A collection of wadded tissues covered a nearby end table. Some of them had dropped to the carpet below, where an empty carton of Blue Bunny hot fudge sundae lay on its side.

"He said you two were going out last night, but I didn't know he was planning to break up with you."

"Really? He didn't say anything?"

I shook my head. "Nothing."

"So you don't know about her?"

"Her?"

"His new girlfriend." Her voice rose. "You're telling me you don't know anything about her?"

"Oh, uh …" Perspiration collected in the creases of my palms and a guilty look must have covered my face.

"That's what I thought," she said with a glare. "So how long has he been seeing her?"

"I don't know."

"What do you mean you don't know? Don't do this to me, Boo. I've been lied to enough lately."

"Really, I didn't know he was seeing her."

"But you've met her?"

I hesitated as my eyes darted away.

"I knew it!" She slammed her fist on the end table. "All you guys have been playing me for a fool."

"No, Eileen. It's not like that." I wiped my palms on my jeans. "Yes, I met her. Once. She was waiting for Sam after a game. We were walking out of the clubhouse when she introduced herself."

"When was that?"

"Fourth of July." I glanced at the issues of *Sports Illustrated* and *Cosmopolitan* lying on the coffee table.

Wheels turned in her head. "Almost a month ago. When did they start getting together? Probably that night."

"I don't know. He started acting a little different a couple weeks later. Not wanting rides from me as much. Not showing up at JK's. So maybe sometime around then."

"Great."

"Eileen, I didn't know he was seeing her. Yes, I *suspected* something was going on, but he didn't tell me anything. And I never saw them together."

"Really?" An inquisitive look replaced some of the pain in her eyes.

"Well … that night he threw the perfect game, I saw her in the stands. But that's the only other time I've seen her."

She eyed me for a few moments and then shook her head. A tear rolled down her cheek. I wanted to say something, but no words came. A minute or two passed before she spoke. "This is just like what happened to me in high school." Her quivering face strained against a building wave of emotion. "Why wasn't I enough for him?"

My heart broke. "Sam is hard to understand. I don't know what's going through his head."

"I bet she's really pretty." Her eyes fell on me, expecting an answer.

Not as pretty as you. "Enh." I shrugged. "I don't know about that."

She sniffled. "You know she is, Boo. Just say it."

"She's not my type."

Another crumpled tissue joined the others on the floor. "I've been trying to figure out why he dumped me. Did I say something? Did he want more space? But I bet it's all physical, right? That's the way it is with all you guys. I bet she's such a hot babe he can't keep his hands off her … and I'm just a big sow."

"Eileen, no. You're—"

"You said so yourself." Her words sliced through the air.

"What? I never said that."

"Yes you did. When we met at The Watering Hole you said I was fat."

The roof crashed down on me. "No! I didn't say that. I ... I think you're—"

"It doesn't matter," she interrupted. "He's made it clear that I'm not what he wants. I should've seen it coming. He drifted away from me this summer ... it's just, I was so into him. I couldn't stand to think that he didn't feel the same about me." The dam broke.

"Eileen, he cared about you." That was all I could say as she continued sobbing.

Time crawled by while I sat helplessly with no remedy for the hurt. She eventually regained her composure and pulled up the bottom of her shirt to wipe her face. "No, he didn't," she said with a sigh. "Oh well. That's life, right?"

I had no reply.

More time passed before she spoke again. "Well, I guess you've seen enough of how pathetic I am."

I could've said a lot of things. *Let's get a pizza ... go out for a beer ... watch a movie.* But my nerves failed me again. I said nothing. Not a word.

She looked at me with a pained smile. "Thanks for coming over. Sorry I grilled you." She got up and walked to the door.

I followed her. "It's okay."

Her wounded blue eyes gazed up at mine. "It's safe to say I won't be going to any more Giants games this year. So I probably won't see you much anymore."

"Oh." I begged my mouth to say something more, just one lousy sentence to let her know I cared about her. But of course, nothing followed.

"Goodbye, Boo."

A light rain fell as I drove home. At some point, I punched the passenger seat. Then came a honking horn, screeching tires, headlights, and a jarring stop. Looking ahead through the steam, I saw a telephone pole rising from the hood of my car.

"So you were wearin' a seatbelt?" Fender asked.

"Yeah."

"But the car's totaled?"

"Yep."

"It was a piece of crap anyway." He spotted a girl at the bar and tipped his Stetson.

"But don't worry about me," I said. "I'm not hurt."

He flipped his hand in a *"who cares"* gesture.

"The real question is," Weed said, "who's gonna be carting you around now?"

"Randal gave me a ride today. I'm sort of on his way to Sherman."

"Don't get used to it," Randal said, raising a glass to his lips.

Weed snickered. "You could ride with Sam and his new honey."

"Yeah right," I said. "He took off with her right after the game. Might not see much of him the rest of the season."

"Eileen took it pretty bad, huh?" Kenny asked.

"You could say that."

Fender returned his attention to the table. "So you was comin' back from her place last night when you wrecked your car?"

"Yeah, like I told you. She thought I knew something about when Sam and Danika started getting together."

"Did you comfort Blondie in her distress?" A grin cut across his face.

I glowered at him. "No, we just talked."

"Ah, I see what happened," Weed said. "You tried to get it on with Sam's ex, and she shot you down. You were so frustrated, you drove your car into a telephone pole on the way home." He and Fender high-fived.

"Shut up, pothead."

The conversation thankfully moved to another topic. A while later, Weed and Fender went over to the pool tables to shoot a game.

"Do you know what Cathy and Eileen are doing tonight?" I asked Randal.

He shook his head. "Nope. Eileen called before the game and asked Cathy if she wanted to do something. That's all I know. Guess she didn't want to be home alone tonight."

"Yeah." My uselessness at Eileen's replayed in my head. I felt worse about that than the loss of my Taurus.

"Eileen's a tough girl," Kenny said. "She'll be alright."

Moments later I glanced up at a sight that nearly knocked me from my chair. Sam and Danika approached. "Gentlemen," he said. "And I use that term loosely." They claimed the chairs that Weed and Fender had vacated. "This is Danika," Sam announced. "And this is Randal, Kenny, and Brian." He pointed to us in succession.

During the greetings, she acted like we'd never met. Her gaze fell on me for just an instant before moving on. While Sam grabbed a pitcher and filled their glasses, I couldn't help gawking at the purple top that hugged her torso.

"Did you see the game tonight?" Randal asked her.

"Nope." As she shook her head, two silver ankh earrings swung back and forth below her tossed-to-the-side updo. "Didn't make it."

"Didn't miss much," he said. "We were terrible."

"Is LaVelle pretty worried?" Kenny asked Randal.

"Yeah, he is. After that pounding St. Cloud laid on him tonight, his numbers aren't much better than Clyde's." He and Kenny then started a conversation about the Giants pitching situation. They talked as if Sam and Danika weren't there. Though I understood why, it seemed a bit rude to me. The return of Weed and Fender actually came as a welcome tension-breaker.

"Well, howdy howdy," Fender said, his eyes feasting on the visual treat that was Danika. "I didn't know y'all were gonna show up here tonight." He and Weed both eyed her like a kid peering through a candy store window.

After the introductions, Fender and Weed pulled up chairs and started chattering away. With every quip and comment, they tried to outdo each other at impressing Sam's guest. She barely paid them any attention. Randal and Kenny, meanwhile, left to shoot a game of pool.

When Sam emptied his glass, he asked, "We gettin' another pitcher?"

"Sure are," Fender said.

"Actually babe," Danika said to Sam in a soft voice, "isn't it about time to go?" She pursed her lips and kissed his cheek.

He sprang to his feet. "Alright boys," he said to us, "we gotta take off. See ya tomorrow." Holding hands, they disappeared out the front entrance.

Chapter 9

I woke up just before 9:00 Tuesday morning. Sunlight streamed around the beige curtains to cast a pale light into the room. Sam lay sprawled across his bed snoring like a freight train. I had no idea when he'd stumbled in the night before. With the professor out to breakfast with former colleagues, I went downstairs to a quiet house. A pungent aroma emanated from the nearly empty coffee pot in the kitchen. After a bowl of Rice Krispies, the only cereal in Hornsby's bran-heavy pantry I found edible, I decided to make a call.

Sitting in the stuffed armchair in the den, I punched the digits from my calling card into the phone and dialed the number. A familiar voice said hello.

"Hi. Got a minute?"

"Yes. I don't have to clean the Brinkmeyer's place for another hour."

"Alright."

"Everything okay?"

"Yeah, you know. Team's in second place."

"I saw that in the paper. You're pitching tonight, right?"

"Yeah. Against St. Cloud."

"Are you ready?"

"I think so. Tony's got a good scouting report on them."

The line went silent for a few moments. "So what's wrong, Brian?"

"Nothing. Why do you think something's wrong?"

"Brian."

"Alright … I got in a car accident."

"Oh no. Are you okay?"

"I'm fine, Mom. But the car's totaled."

"Oh dear. What happened?"

"It was raining. I went through an intersection and this car almost hits me. I swerved, the tires skidded, and I hit a telephone pole." I didn't mention that I initiated that sequence of events by driving through a stop sign.

"Oh no. Are you sure you're okay?"

"Yes. I had my seatbelt on."

"Thank heavens ... but your Taurus is completely wrecked?"

"Yeah."

"How are you going to get to your games? Sam still doesn't have a car, does he?"

"No."

During the following pause, my eyes examined the large antique globe across the room. I hoped she would be the next to speak.

"Do you want the Buick?"

"Is anybody using it?"

"No, your brother is still driving his pickup."

"And you and Dad don't need it?"

"No, our cars are fine. The old Buick is just taking up space in the shed."

"Think it still runs?"

"Sure. Your dad and Mark worked on it last spring. It started okay then."

"That's good."

"Guess we would need to get it out there to you." The sound of a faucet running came though the phone. For a moment I was back in the house where I grew up.

"Yeah."

"Well ..." I knew she was walking over to the Campbell's Soup calendar on the kitchen wall. "There's nothing going on Friday. We could bring it out to you then. Too bad you won't be pitching that night."

"Yeah. After tonight my next start won't be until Sunday in Columbia. Friday's fine. You guys wouldn't have to stay for the game."

"Okay. I'll talk to your dad. Mark might want to come out there too."

"Alright. Hey, I really appreciate this. There's only about a month left in the season. I'll bring your car back then."

"You can keep it longer than that. It's been years since anyone's driven it regularly. Somebody might as well be getting some use out of it. The poor thing."

"Thanks."

"So everything else is going okay?"

"Sure." I didn't want to tell her about my conversation in Angley's office a few days ago.

"That's good. Hope all goes well for you tonight."

"Thanks."

"We'll be listening."

My start at Sherman did in fact go well that night. The slider had a nasty break and my fastball, though still lacking velocity, moved enough to keep batters from making solid contact. We led 4-1 heading into the seventh. I felt like I had a shot at my first complete game. Then the umpire started squeezing the strike zone. A couple walks put two on with two out. When the next guy hit a ground ball to third, I thought the inning was over. But Matt muffed it to load the bases.

Angley came out to the mound and asked if I could get the next guy. I assured him I could. Sarge nodded in agreement. The man at the plate was St. Cloud's designated hitter, a big Buddha-shaped redneck who had already twice struck out. He had some power, but his average lingered in the .230s, and he often chased crap.

Two sliders and a changeup, none of them in the strike zone, put him in a 1-2 hole. Sarge flashed the sign for another slider, low and away. I checked the runner at third and moved my fingers into the appropriate grip. When my arm whipped around to send the ball toward the catcher's mitt, something stabbed my elbow. The twinge caused me to release a fraction of a second too soon. The pitch floated languidly over the heart of the plate, about waist high.

Fans often describe the resonant crack of a wooden bat crushing a baseball as beautiful. I myself have shared those sentiments on occasion, like when Vince unloads on a hanging curve. But this time, the sound was not so beautiful. It actually made me a little sick. Angley had already arrived at the mound by the time the ball finally landed somewhere in the next county.

As I approached the dugout, our loyal fans consoled me with a chorus of boos.

Wednesday night the Bismarck Hawks came to town and pinned another defeat on the Giants—our third in a row. The next morning Kenny called and asked if Sam and I wanted to come over and hang out. His host family had gone on vacation, so he had the house to himself. I said I'd be over if I could get a ride. When I went upstairs to ask Sam if he wanted to go, his head remained buried under his pillow. I figured he wouldn't be interested in going anywhere before noon.

Kenny had also invited Randal, so I caught a ride with him. Kenny's hosts, the Bush family, lived in a split-level in northwest Lincoln. After answering the door in a tank top undershirt and ragged Colorado Buffaloes knee-length shorts, Kenny led us to one of the bedrooms, where he sat in front of a computer. "You guys have got to see this."

"You playing a game?" I asked, though nothing on the screen looked familiar to me.

"Nah, I'm checking out the Internet."

"The what?"

"The Internet. You do know what that is, don't you?"

"Yes, I know what the Internet is." I actually didn't.

"It's pretty useless from what I've heard," Randal said, pulling up a chair next to Kenny. "Doesn't it take about ten minutes to get anything to appear on the screen?"

"No," Kenny said. "You just need a little patience."

"Do the Bushes know you're using their computer?" I asked, sitting on the bed.

"Oh, they won't mind. This is Clark's machine. Geeky kid, but he can be kinda cool sometimes. He gave me his password and showed me how to log on to this Mosaic thing."

"I see." Posters of *Weird Science*, *Krull*, and *Monty Python and the Holy Grail* graced the dark blue walls of Clark's room. A collection of *Star Wars* action figures and other sci-fi paraphernalia cluttered the tops of his dresser and nightstands. Trophies from school science competitions stood proudly on mounted shelves.

"And the Bushes won't be back for three days," Kenny said.

"That's about how long it will take this thing to load," Randal quipped, clasping his hands behind his head.

"So what are you trying to do?" I asked Kenny.

"Tryin' to find out if there's anything about the Giants on here."

"The Internet has baseball stuff?" The screen seemed to be frozen.

"It has stuff about everything." Kenny turned his spiky head to me. "It's really cool. Clark showed me this astronomy site that has a 3-D model of the solar system. You can click on the planets and see what they're made of and how far they are from Earth."

"Sweet."

"Yeah, so I'm thinkin' there may be baseball info on here. Like that grand slam you gave up the other night. We could maybe find out if it set any distance records."

"Shut up."

A grin spread across his face. "Seriously, did you see where that thing landed? I bet it cleared the railroad tracks by twenty feet."

"At least," Randal agreed. "The air traffic controllers probably saw it on their radar screens." He snickered. "But actually, that wasn't the longest home run hit at Sherman Field. Back in the '50s, Dick Stuart jacked a tater that landed in a railcar headed to Chicago. So that ball would have traveled five-hundred miles or so. The one Boo gave up couldn't have gone quite that far on the fly. But I'm sure it was close."

The Web page finished loading. "Check it out," Kenny said, pointing at the screen. Rows of Lincoln Giants statistics appeared before us. Sam's numbers, of course, were at the top of the pitchers' section. My totals were several rows below.

"That's it?" I said. "Just statistics. We can get these at the ballpark. This is supposed to be progress? Waiting all morning for numbers we already have."

Ignoring me, Kenny leaned closer to the screen. "These aren't up to date here. They got me at .239. I'm hitting .242 now."

Randal scanned the stats with a grim expression. His batting average had plummeted to .247, forty points lower than when he'd hurt his hamstring six weeks ago. "Yeah, this is boring," he said. "Let's check out something else."

Kenny clicked the mouse and typed something into a bar that appeared. Another page began a slow crawl into view, but it contained nothing of interest. After checking a few more sites (a process that took several minutes), we concluded that the Internet didn't have much to say about the Giants or any of the other teams in the Central States League. Kenny then typed Angley's name and clicked the mouse. He eventually found a brief biography of Skip on a "Minor League Managers" website.

"Check this out," Kenny said. "Skip's first year with Lincoln was 1974. Before that he managed a team in Springfield, Missouri."

"Isn't that where the Simpsons live?" I asked.

"Aye Carumba," Kenny replied, scrolling and reading. "Look at all the places Skip's been. Pitching coach for the Lancaster Red Roses … oh, no way. From 1949 to 1951 Don Angley pitched for the Boston Red Sox. I didn't know he was in The Show."

"Really?" Randal asked in disbelief. "Geez Kenneth, the man is only your manager." He turned to me. "Did you know?"

"Yeah. The professor told Sam and me."

"Let's see if we can find out how the old man did for the Sox," Kenny said. After more clicking and waiting, he found a page chronicling the history of the Boston Red Sox. He read aloud, "As the 1949 season entered the final weekend, the Red Sox held a slim lead over the Yankees. Boston needed just one victory in its final two games at Yankee Stadium to win the pennant. New York, however, prevailed in both contests to claim the American League crown."

"That sucks," Randal said. "Wonder if Skip pitched in either of those games."

"Don't know. It doesn't say."

"I could check Hornsby's baseball books," I said.

Kenny searched for a few more minutes before giving up. "Hey, think they got any pictures of girls on here?"

Randal frowned. "No. Nobody's going to waste their time putting stuff like that on the Internet."

"Oh cool." Kenny's eyes lit up as he clicked a link. "Let's see what 'Naughty Vixens' is all about."

The three of us watched as the top of a woman's head appeared on the screen. Then her forehead; then her eyes; then her nose. When her puckered lips appeared, Randal sprang from his chair. "I gotta make a call," he said, leaving the room.

"What's his problem?" Kenny asked.

"He *does* have a wife and a daughter," I replied.

"So what's your point?" He leaned closer to the screen as the woman's neck came into view. "Alright, now we're gettin' somewhere."

A rectangular box with a small phone icon suddenly appeared in the middle of the screen: "You have been disconnected from the Internet. Would you like to reconnect?"

From another part of the house, Randal yelled, "Hey, what's with all this static and beeping on the telephone?"

"Damn it," Kenny exclaimed. "I forgot to tell you guys we can't pick up the phone when we're on this thing."

That night, Sam tossed another complete game victory to end our losing streak. He plowed through the Bismarck hitters so fast that the game was finished in just under two hours. Friday morning my parents drove in from North Platte. My brother Mark followed in the old Buick that would be my new set of wheels. We all went out for lunch at King's Drive In, a 1950s-style restaurant on South Street.

"Did you invite Sam to join us?" Mom asked as we scanned our menus.

"Yeah, I asked him. He's with his new girlfriend. They spend a lot of time together."

"He's doing really well, isn't he? Chip Sandquist said last night that he'll probably be pitching in the majors next year."

"Could be. At least Triple-A I'd think."

"Are you still working with your first baseman before practice?" Dad asked.

"Yeah, Vince and I still get together."

"So will you need to leave soon?" Mom asked, checking her watch.

"No, we're not meeting today."

"Why not?" Dad asked.

I didn't want the conversation to head in this direction. "Tweaked my elbow the other night. Our trainer wants me to rest it." They both looked concerned. "I'll be fine for my start on Sunday."

"So that explains it," Mark said. He sat next to me in the booth, his eyes roaming the restaurant.

"Explains what?"

"Your pitching."

"What about it?"

"It's been a month since your last win. Must be the elbow."

"My elbow has been fine all season. Just felt a twinge at the end of my last start."

"Then what's the problem?" A condescending look spread from his high forehead to his stubbly chin.

"There hasn't been a problem, Mark."

"Ok*aay*. You just decided on your own to take something off the fastball so hitters can knock you around the park. Good move. Scouts just love ERAs over 5.00."

"Mark." Dad frowned at him as the blood in my veins heated.

"I'm just pointing out facts," Mark said. "If he wants to keep his little pipedream alive, he needs to get it together. He's twenty-five and fast running out of shelf life."

A waitress came over to take our order, but the tension returned after she'd left.

"Brian, you've done very well this year," Mom said, breaking the silence. "You've been in the starting rotation all season and won several games." Dad nodded in agreement.

"Thanks," I mumbled, glancing out the window.

"Playing professional baseball is a big accomplishment," she continued. "And we're all proud of you, right Mark?"

"Yep," he said, eying a young waitress a few booths away.

Dad then steered the conversation to the upcoming Husker football season and we ate our lunch in relative peace. Afterwards, while our parents got in line to pay the bill, Mark and I went out to the parking lot.

"Try not to wreck it," he said as we neared the Buick, its dull brown paint soaking in the midday sun.

"I won't wreck it."

"I'm just sayin'. I put a lot of hours into this car and I don't want you to mess it up."

I glared at him. "Dad put a lot of hours into this car and you don't even drive it. You never liked the Electra."

He snorted. "Yeah, it's a heap. But it's the Carter family heap. Been in the family since the Civil War. It deserves a proper fate when the time comes. So don't you go wrapping it around any telephone poles." He held out the keys.

"Fine." I snatched the ring from his hand. "Does it still belch up a cloud of smoke when you start it?"

"Of course. And the oil light kept flickering on the drive here, so you're gonna want to keep an eye on that. There's a case of Quaker State in the trunk."

"Great … thanks."

He tapped the front wheel with his toe. "You got work after the season?"

"Haven't thought about it." I peered through the driver's side window at the tear in the front seat.

"Season's over in a month, Brian."

"We got the playoffs after that."

"Not the way you guys have been playing. If you fall out of second place, there won't be any playoffs. Judge can't pitch your games, you know."

"Too bad, huh."

His fingertips brushed across the hood. The bulging midsection of his tall frame flowed over the front waist of his Wranglers. "You might think about starting at the rail yard this fall. Nellie's retiring in October. We could get you on full time."

"Can't take a full-time position," I said. "I'll be pitching next year."

He squinted at me the same way he'd been doing since we were kids. "I know it's hard to let it go, but you've got to wake up someday. Man, I spent six years in the minors. I know what it's like. Crappy food. Crappy motels. No money. No appreciation. But I was chasin' the dream. Well, one day I'm layin' in my bed in some flea's nest motel in Fargo and I realized something. The dream ain't gonna happen for me. Not ever. I was twenty-six. And I had better numbers then than you do now."

I drifted to the front of the car, eyeing its many imperfections. "I had some good starts this year. Real shutdowns. I just need to find a consistent release point for my slider and adjust the arm angle on my heater. I'll get the speed back. Been working on a curve too. Throw that in the mix and I could make Double-A next season."

"You've been bouncing benders in the dirt since Little League." He smirked. "Maybe if they move the mound in six feet you might get a curve over."

"We'll see."

"Brian, it was the toughest day of my life when I quit pitching. But I was smart enough to realize it wasn't in the cards for me. I coulda kept slogging it out for another year or two. Heck, I could probably toss a couple scoreless innings for the Giants tonight. But what would that prove? Tomorrow morning I'd still be a million miles from the majors. Smartest thing I did was leave baseball and take a job at Bailey Yard."

My eyes lingered on a rust spot above the right front tire.

"I know staying in North Platte wasn't something either of us dreamed of," he continued, "but you can make good money at the yard. Yes it's hard work, but you'll be bringing in way more than you are now pitching in this league."

"Yeah." I was glad I hadn't told him about almost getting cut. "I may not have much of a chance at The Show. But I'm still gettin' paid to play baseball. I kinda like that, you know. And as long as some manager is fool enough to give me the ball, I want to keep pitching."

Our parents approached. After the goodbyes, the three of them got in Dad's Dodge and started the three-hour trip back to North Platte. The Buick squeaked in protest when I opened the door. As I settled in behind the wheel, childhood smells filled my nostrils. For an instant, Mark and I were in the backseat with our gloves, riding to Little League.

That evening Ted Pottebaum made his second start for the Giants. The Hawks roughed him up, but Lincoln prevailed with a late rally. The next morning we traveled to Columbia for a weekend series against the Patriots. Rain washed out the Saturday game, so we played a doubleheader on Sunday. The Giants won the afternoon contest, 6-1. I was supposed to pitch the nightcap, but Angley skipped my spot in the rotation to give my elbow more time to rest. George Lazzari took my place and got shelled. We next traveled to Council Bluffs, where we took two of three from the Black Squirrels. Sam started the second game of the series, pitching into the eighth and notching his 14th win of the year.

The road trip marked the end of our games against the Eastern Division. The remainder of the season we would be playing teams in our own division. Lincoln was tied for second with Cheyenne, two games behind Pierre. We controlled our own destiny.

The Giants didn't play on Thursday. Angley made it a true day off by canceling practice so we could rest up for the stretch run. Around 9:30, I stumbled into the kitchen to a rare morning sight. Sam was already sitting at the table, eating breakfast and reading the paper. After I finished my cereal he asked me to drive him to the mall.

Tendrils of grey smoke escaped from under the hood as the Buick coughed to life. When I shifted into drive, the brown tank lunged forward with a thundering growl.

"Nice wheels," Sam said, rolling down his window.

"Thanks."

"Yeah, this is a beast." He slapped the outside of his door. "Sounds tough. I like it."

"I think General Patton rode in this car as his army advanced across France during World War II."

"I bet the Krauts were terrified."

"Just like those little kids." I pointed to a group of young children fleeing to their backyard as the Buick rumbled down the street.

He chuckled. "So, aren't you curious?"

"About what?"

"Why I want to go to the mall."

"A little, now that you mention it."

"Sartor Hamann."

It took a few seconds for the words to sink in. "The jewelry store?" My head jerked toward him. "Really?"

"Yep." The corners of his mouth curved.

"Engagement?"

"Yep."

"Isn't this, uh, fast?"

"We've been together long enough for me know that she's the one. Never had a girl make me feel this way before."

I considered mentioning Felicity, but decided against it. Then I thought about Eileen. "Oh."

"Yeah, Danika is like … unbelievable. Honeys like her don't come along very often. When they do, you gotta make sure they don't get away."

"Hmm." I stopped at a red light. "Think she'll say yes? I mean, is she ready for this type of commitment?"

He brushed the tops of his fingers under his chin. "Yeah, this girl knows how to commit. I can guarantee you that. Plus, I won't be askin' right away. Don't want to distract the team while we're fighting to make the playoffs."

"You told your parents yet?"

"No."

"Do they know you're with Danika, and not …"

"No, Brian." Ice accompanied his words. "I don't need any more grief from the old man. I'll tell 'em later."

I turned east onto O Street. "So where you getting the dough for this ring?"

"Might need to get creative with that." He used the front of his Metallica T-shirt to rub a smudge from his shades. "I got a hundred for a down payment. Then I'll see if my status as a sports hero can get me a deferred payment plan."

"Sports hero? You gonna tell 'em you play football for the Cornhuskers?"

"Funny. They'll know who I am. Everybody in this town does. And if they know anything about baseball, they'll know I'll be pullin' down plenty next year. So that should give me some leverage."

"Maybe we should have worn our uniforms."

"Yeah." He chuckled. "Hey, you wouldn't believe what my crazy girl suggested as a way for me to make some extra bread."

"Posing in *Playgirl*?"

I glanced over to catch a trace of levity on his face. "No, smartass. But if I did pose, that'd be their top-selling issue." He flexed his bicep.

"It'd get you some exposure too."

He shook his head. "Thing is, she's got an uncle in Omaha who's big into gambling. Likes to bet the ponies and whatever teams are playing."

"Think he bets on our games?"

"He does. And not only that, he told Danika there's this book up there that posts odds on how many runs I'll give up. You believe that? He tells her it's ten to one that I'll give up three earned runs or more in a game."

"That makes sense," I said. "It's only happened twice this year, right?"

"Something like that. So Danika gets the idea that the next time we face a pitcher we're sure to rough up, I oughta take it easy and let the other team get three runs. She'd call her uncle beforehand and have him put down some money for us. Fifty or a hundred. At those odds we'd clean up. I'd still get the win and me and her would pick up a quick five hundred. Maybe even a grand."

The Buick rolled past the stones and monuments in Wyuka Cemetery. "You're not seriously thinking about doing that, are you?"

He hesitated. "Nah. I don't want to mess up my ERA or jeopardize the perfect record. No big league team can ignore a guy who puts up sixteen or seventeen Ws against no losses. Throw in a buck-thirty ERA, and that's just too sweet for the scouts to miss."

"Right. You don't want to mess around with that. Intentionally giving up runs. Getting involved with bookies. Man, that could get out of control in a hurry."

"Yeah, it's crazy," he said. "She was probably just kiddin' around anyway."

"Hope so." A while later we reached Gateway Mall. After about an hour in the jewelry store, Sam bought an engagement ring for a girl he'd met five weeks ago. It was a nice rock—big and sparkly. A couple of the clerks said they recognized him, though I don't know how much that helped. The payment plan seemed a little out of his range. But I kept my mouth shut. Exiting the store, he seemed unconcerned about the financial obligation to which he'd just committed himself. His face beamed, much like after he'd thrown the perfect game.

That afternoon, we ate crisp meat burritos at Amigos, caught a matinee of *Forrest Gump*, and lifted weights at the Y. Then we headed home so he could get ready for his date with Danika. I spent the evening at Randal's playing Risk with the usual suspects. While the rest of us battled for supremacy in Africa, Europe, and North

America, Kenny hoarded his yellow armies in Australia and then swooped across Asia and the rest of the world.

The next day was Friday, August 12th. The day major league baseball ended. For how long, nobody knew.

Chapter 10

The Pierre Cavaliers came to town and beat us Friday night and Saturday afternoon. That evening, Randal and Cathy invited the gang to a cookout at Pioneers Park. Sam not surprisingly had other plans, so I drove alone. After wandering through a few Frisbee tossers and kite fliers, I spotted Randal across the grassy expanse at one of the black grills. When he looked up from the flame he'd just created, I raised a package of hamburger buns with one hand and a package of hot dog buns with the other.

"Good," he said. "You remembered to get potato buns."

"You know it."

"Just got this going, so it'll be a while before show time. The children are over there." He pointed to an open space where Kenny and Haleigh were playing catch with Freddy.

"Weed and Fender coming?"

"No. Weed called right before we left the house. They met a couple girls at the mall."

"The mall? Are these girls legal?"

"Dunno. Think it matters to them?"

"No. I'm sure it doesn't."

He shook his head and eyed the packages I still held. "You can set those over there." He gestured to a picnic table, where Cathy sat talking to Eileen.

I tried to suppress a gasp. "Oh, Eileen's here."

"Yeah. She and Cathy have been hanging out more since the break-up. I knew Judge wouldn't be coming, so I figured it was safe to invite her."

My throat tightened as I crept over to the table. Eileen's summer blond hair contrasted gorgeously with her tan skin. I barely made eye contact as I flipped the buns onto the table and pushed out a quick "hi" to the two of them. They returned my greeting with a passing glance and resumed their conversation. Like a shooed fly, I buzzed away.

When the burgers and hot dogs were ready, the six of us gathered around the picnic table. Our supper conversation focused mostly on the baseball strike, how long it would last and who was to blame. All of us sided with the players, of course. Cathy then asked how the strike would affect the minor leagues.

"Well," Kenny said, "people might see this as a struggle between greedy millionaires and greedy billionaires. Fans could get resentful of everybody associated with baseball. Then our attendance would fall."

"But the minor leagues are all that's left for baseball right now," Cathy said. "Wouldn't that help Giants attendance?"

"Maybe but—"

"The bottom line is," Randal interrupted, "we need to start winning. That's what will determine if people come to our games or not." He squirted a circle of ketchup onto his second burger. "Like this series against Pierre. This was a big opportunity for us to gain ground on them. With a sweep, we'd have moved back into first place. But no, we drop the first two and now we're four games back."

Unpleasant memories from that afternoon's game returned. I was the starting pitcher. The good news was my elbow didn't give me any trouble. The bad news was Pierre pounded me for ten hits and five earned runs before Angley sent me to the showers. A whine from Freddy, who'd been staring up at me, halted my mental replay of the game. I flipped a bite of hamburger to him, hoping that would send him on his way. But he devoured the offering and kept his black snout pointed at me, waiting for more.

"We lose tomorrow and get swept at home," Randal continued, "we can forget about the division. And now we're two games behind Cheyenne for second, so the Wild Card is slipping away too. Angley knows it. You see how red his face got today before the umpire ejected him?"

"We'll win tomorrow," Kenny said through a full mouth. "The big guy's going."

Eileen's expression darkened as she lowered her eyes to her food. An awkward silence blanketed the table. Cathy then took the wheel and started raving about the food, including the fruit salad Eileen had brought.

After we finished off the cupcakes Cathy had baked for dessert, Haleigh and Kenny ran off to play with Freddy again. Randal and Cathy went over to the grill to gather their stuff. So that left Eileen and me alone at the picnic table. As we started picking up the paper plates and other trash, I begged my brain to think of something clever to say. But what it came up with was, "When does fall softball start?"

"In about a month."

"Cool. You're probably ready to get back out there."

"I guess. I've been enjoying the time off though." A smile flickered and vanished.

We carried the refuse to a nearby trash barrel. I again summoned my brain to come up with something. "Wish I could hit like you." *Thanks brain.*

She crinkled her forehead. "You don't bat."

"Ah, but if I did." I raised my index finger as if making a point.

She snickered. "Heard you got a new car."

"Well, *new* isn't quite the right word."

"You know what I mean."

"Yeah, I wrecked the Taurus." I hoped she didn't know it happened while driving home from her place. "So now I've got my parents' old Buick. I know, it's a piece of—"

"Hey, it gets you around. That's the important thing." Her azure eyes gripped me.

"Yeah."

"Hey Boo … thanks for coming over when Sam broke up with me." She winced when saying his name. "I was a mess that day and I'm glad you were there for me." She placed a hand on my shoulder, sending tingling sensations shooting through my body.

"Uh, sure. I'm glad I could … uh …"

"Leenie! Leenie!" Haleigh came running over. "Come see the trick I taught Fuzzy." The little girl clutched Eileen's hand and started towing her away.

"Gotta go," Eileen said with a giggle.

Standing motionless, I took in the spectacle of her departure. *I love capri pants.*

"You really shouldn't wait much longer," said Cathy, now standing beside me.

"Huh? What?" My head jerked around.

"If you're going to ask her out, you'd better do it soon."

"What? I don't like … what makes you think I want to ask her out?"

A knowing grin appeared. "Well let's see. One clue might be how your eyes were just glued to her ass as she walked away."

"No." I looked at the ground. "I wasn't doing that. I was watching Kenny and the dog."

"Boo, I can spot these things. I've known for a long time. The way you acted around her when she was with Sam. The boys may not have noticed, but I did."

Embarrassment heated my face as I debated how vigorously to deny. "Nah, you're crazy." I continued to avoid her eyes.

"Sure I am. And you're crazy if you keep wasting time. She just told me about this guy at her church. She sounds kinda interested."

It took me a second to recover from that punch to the gut. "That's, uh, none of my concern."

"Okaay. Just trying to help." She turned to walk away. "You guys would make a cute couple."

"Cathy … does she know?"

"Don't think so."

"Think she likes me? You know, would she say yes if I asked her out?"

"One way to find out, Boo."

I was never again alone with Eileen at the park Saturday night. Didn't matter. I was nowhere near mentally ready to ask her out. But Cathy's revelation did ignite a flame of urgency inside me. This soon spread into an inferno of anxiety. I twisted in bed that night imagining who this guy was at Eileen's church. For months I'd wanted Sam to get out of the picture. Then it finally happens and this other guy shows up. My mind conjured image after image of what he might look like—a cross between Tom Cruise and one of the Baldwin brothers popped up most frequently.

A little after 3:00 a.m., Sam lumbered in and found his bed. Since he'd be starting that afternoon, he came back earlier than usual. When he wasn't pitching the next day, he rarely came home before sunrise. Bullhorn snores soon commenced, shattering my world of silent contemplation. My wide-open eyes examined the ceiling, which through the dimness reminded me of the surface of the moon. Finally, the noise and angst drove me from my bed.

In Hornsby's study downstairs, I pulled the chain on a table lamp and scanned the shelves for something to read. *Baseball: The Early Years* by Harold Seymour caught my eye and immediately sucked me in. Four chapters later I'd learned how baseball began in America (it wasn't Doubleday) and spread across the country in the mid-nineteenth century.

The grandfather clock chimed five times. I thought I should try to get a couple hours of sleep, so I put the book back on the shelf. That's when a thick volume titled *The Baseball Encyclopedia* caught my eye. According to the subtitle, it was "The Complete and Official Record of Major League Baseball." I opened to the Pitcher Register in the second half of the hefty book. On page 1567, after Norm Angelini, was the entry for Don Angley. Full name: Angley, Donald Elias; Born Oct. 10, 1927, Richwood, Ohio; BR TR; 5'10" 200 lbs (his playing weight). In his three years with the Red Sox, he compiled a career 12-17 record, 19 saves, and a 4.68 ERA. He never pitched in the postseason. I flipped back and forth through the encyclopedia, but could not find any information about the final games of the 1949 season.

I returned to the armchair. Shutting my eyes for a moment, I tried to picture Angley on the mound at Fenway Park pitching to Joe DiMaggio. My thoughts then drifted to Eileen. An idea materialized. *I will go to her church. Then I can check out the competition. I'll sit in back to remain inconspicuous, and then maybe I can just happen to run into her after the service. A coincidental meeting.* At some point while reviewing this plan, my thoughts faded into a dream.

The sun shone brightly though the windows when I woke up slouched in the armchair. The hands on the clock pointed to 10:47. Too late to make it to church. While adjusting to consciousness, my brain assailed me for missing an important opportunity with Eileen.

Now you've blown it. She'll probably be engaged the next time you see her. A fog of depression settled in.

"Finally awake?" Sam said, entering the room. "The prof said he saw you zonked out in here. You missed breakfast. Crepes. Good stuff." He dropped into the chair in the opposite corner.

"I must have fallen asleep. Crud."

"Get up early to do some reading?"

"Something like that."

His eyes roamed a row of books. A few moments passed.

"So you ready to get this 'must win' against Pierre?" I asked.

"Hell yeah. They won't get nothin' against me."

"Will it bother you when Harvey comes to bat?"

"Not a chance. He's just another guy gonna be wearin' a collar today."

"What if Felicity's in the stands?"

He scoffed. "Who cares? She's nothing to me. I've got Danika now. She's more woman than Felicity will ever be."

"Well alright then." I yawned. "Sounds like the Cavaliers are toast."

He grunted in affirmation, though his brow wrinkled with concern. I wanted to go to the kitchen to see if any crepes were left, but figured he might want to talk about something. After about a minute, he spoke.

"That girl won't let it drop." His gaze moved to the window.

"Oh yeah?" I didn't know what he was talking about.

"Yeah. She wants me to give up three runs today. Says Pierre's got a bum on the hill, so this is our big chance. The Giants will win and she and I can score a grand or more."

"Sam, no. You can't do that."

"I know." He shook his head. "There's no way."

"Good."

"She's really pushin' though. Said she's putting a hundred down, even though I told her not to." He started fidgeting with a bundle of locks that hung down to his chest. "She can't afford to be dropping that kind of cash. But the Giants have got to win this one."

"I know it. Angley will have a coronary if we get swept at home by Pierre."

"No way I'm lettin' that happen." His face turned to granite. "No way."

A sellout crowd packed Sherman Field that afternoon. And they got their money's worth. True to his word, Sam shut down the Cavaliers. Harvey struck out three times. His teammates didn't fare much better, managing only two singles and a walk for the entire game. Sam racked up 15 strikeouts and his league-leading seventh shutout of the year. The Giants closed to within one game of Cheyenne and three games of Pierre.

Sunday evening we boarded the bus for an all-night trip to Bismarck, North Dakota. Since the sub-.500 Hawks were out of the playoff hunt, we had hopes of taking three of four, if not a clean sweep. After Monday's game the Giants appeared well on their way to meeting that goal. Randal's towering three-run homer capped an eighteen-hit attack in our 13-1 victory. But then Bismarck deviated from the script by taking the next two. Angley was overjoyed, especially with the four errors and blown save that accompanied the Wednesday night defeat.

After the game we moped around a bar near the motel, still smarting from the verbal evisceration delivered unto us by our manager. Weed at some point went to a payphone. Minutes later he returned with a goofy grin. "Good news, boys," he said, fully opening his perpetually half-closed eyes.

"Score some high quality North Dakota grass?" Kenny asked.

"Even better," Weed replied. "Just got ahold of a dude. Got us into a game." He motioned with his hands like he was dealing cards.

"Texas hold 'em?" Fender asked, his face brightening.

"You know it." Weed and Fender slapped hands.

"So who's the dude?"

"Spyder Crowley. Pitched for the Giants last year. Randal and Sam remember him."

"Yeah, I remember him," Randal said. "More like a squirrel than a spider if you ask me. Wouldn't trust him." Sam nodded at that assessment.

"Sure," Weed said. "But he's also the worst card player alive. Remember? His friends are even dumber, I bet. We'll make a killing. Come on."

Fender gulped down a final swig of beer and slammed his glass on the table. "Let's do it."

"You know we'll miss curfew," I said. "Skip's already royally pissed at us. Remember his little speech about an hour ago when he promised to cut any and every numbskull who breaks another team rule?"

Weed shrugged. "Yeah, he's just blowing off steam. Nobody's gonna check our rooms tonight."

"We can't afford to get caught, not with him on the warpath like that."

Randal and Kenny expressed their agreement with me, but finally relented to Weed's pleading. "How about it, Boo," he then said to me. "You in?"

"Can't. I'm starting tomorrow night. It's kind of a must game for us."

"Don't give me that crap. This will only take a couple hours. The distraction will be good for your head. And the moolah we're gonna win will be good for your wallet." His eyebrows moved up and down.

"It's late already."

"Spyder's place isn't even a mile away. We'll walk in, clean up, and be back by 2:00 at the latest."

"Not a good idea, man." I took a drink of Budweiser.

"Boo, don't be a chicken." At that, Weed and Fender started making clucking noises. It was juvenile, moronic, and effective. Against my better judgment, I agreed to go.

We threw down some money and headed for the exit. "You coming, big man?" Kenny asked, looking back at Sam still seated at the table.

"Nah. Gotta make a call." Knowing it would be fruitless to try to convince him to skip his nightly talk with Danika, we were off.

For a half hour, Weed led us on a winding journey down streets and sidewalks until we found ourselves in a dilapidated area of Bismarck that the chamber of commerce certainly did not feature in its brochures. We traipsed through an alley to a rotting door in a brick wall. After exchanging pleasantries with the guy who eventually answered, we entered and filed down a narrow staircase to a dim cave-like chamber. A cursory survey revealed a bar, a big round table, fake wood paneling, a couple of ripped couches, and several yellow milk crates. It appeared that someone had long ago intended to turn the basement into a lounge, but then lost interest and let the space atrophy.

Spyder was a tall twitchy guy with dark greasy hair parted down the middle. His cheek bones jutted and track marks lined the inside of both arms. Clearly he was not preparing for a return to organized baseball anytime soon. His four associates varied in shape and size, though each exuded the same surly demeanor. The dress code apparently called for dirty wife beaters and ripped jeans. More than a few tattoos (one of them a swastika) covered arms, faces, and necks. On the bar, a razor blade rested on a mirror. The stench of cigarettes and other foulness hung in the air. It was an ambiance that whispered, "Hepatitis."

With a wave of his arm, Spyder directed us to our seats around the huge table. I didn't like that all of our hosts sat on the side of the table between us and the lone exit from this gloomy dungeon. After Spyder distributed cans of Black Label beer, the game began. My cards repeatedly amounted to nothing but crap. It took only five hands to rid me of the entire $57 that I'd carried in my wallet. I didn't want to remain in the haze of pollution flowing from the ashtrays on the table, but the couches looked like breeding grounds for lice, ticks, rats, or worse. An acceptable alternative appeared when I spotted an upside-down milk crate near an ancient turntable stereo in the corner.

Randal exited the game after the following hand. Sputtering to himself, he came over and pulled up a crate next to mine.

"Me thinks Weed's scouting report was a bit off," I whispered.

"That moron," he muttered, glaring at the table bathed in the weak glow of the single overhead light.

"What'd you drop?"

"Hundred."

"Ouch. Gonna tell Cathy?" We kept our voices low, even though none of the card players paid any attention to us.

"That's not the problem." He bowed his head and issued a long exhale.

"What is?"

He squinted at me like I was an idiot.

"Oh, you're still …"

"Yes, Boo. I am."

"The hammy's about healed, isn't it? You still need that stuff?"

"Yes, the leg is better. But I still need the juice."

"Why?"

"You see how far I hit that ball Monday night? That's what I need to keep doing to get the scouts to notice me."

I glanced at his forearms, which had noticeably thickened since the start of the summer. "I guess."

"It's now or never for me, Boo. I've got to tear it up from here on out. And to do that I need the edge. But now, thanks to that pothead, I won't be able to make the payment for my next cycle. I was thirty short before tonight. That's why I came here. Now I'm screwed. Don't even have meal money for the rest of this trip."

"Me neither." I wondered what we would do for food the next three days.

Over the following hour, the players one by one ran out of money. When Fender bowed out, there was just Weed, Spyder, and the burly skinhead with a swastika on his shoulder still in the game. The neo-Nazi was dealing the next hand when Fender shot to his feet. "He's cheatin'! I saw it. The dawg's slippin' in extra cards."

The room fell quiet for a few beats, after which, we were all on our feet. The five Giants stood on one side of the table; our hosts faced us from the other side. "Now that's a heavy allegation, friend," Spyder said with a faint grin. "Remember you are guests here. And Eddie don't like it when guests start gettin' rude." Eddie aimed his war face at Fender. I really wished Sam had come along.

"I saw him with my own two eyes," Fender shouted. "You boys have been playin' us."

"Now that's not true," Spyder said. "But even if it is, what do you think you're gonna do about it?"

"We're gonna git our money back," Fender growled.

"I don't think that's gonna happen," Spyder replied in a chilly voice. A series of five clicks followed. Four switchblades glinted at us from across the table. I didn't know what had produced the fifth click until I spotted the pistol Spyder held low in his right hand.

After an instant of shocked silence, Randal pushed out his palms and said, "Whoa, easy guys."

"See now, I didn't want it to come to this," Spyder said, the twitch in his eye accelerating. "We was just playin' a friendly game of cards, when the cowboy here had to ruin it by making wild

131

accusations." He waved the gun barrel at Fender. "And now you have offended us."

Nobody spoke. The prospect of dying in this rat cellar loomed large and likely. And our bodies would never be found.

"What are we going to do about that?" Spyder asked, shaking his weapon.

"Forget about the game," Weed said. "Just keep the money and we're gone. Cool?"

"I wish it was that easy, but Eddie has been slandered. And my hospitality has been abused. Something must be done to make up for these offenses."

"We don't have any more money," Randal said.

"Maybe not, but you boys owe a reparation before you can leave." His eyes fell on my watch. "I bet you each have *something* that could right the wrongs committed here tonight."

"Come on, man," Weed pleaded. "I thought we were tight, Spyder. I mean, we were teammates last year."

Spyder smiled. "This is just business, Weed. We're still friends. Just like the good old days in Lincoln."

And so we each paid a "reparation" to get out of the dungeon. The items included: Kenny's stud earring, Fender's beloved black Stetson, a small bag of marijuana from Weed, the Timex my parents gave me for high school graduation, and Randal's leather wallet. Eddie had demanded his wedding band but Randal refused, saying he'd have to kill him first. The standoff ended when Spyder, wanting loot more than bloodshed, suggested the wallet as a compromise.

The five of us made our way through the dark streets back to the motel.

Sam blew his stack the next morning when we told him what had happened. "Show me where they are," he fumed. "I'll get your stuff back." With most guys, such talk would've been bravado. But Sam was deadly serious—even if he had to fight all five guys by himself. Despite our anger, we didn't tell him the address. The combined value of what we lost—cash and possessions—totaled less than $1,000. Sam had a million-dollar arm, and nobody wanted him to damage it in a fight.

"You gotta tell the cops then," Sam said.

"Can't," Randal said. "We were out way past curfew. We bring in the cops, Angley will find out what we did. And then the five of us will be turning in our uniforms."

After much grumbling, and profanity directed at Weed, we agreed to let it drop. The events of the previous night nonetheless remained on my mind. And not being able to afford any lunch left my stomach growling all through practice. There was a silver lining though, since the gnawing hunger kept me from fretting about my start that evening.

Angley sat in while Tony went over the plan for how to pitch the Hawks. The wrinkles on the old man's face were more pronounced, evidence of the stress he'd been feeling from the team's recent inconsistency. Having not recorded a win in almost six weeks, I felt awful seeing him like that. He remained quiet though the whole meeting. At the end, he stood and grabbed my shoulder. "We need this one, Carter. Go get 'em."

Only a few hundred fans showed up for the game, and I kept them quiet by shooting down Hawk after Hawk. While throwing to Vince before practice, I'd worked out a new arm angle for my fastball, which now had a little more zip. And an adjustment I'd made to my slider grip gave that pitch a sharper cut. At the end of five, I'd struck out eight batters and surrendered only three hits. Lincoln led 5-1.

But then came the sixth. A walk, an error, and an infield hit loaded the bases with two outs. Angley tottered out and asked if I could get the next guy. I said I could. "Good," he muttered, "the bullpen needs a rest."

The batter was a stocky third baseman who led his team in runs batted in. Sarge called for a changeup to start him off. It crossed the plate for strike one. A slider missed outside, and a fastball got fouled straight back for a 1-2 count. Sarge then put down four fingers—a sign I rarely saw. The curve. I hadn't thrown a bender all night, so I shook him off. Sarge remained adamant, again flashing the sign. Reasoning that the pitch would be unexpected, I reluctantly nodded. My fingers found the laces and I went into the stretch. With a twist of my wrist the pitch spun toward the batter's head. He flinched back just as the ball changed directions and curled over the inside corner at his knees. Strike three. I was shocked.

"I can't remember the last time I threw a curveball for a strike," I said to Sarge as we approached the dugout.

He slapped my back. "Homes, you always trust the Sarge. He knows what you can do."

Lincoln added three more runs in the top of the seventh to break the game open. Angley left me in for the seventh, eighth, and ninth innings. The big lead removed the weight from my shoulders and the fire from Bismarck's bats. When their catcher lofted a routine fly ball to Willie Small to end the ninth, Lincoln had a 10-2 victory and I had my first complete game as a Giant.

In the locker room, Angley gushed (or the closest he gets to gushing) with praise about my performance. It felt good to be the hero. As I sat there with my arm wrapped in ice, my thoughts drifted to home. I knew Mom and Dad had listened to the game. So too did Mark. He denied it, but I knew he listened to Giants broadcasts whenever I was starting. A smile crossed my face.

With no money though, I had little hope for any kind of postgame celebration. But then Jamario, Willie, and Bobby offered to buy me a beer and some nachos. Some of the other guys said they'd help cover us poker losers too. So it was nearly three-fourths of the Giants roster that went out together that night to celebrate.

I fell asleep almost immediately after returning to the room for our 1:00 a.m. curfew. But the sound of talking woke me up a while later. A glance at the clock revealed that it was 2:13. Sam lay on his side in the other bed with his back to me. I soon realized that the voice I heard was his.

"I can't," he said in a hushed tone. "No. Not tomorrow. We need this game." Pause. "Baby, it's Pierre. We can't mess around."

A longer pause followed. I pretended to snore so he wouldn't catch on that I was awake.

"I know it's easy money," he said, "but forget the thousand. We'll be making hundreds of thousands next year at this time." His words came out slightly louder. "Baby, please. It's not that ... come on."

The conversation went on like this for another half hour. Finally, his weariness got the best of him. "Alright. I'll think about it. What do you mean that's not good enough." Pause. "Okay fine," he hissed. "Make the bet. I'll give up three."

Sam spoke nary a word on the bus ride to Pierre the next morning. Barely moving in his seat, he stared daggers out at the passing Dakota countryside. I wanted to ask him about Danika, just to get the chance to talk him out of what he'd agreed to do. But I kept silent, hoping that the Giants would put up a bunch of runs that night.

They didn't. Lincoln managed only two runs against Pierre's ace, Arthur Widhalm. But that turned out to be enough. Apparently having a change of heart, Sam torched the Cavaliers lineup for eighteen strikeouts. Tony and Angley must have uttered the word "masterful" fifty times while watching him pitch. When the smoke cleared from Sam's barrage, Lincoln had a 2-1 victory over the division leaders.

After our postgame libations, Sam and I returned to a ringing phone in the motel room. He told me not to answer it—we both knew who it was. When the sound stopped, he took the phone off the hook.

Saturday afternoon, Lincoln's bats came alive late to pull out a 7-6 victory over the Cavaliers. Vince hit for the cycle while driving in four runs. Now riding a three-game winning streak, Lincoln had reclaimed second place, one game ahead of Cheyenne and just two games behind Pierre.

An upbeat group of Giants boarded the bus for the ride back home. Not everybody joined in the levity though. Angley, Randal, and Sam sat brooding, deep in contemplation. Skip faced the challenge of preparing his team to meet Cheyenne in a crucial four-game series. Randal faced the dilemma of how to increase his productivity without his special "edge." And Sam faced his first big fight with the woman he wanted to marry.

Chapter 11

The driver of the pickup I'd been following pulled to the side of the gravel road and killed his lights. I did the same, stopping a few feet behind. Sam, Kenny, and I got out of my car while Randal, Fender, and Weed exited the truck. The pale moonlight allowed my eyes a dim survey of the countryside around us. "Let's do this," Fender said, beckoning us into a roadside ditch. Upon traversing the grassy trench and navigating a low barbed wire fence, the six of us started our trek across a large pasture.

"Gotta hand it to you, Fender," Randal said. "I didn't think anybody could come up with a dumber idea than Weed's poker game in Bismarck. But somehow you've done it."

"Faith, partner," Fender said. "Gotta have faith. This'll work, gar-un-teed."

"We have to try something to exorcise the demons from this afternoon," Kenny said. "That was a big time ass-kicking Cheyenne laid on us. I've never heard our fans boo so loud."

"I thought they were calling for Boo to come in and pitch," Weed said.

Kenny chuckled. "That's funny. Shoulda said that to Skip when he was tearin' us a new one after the game."

"No way. The old man's got no sense of humor anymore."

"Funny how losing 9-0 to start a crucial series will do that to a manager," I said.

"Yeah, that was bogus. Ted had nothing on his pitches today."

"Wish we had Clyde back," Fender drawled, his eyes scanning the dark field ahead of us. "That boy knew his cigars."

"So what's our sitch now?" Weed asked.

"We're tied with Cheyenne," I said. "Three back of Pierre. Nine games left to play."

"And so that's why we're here," Randal said. "Hiking through a cow pasture ten miles outside town at two a.m. Unbelievable."

"This'll work," Fender said. "I keep tellin' y'all."

"Actually I was a little buzzed when you told the story," Weed said. "What is it we're doin' here?"

"Fender's high school team needed three straight wins to make the tournament," I said. "So the night before the first game, he and his teammates went out cow tipping."

"That's right," Fender said. "Knocked three of 'em over that night. Then we won three in a row, got in the tourney, and rolled on to the Texas 2-A state championship."

"Three cows, huh," Kenny said. "Sure it wasn't three cases of Lone Star you and your boys knocked over?"

"Well that too. But we tipped three prime Texas Bossys to the ground that night. And the cow gods rewarded us with a championship. Just like what's gonna happen with the Giants."

"The cow gods?" Randal scoffed. "Couldn't we just get Weed to pray to Scott Baio?"

"It's Willie Aames," Weed retorted. "And I pray to him every night to bless us with runs. Eight, to be exact. For as the holy one has decreed …"

"Yeah, we know," Kenny said. "But I don't think Buddy Lembeck can hear you with all those community theater auditions he's got now."

Weed tilted back his head and lifted his hands to the sky. "Oh great Willie, please forgive these simple heathens. They know not the folly of their ways."

Fender stepped ahead and extended his arm like a crossing guard. "Hush now. We're gettin' close." We all stopped, the buzzing of insects the only sound in our ears. Up ahead through the gloom, I saw about three dozen large shapes. Cattle. Some were standing and some lay on the ground. We crept closer. Fender gestured to the right where a fawn-colored Guernsey stood by herself. Then he pointed to the left where a spotted cow, similarly isolated, stood unmoving.

"Okay," he whispered. "Me, Weed, and Haldeman will get the one on the right. You guys take the spotted Bossy over there. Then we'll move in on the herd and get the third one. Remember, we gotta get three."

Lowering into a crouch, Fender, Weed, and Kenny tiptoed toward their target. They reminded me of Elmer Fudd hunting wabbits. After a few steps, Kenny started hopping. "Aw man, I just stepped in—"

"Shhh!" Fender turned and swatted him with his Giants cap.

With arms crossed, Randal, Sam, and I stood watching them. "So why did we agree to come out here?" Randal asked.

"Eh, they're just blowin' off steam," Sam said. "It's good for 'em." Those were the first words he'd spoken since the game ended that afternoon. Figuring he'd go out with Danika, the other guys were surprised he'd agreed to join us on this outing. I, on the other hand, was not.

When Fender, Weed, and Kenny had closed to within ten feet of the cow, she turned her head to them. A curious *moo* followed. "Now," Fender hissed. As the three stalkers lunged forward, the cow strode away at a brisk pace. Remaining just ahead of her pursuers, she moved among two other bovines that also took flight. One of them wore a bell, alerting the entire herd that strangers were in their midst.

From a safe distance, Randal, Sam, and I watched our three idiot teammates dart vainly after the scattering herd. Each of them slipped to the ground multiple times while trying to zero in on a target. "How is it those three morons are allowed in public without adult supervision?" Randal asked.

"Amazing, isn't it," I said. Sam grunted.

The commotion of pounding hooves, anxious moos, and clanging bells increased as Fender, Weed, and Kenny continued their pursuit. Not once did they get close to pushing over a cow. A light came on in the farmhouse about a hundred yards away. The three idiots froze. Kenny uttered a barnyard expletive appropriate for the occasion. An instant later all six of us were sprinting across the pasture back to the gravel road.

The Buick mercifully did not protest when I turned the key in the ignition. After Kenny stumbled through the ditch and dived into the backseat, I hit the gas and wheeled the car around. Gravel flew back at Randal's truck, which trailed close behind. Way out of breath, Kenny never stopped panting the entire trip back to Lincoln.

Even with our windows rolled down, the stink of his manure-caked shoes nearly gagged us. The odor remained after I dropped him off.

"Man, I'm gonna have to get the backseat fumigated," I said.

"Yep." Sam leaned his head farther out the window.

I steered the Buick down the empty streets of Lincoln toward home. "So, you talked to Danika since we got back in town?"

"Nope."

"Everything cool?"

"It will be. We just had a little disagreement. I'll catch up with her soon enough."

Soon enough turned out to be sooner than either of us expected. We walked up the front sidewalk at Hornsby's to find Danika sitting on the porch steps. It had to be close to 3:00 a.m.

"Are you ever going to talk to me again?" Her voice quavered with emotion.

"Yes."

"I've been calling you for three days." A sniffle trailed her last word.

"Yeah."

She stood. "Sam, you can't shut me out like this. Whatever disagreements we have, we'll work through them. Just don't shut me out. That's the worst." Tears trickled down her cheeks.

Sam looked over at me. "Oh," I said, "uh, I'll be heading in now."

As I passed through the front door, Danika flung herself into Sam's arms.

Monday night Burke pitched eight strong innings and Lincoln evened the series with Cheyenne. Tuesday night I took the hill. My slider still had a nice cut, but it didn't stay in the strike zone. To make matters worse, the Mule base runners picked up on something in my move to the plate, so they knew exactly when to take off to steal. Sarge was one of the best in the league at throwing out base stealers, but even he couldn't do anything to stop runners who were almost on second by the time I'd released the ball. Angley pulled me in the fifth inning with men at second and third and Cheyenne leading 4-3. The guy on third later scored, adding to our deficit. But Lincoln plated runs in the seventh and eighth to tie the game, and in the bottom of the ninth Matt Thompson drilled a shot into the left field corner to drive home the winning run.

Wednesday morning, I tried to convince Sam and Randal to come to Bible study. Sam said no. Randal said maybe, but didn't sound interested. Surprisingly, he was the first one there, waiting in the stands at Sherman Field, Bible in hand. Without his chemical edge, he must've figured that appealing to a higher power might help his swing.

After we completed our discussion of David and Bathsheba, Vince asked us (me, Randal, and Bobby Evans) for prayer requests. Bobby opened up and said he'd been battling homesickness. He was nineteen years old and this season was the first time he'd been away from his family in South Carolina for any length of time. Randal asked for prayer about an unnamed issue, a fairly common type of request at our studies. I thought about making a similar prayer request for Sam. From the tidbits he'd revealed to me the past couple days, Danika was once again pressuring him to give up runs in his next start. I nonetheless decided to keep my mouth shut.

Later on, Vince and I went out to the field so he could help me figure out why base runners were getting such a big jump off me. He stood on first, while I practiced my pickoff move. "Hey Brian," he said, after a few throws. "Is Sam doing okay?"

"Yeah, sure."

"I know he's been pitching lights out, but uh, how's the rest of his life?"

"He's doing all right, I guess."

"This new gal he's with, think she's the reason he doesn't come to study anymore?"

"Possibly. They spend a lot of time together." I looked over as if checking a runner and then fired a pitch into the cage behind the plate.

"I don't mean to pry, but do you think she's good for him?" He walked toward me.

I drew a breath and scanned the empty stands behind him. "I dunno. Maybe, maybe not. But he's hooked on her. Big time."

He nodded as his gaze fell to the grass below. "Brian, we got to look out for our brothers. I may be outta line, but I got a bad feeling about this. I know I'm not as close to him as you are, so maybe I'm wrong. I hope I am."

"I know what you mean. She concerns me too. But Sam does what he does, you know. I always invite him to study, but his mind is elsewhere."

"Well, we'll keep praying for him."

"Yeah. Ready to watch a few more pickoff moves?"

"Oh, I already figured out what you're doing. See, you're telegraphing with your glove when you're gonna throw to the plate and when you're gonna throw to first. Here, let me show you …"

Watching Sam warm up that night, I wondered what he was going to do during the game. We were two up on Cheyenne and could create some nice breathing space with another win. But Danika might've swayed him, especially since he reneged on her in his last start.

He struck out the leadoff hitter, but walked the second guy on four pitches. He then threw four wide ones to the next batter and the guy after him. Bases loaded. Yet Sam didn't look flustered as if he'd lost his command. His body language told me he was putting the ball right where he wanted. My fears were confirmed—he was going to intentionally give up runs.

While Tony trotted out to the mound, the Cheyenne players amped up their chatter. "Whatsa matter, Bigfoot? Can't find the plate? Get a haircut, Metalhead. The eighties are over. Major league prospect, my ass. This hairball ain't ever leaving Lincoln."

The big man heard them loud and clear. Smoke wisped out from under his purple cap as he glared into the visitors' dugout. A switched flipped inside him. His next fastball was nearly invisible. A wicked slider followed, and then another fastball finished the strikeout. The next batter went down in a similar fashion.

In the subsequent innings, Sam sent Mule after Mule to the glue factory. The way he painted the corners and changed speeds was truly a thing of beauty. In the fifth, he issued a walk. And that was the only Cheyenne batter to reach base after the first. At the end of the game, Sam had not only notched another shutout, but he'd tossed his third no-hitter of the year. His 18 strikeouts gave him a season total of 221, a new league record. And Lincoln had taken three of four from Cheyenne to drop them three games behind us with six left to play.

Sam passed on a postgame celebration with the boys to go out with Danika. I'm sure the two of them had plenty to talk about. Weed, Fender, and Kenny headed to the bars downtown to hit on the college girls who'd just arrived in Lincoln for the fall semester. Not interested in playing the wingman, Randal asked if I'd join him elsewhere. We ended up at the Coin Fun video arcade on Q Street next to Nebraska Bookstore. After a couple games of air hockey, we moved over to the skee ball machines.

"Did Cathy ever find out about the money you lost in Bismarck?" I asked.

"Yeah, I told her."

"How'd that go?"

"She wasn't thrilled." He winced as one of his balls bounced out of the *50 points* hole at the top.

"She's probably glad you're off the juice."

"That makes one of us."

"You had a nice series against Cheyenne. Five for sixteen. You don't need that stuff."

"Four singles and a double. No dingers. That's not gonna cut it with the scouts. I still need my edge."

"You can't afford it though, can you?"

He eyed me for a second. "I might have something worked out."

"What's that?"

He turned his back to the skee ball machine and scanned the noisy arcade. "Hey, let's go play Galaga."

"Randal." I put a hand on his chest. "What's going on?"

"Don't worry about it." His eyes locked on mine. "It's covered."

"How?"

He looked away. "Cornhuskers."

"Huh?"

"Football."

I paused to contemplate what that meant. "You put money on the Kickoff Classic? Danika get you into this?"

"Danika? No. What, is she a bookie?"

"No, but her uncle in Omaha knows one."

"Really? Hmpf. Well, I know a guy here." He started walking across the room.

I followed. "How much you got riding?"

"Grand."

"You don't have that."

"I know." He pushed a quarter into the Galaga machine. "Huskers better cover."

There was no game Thursday, but we still put in a full day with practice, weightlifting, and a two-hour autograph session at the UNL Student Union. Colorado Springs came to town Friday for our final home series of the regular season. The Giants took the first two games, 7-4 and 9-6. Sunday afternoon was my turn to start. A win would guarantee us no worse than a second place finish, thereby clinching a spot in the playoffs.

Though it was Fan Appreciation Day, fewer than 500 fans showed up to be appreciated. Even a performance by a Rolling Stones cover band and a T-shirt giveaway sponsored by NBC Bank weren't enough to fill the seats. The prospect of the Giants making the postseason for the first time since 1989 also did not wield much drawing power. On this afternoon, there was just too much competition for the hearts of Lincoln sports fans. This is because the Cornhuskers faced West Virginia in the Kickoff Classic in East Rutherford, New Jersey. Football season in Nebraska had arrived.

The show still went on at Sherman Field. Fans cheered, cowbells rattled, stilted Lincoln staggered, and I pitched. Though my fastball didn't have great velocity and my slider didn't move much, my control returned. I couldn't put much on the ball, but I could put it where I wanted. And when the Pikemen hit the ball hard, their shots more often than not found their way into a glove. Sarge also helped keep them in check by gunning down two would-be base stealers. My line for the day sparkled: 8 innings, 6 hits, 0 walks, 1 earned run, and 4 strikeouts. Fender sent the Pikemen down in order in the ninth to get the save. The win brought my final regular season record to 7-7. And more importantly, Lincoln was in the playoffs.

The fans gave us a standing ovation as we strutted around the field waving and tipping our caps. While some of the spectators moved to the front railing to get autographs, others remained in their seats listening to the Husker game on their headphones. Randal, likewise, had been keeping tabs on the football score with a small transistor radio in the dugout. He needed Nebraska to win by

14 points or he'd be in trouble. Fortunately, quarterback Tommie Frazier had little trouble carving up the Mountaineers defense, and the Big Red rolled to a 31-0 victory.

The Giants locker room celebration was short. Only two hours after our game ended, we were to meet at Misty's Steakhouse for a banquet with team boosters. And at 6:00 the next morning, we'd be hitting the road to Pierre for our final series of the season. The Cavaliers had lost to Cheyenne that afternoon, moving us into a tie for first place in the West. So, in effect, we'd be playing a best of three series against Pierre to determine the division title. Though both teams had already clinched playoff berths, winning the division was still important. The first place team opened the postseason at home, while the second place team would face the Eastern Division winner on the road to start the playoffs.

I headed to Hornsby's to pass the time until the banquet started. Just minutes after I stepped through the door, the phone rang. The professor answered and handed it to me.

"Hey Boo!" The voice in the receiver shot currents of electricity through my body.

"Eileen. Hey. Great to, uh … what's up?"

"I listened to the game today. You were awesome. Congratulations!"

"Thanks. You mean you weren't watching the football game?"

She giggled. "Well, some friends came over for the Husker game. So yes, I watched. But I also put on my headphones so I could hear the Giants game too."

"Cool."

"That has to be a great feeling to get the win that sends your team to the playoffs. I'm so proud of you."

"Thanks. It was fun today, definitely." My confidence surged. *I am asking her out. This conversation. It's going to happen.*

"I'm sure. I remember how exciting it was for us when we made it to the NCAA tournament last spring."

"Oh yeah, I remember that." She didn't say anything more, so I quickly broke the silence. "Classes just started for you, right? How's that going?" I figured I'd engage in some casual chatting before delivering my most important pitch of the day.

"Great," was her reply. She then described her classes, her professors, and how much homework she was going to have, especially in Business Management. I said "uh-huh" in all the right places, though my mind kept rehearsing the words I'd use for my big question.

And then I heard it. A male voice in the background. "Okay, I'll be done in a minute," Eileen cheerfully told this person.

"You have company," I said.

"Yeah, that's Chad. He's taking me to a movie tonight. *The Mask.* You seen it?"

"Chad?" I didn't mean to say his name out loud.

"Oh, yeah. He goes to my church. We're kinda seeing each other now."

The pieces of my shattered heart rattled across the hardwood floor in Hornsby's den. "Oh" was all that escaped from my voice box.

"So have you seen the movie?"

"No. Haven't heard much about that one." A giant vice squeezed my head.

"Jim Carrey's in it. He is so funny. Do you like him?"

"Uh-huh. Sure." *What are we talking about?*

The conversation dragged on for another five minutes, about what, I didn't care. With each word, air rushed out of the popped balloon that was me. By the time we hung up, I was nothing but a shriveled piece of latex lying on the floor. The grandfather clock ticked away the seconds. NPR filtered in from the professor's kitchen radio. Needing to clear my head, I went out to the backyard, where two large oaks provided a vast canopy of shade. An old wooden shed with chipped paint occupied the back corner of the lot. Along the side wall facing the yard stood an iron park bench. Wanting to hide, I walked past the bench to the rear of the shed. About three feet separated the back of the structure from the chain link fence running behind it. Vines and tall weeds grew all along the fence, creating a green barrier that concealed the narrow space from the adjacent yard.

So there I sat behind the shed, knees pressed to my chest, contemplating the ruination of my life. Barely an hour earlier, I basked in the glory of my biggest win as a pitcher. And now I wallowed among the bugs and weeds, wondering what had just happened. After an unknown amount of time had passed, I heard voices in the backyard. They got closer. It was Sam and Danika.

They sat on the bench just around the corner of the shed. I couldn't see them and they couldn't see me.

"This is nice," she said. "Shady. Good place to come out and read."

"Yeah, I think the professor does that sometimes."

A silence followed. I didn't move a muscle.

"Do you love me?" she asked.

"What? You know I do."

"I know what you say, but sometimes I wonder."

"What's that supposed to mean?"

"Nothing."

"Is this about the money again? I thought we were done with that."

"I'm sure it's easy for you to forget. You didn't lose two-hundred dollars on bets you thought were a sure thing."

"I told you, I'll pay you back."

"That's not the point." Her words came out as a sob.

"Hey, come here."

"Don't touch me." I heard movement on the bench.

"Come on, baby. We'll have plenty of money next year. More than we'll know what to do with."

"Don't." There was a smacking sound. Possibly her swatting his arm away as he tried to put it around her.

"What's wrong?"

"You treat me like a child. Like my opinion doesn't matter."

"That's not true."

Her crying increased. "I just try to do one thing for us, get us a little money now when we can really use it, and you make me look like a fool."

He didn't respond for a few seconds. "I'm sorry," he said meekly. "You matter more to me than anything. You know that."

"Do I? Those are just words, Sam. Like when you tell me you love me."

"Hey, I mean what I say to you."

"Right. Remember what you said to me before the last game you pitched? And the time before that? And ..."

"I was going to do it last time out. Then the other team started lipping off. I got mad and had to put them in their place. I'm sorry. I'll get back what you lost. I promise."

"It's not about the money, Sam. It's about you and me. You have to call all the shots, and you won't let me do this one thing for us. I'm just a dumb girl that you can lie to whenever you want."

"That's not the way it is. You're my world, baby."

"Prove it."

"How?"

"Tomorrow's game. The odds are fifteen-to-one now."

A silence followed. "Three runs?" It sounded painful for him to say the words.

"That's all. And the way the Giants have been hitting lately, you'll still win easily. Plus, you guys are already in the playoffs. So there's nothing to lose, really."

"We're still fighting for the division."

Her sigh seemed loud even in my weedy hiding spot fifteen feet away. "Forget it, Sam. You love baseball more than me. Maybe we should just stop—"

"No! I'll do it. Promise. And I've got eighty-six dollars. That's all that's left in my savings right now. Put that down too when you call your uncle."

"You're going to bet your own money? With me?"

"Yeah. We're in this together."

"Oh Sammy, I love you."

An ill feeling crept up my throat.

Monday morning the Giants rode seven hours to Pierre, South Dakota. After we checked into our motel, the bus carried us to the ballpark where a small crowd had gathered. The people appeared to be waiting for us. Or rather, one of us. Sportswriters from newspapers around the region were there, as were scouts from at least a dozen big league teams. *Baseball Tonight* had even sent a reporter. After Sam's last no-hitter, word had spread among the national sports media that a pitcher for the Lincoln Giants was on the verge of making history. In a nation now devoid of major league action, those who made their living covering baseball hungered for compelling on-field stories. They found one in Sam Judge.

Heading into his final start of the season, Sam's record stood at 17-0. Only two minor league pitchers had ever posted a better season record: Tony Napoles for the Peekskill Highlanders in 1946 and Billy Macleod for the Pittsfield Red Sox in 1965. Both of those pitchers finished their regular seasons with 18-0 marks. But Sam's ERA, a sparkling 1.18, was more than a run better than Napoles's and Macleod's. So if he picked up his 18th win that night against Pierre, Sam Judge would complete arguably the greatest season by a pitcher in minor league history.

The flurry of attention took us all by surprise. Sam especially. He sounded humble, even sheepish, when interviewed before the game. I'm certain he didn't know how close he was to making history when he uttered his promise in Hornsby's backyard. The dilemma had to be eating away at him. Sam had a golden opportunity to wow the scouts and garner praise from the national media, but if he broke another promise to Danika he would likely lose the woman he loved. I had no idea how this evening was going to play out.

Fans poured into the ballpark, filling all 1,500 seats in the stands at Cavaliers Field. An equal number crowded into the grassy standing-room-only areas beyond the foul lines and outfield fences. Those faithful to the home team held a clear majority and they vocalized their desire to see the celebrated Giant go down.

Pierre's Arthur Widhalm retired Lincoln 1-2-3 in the top of the first. The Giants then took the field. Clad in his road gray uniform, Sam stood poised atop the mound like a barbarian prince ready for battle. Flashbulbs popped throughout the stands as the big man unleashed his first pitch.

Picking up where he'd left off in his previous start, Sam sent the home team down in order. Harvey, batting third, struck out on three pitches. The last fastball he waved at clocked in at 96 mph on the radar guns. My hope that Sam would forget his promise to Danika gained new life, but it was still early.

Sam opened the bottom of the second by walking the first batter. The next guy also received a free pass. Sarge went out to the mound. When the third batter stepped in, Sam served up a batting practice meatball. The Cavalier smashed a line drive that Kenny speared for out number one. Sam then issued another walk to load the bases. The anemic fastball he offered to the next batter got ripped up the middle to score two. The crowd exploded. I shut my eyes and lowered my head.

With one out and runners at the corners, Sam likely wanted to let in the third run with a sacrifice fly or a ground out. Then he could bear down the rest of the game. Pierre's second baseman had other ideas, smoking one into the gap to score two more. Backing up third, Sam punched the air in disgust. Tony visited the mound to talk to him. Sam looked away, impatient for his coach to leave.

Having more than covered Danika's bet, Sam went back to his full arsenal. A one-hopper to short and a fly ball to Randal ended the inning with Lincoln trailing 4-0. The fans let Sam hear it as he returned to the dugout. "O-ver-rated!" Clap-clap clap-clap-clap. "O-ver-rated!" Clap-clap clap-clap-clap. He stomped to the end of the bench and slammed his glove to the ground. We all gave him his space. Sarge ended up next to me. Angley came down and asked him what was going on out there.

"Don't know," Sarge replied. "First, he's wild. Then, lollipops down the middle." The catcher shook his head. "Never seen him like this." Skip muttered something under his breath and then trotted out to coach third base.

Lincoln got one back in the top of the third and Sam allowed only a single in the bottom of the frame. We still had hope. This optimism brightened in the fourth when Eduardo Salazar drilled a two-run homer to pull the Giants within one. In the bottom of the inning, Sam walked the leadoff batter. He got the next two guys but then gave up a single. A grounder to Kenny should've ended the inning. Instead, he booted it to put the Cavs up by two.

After finally getting the third out, Sam smoldered on the bench. With a withering gaze he willed our batters to get on base and score runs. But the Giants could muster only a Willie Small single in the top of the fifth. Sam labored in the bottom of the inning, surrendering a walk and a hit before a double play grounder ended the Cavalier threat.

The score remained 5-3 heading into the bottom of the sixth. Though he was done intentionally giving up runs, Sam didn't seem right. As I knew all too well, pitching is a head game. And what had happened earlier still occupied space in his brain. The first Cavalier dropped down a perfect bunt. Sam lunged after it and, even though he had no play, fired it toward first. The ball sailed past Vince and rolled down the right field line, sending the runner to third. Harvey then stepped into the box. Sam hung a slider that his old friend launched over the wall in left center. Sam didn't even turn to watch it land. He just stood alone on the mound, shoulders slumped and head down. Angley summoned a new pitcher. The joyous crowd serenaded Sam with the chorus from that "hey hey hey goodbye" song as he left the field. A few fans added "you suck," and several other choice words.

The Giants scored a run in the eighth to make the score 7-4. And that's how it ended. Filing into the locker room after the game, we found Sam on a bench, his head in his hands. Even though he'd been in there for almost an hour, he still hadn't taken off his uniform. Nobody said a word as they moved to their lockers.

Angley and Tony stepped into the morgue. "Now listen," Skip said. "This was one game. That's all. Nights like this are gonna happen. Shake it off." His gaze roamed from player to player. "You boys have had a helluva week. Won six straight heading into tonight. We got two more games here. Win 'em both and we take the division title. If you woulda told me at the start of the season we'd be in this position, I'd have taken it in a heartbeat." He squinted at us. "The playoffs start Friday. I'd like to open at Sherman Field, so you boys go out and get me that division."

The two coaches left the room.

The next day we moped our way through practice and pregame warm-ups. With the fall of our unbeatable ace, the division title seemed out of reach. Our usual bench chatter was noticeably lacking when our leadoff batter, Jamario Rhoades, stepped to the plate. With an 0-2 count, he dribbled a grounder to third that the fielder misplayed for an error. The next two batters flew out. That brought Vince to the batter's box. After taking two balls he unloaded on a hanging slider, the crack of impact sounding like thunder. Watching the shot sail high into the sky reminded me of the climactic scene in *The Natural*. Except Vince's drive didn't smash into any lights; it actually cleared the bank of lights above the right field fence.

After several moments of stunned silence, the Giants leapt out of the dugout to congratulate our first baseman. With one swing of the bat we believed again. Our opponents, on the other hand, appeared to deflate in the wake of Vince's blast. A bit too much celebrating the night before may have also contributed to their lethargy. It turned out to be a pleasant evening at the ballpark. Reed

Perry pitched into the seventh, and Lincoln cruised to an 8-2 victory.

The final game of the season was Wednesday night. One last battle to determine the division title. The new kid, Ted Pottebaum, took the ball for Lincoln. He responded with a majestically mediocre outing, giving up five runs in five innings. Fortunately, the Giants bullpen stopped the bleeding and our lineup once again brought the heavy artillery. Brad, Vince, and Randal each homered, part of a thirteen-hit attack that powered Lincoln to a 10-6 victory. The Giants finished with a 57-37 record and the Western Division title.

A lively celebration ensued in the dumpy visitors' locker room at Cavaliers Field. A rain of Budweiser sprayed from recently-shook cans to douse the jubilant Giants. Sam, however, remained an island of gloom. Only a few minutes into the postgame party, he got up and left. I squeezed my way through the reveling players and went out to follow. Exiting the ballpark, he trudged to our bus, where he sat alone in the back. I climbed on board and claimed a seat just across the aisle from him.

I waited a while before I spoke. "You know, this division title wouldn't have happened without that monster season you had. We rode your back all year. The Giants are barely a .500 team without you."

He stared out the window at the line of cars exiting the parking lot. "Thanks."

I knew he'd been stung by the articles written about him following his loss on Monday. Many sportswriters speculated that his stock would plummet after that dismal outing. Some reporters questioned if he could ever keep his head straight in pressure situations. The *Baseball Tonight* feature that aired Tuesday evening didn't help. Focusing more on Sam's final defeat than his season of dominance, the analyst belabored that some guys just can't get it done when the spotlight burns brightest. That brought up the old concerns about Sam being a head case who can't control his emotions.

"We're in the playoffs, man," I said. "You're going to be starting Game One. The Trappers won't get nothin' off you. After you tear it up in the postseason, nobody's going to remember your one bad start of the year."

"Yeah."

"What happened Monday won't happen again."

He turned to me with a hard glower. "You got that right."

Chapter 12

The Giants division title celebration was brief, moving straight from the locker room at Cavaliers Field to our bus. Division champions or not, Wright and Mendenhall had no intention of allowing us to stay an extra night in Pierre. By midnight we were all slouched in lumpy vinyl seats, trying to get comfortable enough to sleep through the long ride home. Hours later, a yellow-orange glow spread across the eastern sky as the State Capitol building, Lincoln's tallest structure, emerged from the horizon. In the afternoon we dragged ourselves back to Sherman Field for practice. That evening I went to the Nebraska State Fair with the boys and caught a Collin Raye concert at the Devaney Center. Sam did not join us. He was still out with Danika when I crawled into bed.

Something startled me awake in the middle of the night. It was Sam tromping into our room. This had happened many times before and when it did, I usually drifted back to sleep within seconds. But he dropped heavily onto his bed and kept tossing about. His squeaking mattress springs blocked the resumption of my bungee jumping dream. Minutes later I heard him sit up. Opening an eyelid, I saw the numbers 3:41 gleaming red from the digital clock on my nightstand.

"Going out for a jog?" I asked.

"Sorry. Didn't mean to wake you."

"Nah, I'm not awake. I'm just dreaming that we're talking."

"Sorry."

As my eyes adjusted, I saw him hunched forward on the edge of his bed. "You wanna deal," I asked through a yawn, "or should I?"

"Not up for cards." His words dripped with dejection.

"Rough night with your woman?"

A long pause followed. "You could say that."

I sat up and flipped the switch on my nightstand lamp. "What happened?"

"You know Monday night?" He lowered his face. "I let up on purpose. Just like she wanted."

"You mean for that bet?" I played dumb. "Giving up three runs?"

"Yeah, three. The girl just wouldn't let it go. So I did it. Thought I'd still get the win." He raised his eyes to me. "You saw how that turned out."

"That's in the past, Sam. We got the division anyway. You'll dominate tonight."

He scoffed and shook his head.

"What? Is Danika wanting to make another bet? Didn't she collect big off Monday night?"

"She did win big. I put some money down too. Together we made over two grand."

"Wow. So now she wants you to do it again?"

"No. *She* doesn't."

I leaned forward on the edge of my bed awaiting further explanation that didn't come. "Then what's the problem?"

He stood and paced over to the closet, keeping his back to me. "She says some gamblers found out about what happened. So they're laying a bunch of money on St. Cloud and expecting me to lose."

"What? I don't understand."

He turned, shifting the shape of his massive shadow on the far wall. "Danika placed the bet through her uncle in Omaha. She told him not to let anyone know who it's from. But this idiot, Turk, shoots off his mouth to some friends that my girlfriend put money on me giving up runs."

I scratched my head trying to process it all. "How does that relate to the St. Cloud game?"

"Turk won big off the Pierre game too. Put down a thousand on me giving up the three. Something the smart money wouldn't touch. Not for that amount. When Turk's gambling pals saw his big payoff and then found out about Danika's bet, they figured I let up."

"So the gamblers think they got something on you?"

"Yeah. Danika said Turk told her if I don't tank this next game, these guys will tell everybody that I took a dive in Pierre."

"But you didn't intentionally lose."

"I know, but they're saying I did. Said my performance looked awfully fishy that night." He started chewing a thumbnail.

"You gonna do it?"

He shot a glare at me. "Hell no. They can't prove nothin'. All they got is people talking. They're just trying to intimidate me."

"Is that what you told Danika?"

"Yep. I told her I'm not takin' a dive for nobody. And she can tell her scummy uncle that, and he can tell his friends."

I stared at the floor as he sat on his bed again. "That last game," he said, his voice barely audible, "it made me want to puke." His fists clenched. "Giving up runs in front of all those reporters and scouts, that was crap. I coulda tossed a shutout blindfolded that night."

"I knew something wasn't right."

"And the record, eighteen and oh. I coulda had that. Best season in minor league history." His face contorted with bitterness.

"Forget about it. Your season was still off the charts. And you'll set plenty of records in the majors."

"Yeah."

"Everybody knows what you can do. Fans, scouts, opposing hitters. And if they forget, you'll remind them."

His lips curled into a sneer. "Yeah. I'll show 'em."

The next morning we had a team meeting at Sherman. We all crowded into the clubhouse as Angley went over the strengths and weaknesses of our first round opponents, the St. Cloud Trappers. They had a so-so pitching staff anchored by ten-game winner Parker Teske. None of their other pitchers had great stats, but their lineup had some thumpers. Three guys topped 20 home runs and five guys batted over .300.

Skip told us we were the better team and would prove it on the field. What he didn't mention was that we had split the season series with St. Cloud, and that our regular season record was only two games better than theirs. Angley then surprised us by distributing sheets of paper with our individual statistics. "These are the final numbers from the season," he growled. "I'm giving you five minutes to enjoy your accomplishments. That's it. Then I'm taking 'em back and destroying 'em. These stats don't mean nothin' once Judge's first pitch hits Sarge's mitt tonight."

After grabbing a sheet and passing along the stack, I reviewed the pitchers' section. Even after what had happened in Pierre, Sam still led the league with 17 wins and a 1.45 ERA. His 224 strikeouts in 180 innings were unmatched as well. Moving down to my numbers brought a modest feeling of satisfaction. My last start dropped my ERA to under five, 4.98 to be precise, for the first time all season. And my seven wins were third highest on the Giants staff, behind Sam and Burke LaVelle, who finished at 8-5. Never mind that my seven losses led the team.

Moving to the team's offensive statistics, I read Vince's numbers: .292 batting average, 33 home runs, and 84 RBI. Amazing power productivity for a 94-game season. After a strong final week, Randal had raised his average to .263 with 11 homers and 51 RBI. He credited the juice for his resurgence. I thought it was more of a mental thing. Before I could assess the other players' stats, Tony started snaking his way through the room plucking the papers from our hands.

After Tony had collected all the stat sheets, Angley announced the starting lineup for Game 1. No surprises. Next came the moment I'd been waiting for—the pitching rotation for the playoffs. Sam of course would start the first game. Burke would get the nod for Game 2 Saturday evening. The big question was who would start the third game, a Labor Day contest in St. Cloud. It would either be Reed Perry, Ted Pottebaum, or Brian Carter. Skip's eyes roamed the faces in front of him before fixing on mine. My body flinched when he barked my name. Reed would start Game 4 on Tuesday if necessary.

My mood soared for the rest of the meeting. Having nearly been cut from the team a few weeks ago, it felt good knowing that Skip now considered me the number-three man in his rotation. I resolved not to let him or the team down.

The meeting adjourned around 11:30. Most of my gang scattered. Fender and Weed had dates. Randal was meeting Cathy downtown for lunch. Kenny was getting together with his mom and sister, who had driven in for the playoffs. So Sam and I went to the golden arches. Not long after diving into our food, I noticed a short guy in a grey suit pass through the doors and scan the room. A big grin covered his face when his eyes fell on me. He approached and slid into my side of the booth. Sam and I looked at each other as if to ask, *Do you know this guy?*

"Sam, Boo, good to see you," the man said. "It's nice that you boys are out enjoying yourselves on such a fine day." The high pitch and rolling cadence of his voice reminded me of one of those radio announcers from the 1940s. Above an expansive forehead, his dark hair slicked straight back.

"You got something for me to sign?" Sam asked, trying not to sound annoyed.

The man grinned at me, accentuating the crow's feet on his tanned face. "That's what I love about our Sammy. He's always so confident." I caught a healthy whiff of his cologne.

"Do I know you?" Sam asked, this time not masking his irritation.

"No, you do not," he said, grabbing one of my French fries and popping it into his mouth. "But I know you. And so do my bosses."

Sam looked like he swallowed something unpleasant. "Who are you?" I asked.

"The name's Mercury."

"Mercury? Like the car or the thermometer?"

He smiled again. "Mercury like the messenger. You boys can call me Merc."

"How about if we call you gone," Sam said, crumpling a napkin between his hands.

"Now don't be rude, Sammy." He grabbed a couple more of my fries and shoved them in his mouth. "Remember, I'm a messenger. And that's what I'm here to do, deliver a message."

Sam's glare hardened. "I'm not interested in any message from you."

"Oh I'd recommend you pay attention to what I've got to say," Merc said in a darker tone. "Because if you don't get this message, people could get hurt. People close to you, Sammy."

Sam slammed his fist on the table. "Listen runt, I could snap your neck like a pencil. So don't tell me about who could get hurt."

After a pause, Merc started laughing and turned to me. "The big man doesn't get it, does he? Well, let me enlighten you both about the way things are. See, important people have a vested interest in the outcome of tonight's ballgame. They need the Giants to lose. And you, Sammy, are going to make sure that happens."

"Get out," Sam hissed, thrusting a finger at our unwanted visitor.

Merc sat back and held up his hands like a gun was pointed at him. "Sammy, please. Remember, I'm just the messenger. The words I speak to you are not my own. I personally don't even like baseball. Now soccer, there's a sport."

"Who are these people you work for?" I asked.

"Men of leisure. Good fellas. Sportsmen."

"Gamblers, you mean."

Merc grinned. "It's not gambling the way they do it."

"These are the Reapers, right?"

"That's what they're called in certain circles." He filched another fry.

"I don't care what they're called," Sam said. "I ain't rollin' over for nobody."

Merc sighed and reached into the pocket of his suit jacket. I tensed, expecting to see a revolver. But he grabbed a pack of Lucky Strikes, tapped out a cigarette, and lit up. "See, Sammy, you don't have a choice. The Giants must lose tonight. The Reapers are counting on it."

"I don't care what they want. They're your bosses, not mine. I ain't involved with scum like them."

"But you are, Sammy." Merc chuckled. "When you rolled over against Pierre, you jumped into our world with both feet."

"I didn't do nothin'." Sam glared out at the parking lot.

"Riiight." Merc inclined his head and exhaled a plume of smoke toward the ceiling. "Let me refresh your memory. Five days ago, your girlfriend—who is quite lovely I might add. Very nice, Sammy. Well, she puts $200 of her money and *your* money on you to give up three runs against the Cavaliers. And what should happen that night? The unhittable Sam Judge gets rocked. Unbelievable." A tone of mock surprise dripped from his last word. "Gotta admit, Sammy. That don't look good."

I shifted in the booth. "You don't have any proof."

"Don't we? Let's review what we've got." Streams of smoke shot from his nostrils. "Thanks to our friend Turk, we've got a phone record of Danika placing the bet. I've heard the recording myself. The silly girl even told her uncle that part of the money being wagered was Sam's. We sure wouldn't want that tape to get into the wrong hands." Shaking his head, Merc directed his smug look at Sam and then back to me. "See, Boo, if the baseball people find out that Sam bet against his own team—which is in effect what he did—he will *never* play major league baseball. Ever. Sammy here will be just like Pete Rose and the Black Sox. Lifetime ban … the suits just have no sense of humor when it comes to gambling."

Sam's gaze dropped to his half-eaten Big Mac.

Merc puffed again and tapped his ashes onto my sandwich wrapper. "Don't look so glum, Sammy. It's not like we're asking you to shave off all your hair. This is just one little minor league game. Meaningless in the big picture. Lose tonight and your obligations to us are met. Then you can go on to your superstar career in the big leagues and never will you hear from us again. A small price to pay, if you ask me."

"Nobody tells me to lose," Sam said, his voice low and defiant.

Merc sighed. "Sammy, you're killing me here. You do NOT want to cross the Reapers. See, there's no major league baseball right now, and that *Baseball Tonight* feature broadcast your name across the nation. So there's a lot of action on this game today. Vegas even posted a line. My bosses have wagered a bunch of cash on St. Cloud. And they do not like to lose, especially sums of that magnitude. Makes 'em surly and unpleasant."

"Then they'd better change their bets, because the Giants are winning tonight."

Merc turned to me. "Will you help me out here, Boo? I'm just not getting through to him." He raised his Lucky Strike for another drag and looked at Sam. "Okay, I'll say it one more time, as clearly as I possibly can. Judge, if you don't deliver tonight, some dangerous men are going to be angry with you. And they will express that anger in a very direct manner. They will expose your prior involvement with gambling and end your baseball career. And, for good measure, they may do something physical to you or somebody you know. Get the message?"

"Yeah, and I've got my own message for them," Sam said. "How about if I rip that shiny blue tie off your neck and shove it down your throat. Would that be clear enough for your bosses to understand?"

"Oh Sammy, what are we going to do with you?" Merc's grin returned. "You think about what I've said. Talk it over with Boo here. It's a fair offer. After you've thought about it for a while, you'll see that there's only one play for you. Do the right thing, Sammy."

Merc smashed the remains of his cigarette into the bun of my chicken sandwich. He then sauntered away whistling the theme from *The Sting*.

Sam and I sat in silence, our appetites gone. After a while I asked him what he was going to do. He just stared out the window and shook his head. I didn't know what that meant, but decided not to ask again.

Practice that afternoon was livelier than usual. Wired about the postseason, the guys remained blissfully unaware that our star pitcher had just been ordered to throw the first game. I kept my mouth shut. Sam didn't say anything either, which wasn't much of a departure for him.

As the ballpark started to fill, Angley gathered us in the clubhouse. "All right," he said. "This is it. You've worked all season to get to the playoffs. And now you're here. Sure, this ain't the majors. I know you ain't making much playing in this league. I ain't makin' much coaching here either." His stern face lightened.

"But you are all professional ballplayers. And you all have a chance to be champions. Even though you're only gonna be playin' in front of a few thousand fans, what happens tonight and over the next week matters. You *will* remember it." The old man removed his cap and lowered his head.

"Back in forty-nine I pitched for the Red Sox. Bullpen. With two games left we had the Yankees on the ropes. Just needed one win to get the pennant. I knew we were gonna do it and then go on to win the World Series. Thought I'd be wearing five or six rings before I was through." He sighed and shook his head. "We dropped both those games to New York. Two years later I was in the minors. Never got back to The Show. Never made it to the Series. Some opportunities are a one-time deal." The room quieted as he drifted back 45 years.

Skip's cap returned to his head and his gaze returned to his players. "You boys have had a great season and you can finish it as winners. Don't pass up that opportunity. If you fall on your faces now, that's what you'll remember." He jabbed his finger at us. "It'll stay with you for years down the road." After a few moments, he stepped toward the exit. We remained quiet after the clubhouse door closed behind him.

Tony occupied the space Skip had vacated at the front of the room. "That man has been managing teams longer than you and I have been alive." The expression behind his moustache was as serious as I'd ever seen on him. "In all those years, he's never had a team win it all. Divisions yes, but Don Angley has never claimed the ring. For all he's given to this game, he deserves to be a champion at least once. Gentlemen ..." His voice rose in volume and force. "Go get your skipper that title."

The fired-up Giants looked sharp rocketing the ball around the field before the game. They could barely stand still during the national anthem. A capacity crowd packed the stands at Sherman Field, contributing to a perfect baseball atmosphere. The American flag snapped in the breeze above the outfield wall. Fogerty blared from the speakers. Our tall, truculent Lincoln mascot stomped about with a menacing glare. Purple balloons soared into the sky above. The aroma of peanuts and hot dogs tickled my nostrils.

With muscles bulging and hair cascading, Sam looked as imposing as ever on the mound. For opposing batters, it had to be unnerving seeing him glowering down at them from only sixty feet away with a deadly missile in his hand. But as invincible as Sam appeared, he may have already been defeated before throwing a pitch.

The first fastball smacked into Sarge's glove. Fans shouted and cowbells rattled as the umpire raised his right arm. The overmatched Trappers went down in order. Sam returned his teammates' high fives but said nothing as he sat on the bench next to me. When I held out a bag of sunflower seeds, he waved it away.

Defiance-fueled pistons pumped furiously inside the pitching machine that was Sam. Some of the projectiles he fired streaked by like blurry white lines. Others changed directions like fighter planes, seemingly unbound by the laws of physics. And then out of nowhere came those filthy changeups. Batters nearly burrowed themselves into the ground swinging way early at balls that leisurely glided over the plate.

In the top of the fourth, the Trappers shortstop walked on a 3-2 fastball that came in just low. Sam struck out the next two batters to strand the runner at first. In the bottom of the inning, Lincoln strung together a walk and three hits to take a 2-0 lead. If Sam were going to comply with Merc's orders, he'd need to start giving up runs.

He didn't.

The batter who walked in the fourth turned out to be the only Trapper to reach base. Those St. Cloud boys might as well have been wearing blindfolds. Sam's stellar performance was the first postseason no-hitter in league history. It also served as an emphatic reply to the Reapers.

Sam spent close to an hour after the game signing autographs and answering questions from Chip and the sports reporters from Lincoln's two newspapers and the 10/11 television station. I remained outside the clubhouse leaning against a wall. When anybody asked, I said I was waiting to see if my roommate wanted a ride home. But I was actually scouting the area. If Merc was telling the truth, there could be some unsavory characters lurking in the shadows ready to jump Sam. Nobody looked suspicious, and eventually the only people hanging around were Stan LaFollette, the portly head groundskeeper, and the three teenagers in his crew.

After Sam emerged from the clubhouse, he told me what I already knew. He was going out with Danika. We walked in silence to the gravel parking lot. She waited for him near the gate in her white Pinto. I caught a glimpse of her face under the dome light when Sam opened the door. She wore a grave expression, like the world was ending.

Fans again packed Sherman Field for Game 2 Saturday evening. After nine innings the score was tied at three apiece. Having already used Burke, Lazzari, and Fender, Angley alerted all remaining pitchers to be ready to throw an inning or two if needed. I moseyed to the bullpen and started stretching. Weed pitched the tenth and gave up a hit and a walk before a series of junk balls and knucklers got him out of trouble. In the bottom of the inning, Matt Thompson led off with a single. Randal sacrificed him to second and Eduardo Salazar drove him home with a liner to center. With the win, Lincoln grabbed a commanding 2-0 lead in the best of five series. The other good news was that there had been no sign of the Reapers or Merc. The little creep may have been bluffing after all.

Sunday morning I decided to go to church. Though I had tried to evict her, Eileen would not leave my head. So I thought going to her church and seeing her with Chad would give me closure. Something like a funeral for my unrequited summer love.

My head stayed low as I weaved through the people gathered in the lobby at Lincoln Berean. Slipping into the auditorium, I grabbed a bulletin and found a spot in the back row near the center. From there, I could survey nearly all the seats in this vast hall of worship. The setting was a striking contrast to the small Methodist church I'd attended growing up in North Platte.

The band cranked up an upbeat melody as three men and two women spread across the stage to lead the congregation in a song of praise. My eyes roamed back and forth as the music continued, but I still hadn't spotted Eileen. By the time the pastor took the stage, I had resigned myself to the reality that she wasn't there. In past conversations, she'd said she always went to late service. My brain reviewed the possibilities: maybe she went to early service; maybe she was sick or had gone out of town; or maybe she and Chad had eloped. I felt foolish for coming to church and resolved to banish Eileen from my thoughts once and for all.

I considered leaving, but didn't want to draw attention to myself. So there I sat, sulking. At some point the pastor caught my attention with the words, "Be strong and courageous." Recalling sermons heard in my youth, I remembered that the verse was from the book of Joshua. The pastor continued by describing how the Lord had called Joshua to lead the Israelites against a powerful enemy. Trusting in God's promise to be with him wherever he went, Joshua and his army emerged victorious. The message encouraged me as I thought about facing St. Cloud the next day.

My mind remained on Joshua after the service as I wound through the parking lot toward my car. Someone behind me yelled, "Boo!" My head jerked around to behold Eileen, wearing a violet cotton dress that fell just above her knees. The sight took my breath away.

"I thought that was you," she said, beaming. "What are you doing here?"

"Um, you know. Thought I'd go to church this morning." I quickly scanned the area for any straggling boyfriends. Happily, there were none.

"Oh. Have you ever been here before?"

"No. This is the first time."

"I didn't think you went to church." She shifted her Bible from one arm to the other.

"Well, I need all the help I can get during the playoffs." I chuckled at my weak attempt at humor.

Returning my smile, she said, "Oh Boo, that's not why you should go to church."

"Yeah, I know." My eyes examined the ring finger on her left hand. No rock. *Yes!* "I'd been thinking about going to church for a while, so I decided to check this one out." I hoped the Lord would forgive me for not being completely truthful about my interest in Lincoln Berean.

"Oh, well great." She appeared convinced.

Her gleaming blue eyes set my heart racing. I wondered if she had any idea how I felt. "So you saw me during the service?"

"Oh, no," she said. "I just got out of Sunday School. My class meets the same time as late service, so I go to early now."

"Ah, I see."

"Yeah, I started going to Sunday School last week. It's a college group. A couple friends convinced me to go. I like it, but it's been an adjustment getting up for early church."

Here it comes. Now is when she tells me more about her wonderful boyfriend Chad. But she said nothing more. I didn't know what to say, so I blurted out what was on my mind. "You look nice, er … that's a pretty dress." *Smooth, Brian.*

Her brows rose. "Thanks." She glanced down at her outfit. "It's passable I guess."

I wanted to tell her that everything looked great on her. Or, more accurately, she made everything she wore look great. But I said nothing.

A couple little kids darted past us. She smiled. I fidgeted. "Guess I should scoot," she finally said. "Gotta grab some lunch and then get studying for a history quiz on Tuesday. Can you believe we already have a quiz?"

"Really? Isn't this just the second week of the semester?"

"I know." She rolled her eyes. "I haven't even opened the textbook yet."

"Oh wow. Okay. Uh, guess I should let you get going."

"'Kay. Hey, it was great to see you, Boo." She put her hand on my arm.

"Great to see you too."

And with that, we parted ways. As I navigated out of the parking lot, my mind swirled. *Why didn't she mention Chad? Are they through? Why didn't I ask her to go to lunch? Did I say anything stupid?* The questions kept coming.

Eileen remained in my head the rest of the day and through the entire eight-hour bus ride to St. Cloud. She was still with me when I strode to the mound Monday afternoon. At least having such a powerful distraction kept the butterflies at bay. The message I'd heard Sunday morning about Joshua also helped, as did the 2-0 lead Lincoln held in the series.

Blocking out the crowd noise, I toed the rubber and went to work. My slider had a decent break and the fastball tailed a little just before disappearing into Sarge's mitt. More importantly, my pitches usually went where I told them to go. The Trappers ripped a few of my offerings, but couldn't put together a big inning. We took a 3-2 lead in the top of the seventh. In the bottom of the inning, I retired the first batter on a routine grounder. Then a rare miscue by Eduardo put a man on first. Losing my focus, I served up a tasty fastball over the heart of the plate. It of course got drilled into the right field corner to tie the game. Angley came out and I was done for the day.

I watched from the dugout as Ted Pottebaum walked the next guy, but avoided further trouble after a pop out to Sarge and a soft liner to Vince. Lincoln then tagged the Trappers bullpen for two runs in the eighth to take a 5-3 lead. And that turned out to be the final score.

After briefly celebrating our sweep, we boarded the bus for a raucous trip through Minnesota and Iowa. The boys belted out rock classics and shouted ribald jokes at each other as the movie *Zapped!* played on the TV screen. It was the first time all season that nobody on the team went to sleep on an eight-hour bus ride.

We finally pulled into the lot at Sherman Field just before 2:00 a.m. After Sam and I crept through the front door at Hornsby's, we decided to raid the refrigerator. The phone rang. Startled, I grabbed it after the first ring hoping it hadn't awakened the professor. It was Randal.

"What's the matter with you," I said. "It's the middle of the night. You're gonna wake—"

"Boo, you need to drive Sam over here."

His grave tone sent an icy dread running through my body. "What happened, Randal? Are Cathy and Haleigh okay?"

"Just get him over here. Now." He hung up.

Sam examined me with apprehensive eyes. "What's going on?"

"We have to go to Randal's. I think something bad happened.

Chapter 13

The pavement of the abandoned city streets reflected a soft glow from the lights above, a beautiful sight that I was unfortunately not able to appreciate. My eyes instead remained alert for objects moving into the path of my racing Buick. At red lights, I barely let up on the gas before accelerating through the intersection. Turns were navigated on screeching wheels. At last my smoking tank burned to a halt in front of Randal's house. A living room lamp glowed dimly behind closed curtains. Slightly brighter was the illumination cast from the back porch onto the driveway. Sam and I hurried in that direction toward the backyard.

Randal sat in a lawn chair near the back door. Cathy stood above him, her arms crossed against her body. They both looked over when Sam and I passed through the gate in the chain link fence, but neither of them moved. I sucked in a deep breath. "What happened? Please tell me Haleigh's okay."

They examined me with frigid eyes, then directed their stares at Sam.

My soul shrank in horror. "Oh, no. No …"

"Haleigh's fine," Cathy said. Though laced with distress, her words brought a wave of relief.

"What happened?" Sam asked.

Randal gestured out to the yard. The reach of the porch light extended only a couple dozen feet, beyond which the grass darkened into shadows. I did not notice anything unusual. "Go on," he said. "See for yourself."

Sam and I stepped out into the yard. My nerve endings prickled with trepidation. Slowly my eyes adjusted to the shapes hiding beyond the range of the light—a swing set, a large ball, a tricycle.

To the right, a doghouse. Sam headed over there. Following, I noticed something in the entrance.

We gazed down at Freddy lying on his side. The back half of his body lay outside his house, his head was concealed within. No sound. No movement. Nearby were two empty bowls, one of them overturned. The night breeze blew cold against my skin.

We stood in silence staring down at the lifeless animal. Randal approached. "This was tacked to the front of the doghouse." He thrust a piece of paper at us.

Sam grabbed it and stepped toward the house for better light. I slid in behind him to read over his shoulder. It was a newspaper clipping with the headline, "Judge No-Hits Trappers to Propel Giants in Playoff Opener." Taken from last Saturday's *Lincoln Journal*, the article described our Game 1 victory against St. Cloud.

The accompanying picture showed Vince, Kenny, and Sarge congratulating Sam after the last out. Someone had scrawled over the photo in red marker, "HOPE IT WAS WORTH IT. NEXT TIME IT WON'T BE A DOG." My blood chilled. I looked around at the neighboring yards, wondering who could be out there in the darkness watching us. Sam slowly lowered the article to his side.

"Do you know what this is about?" Randal whispered. "Cathy is freaking out. She thinks this threat is for me. Like I owe somebody something."

Sam nodded. "Yeah, I know what this is about." He moved toward the house, where Cathy waited with arms still crossed. Randal and I followed. The four of us stood facing each other on the back patio. "This has nothing to do with Randal," Sam said to Cathy. "It's for me."

"Don't protect him, Sam." Cathy glared at her husband. "I know he's been buying steroids again and placing bets to pay for them."

"I only made one bet," Randal pleaded. "And I won. I don't owe anybody."

"But you associated with those people. You brought them into our lives. And look what happened."

"This wasn't for Randal," Sam said.

"Then why would somebody poison *our* dog?" Cathy demanded.

"They wanted to send me a message." Sam looked down at the article again. "They're showing me they can get to anybody in my life."

"Who's they?"

"Gamblers," Sam said with a sneer. "They wanted me to take a dive against St. Cloud. I didn't. This is their way of getting back at me."

Cathy and Randal looked confused. He asked Sam if he owed money to a bookie. Sam shook his head and then told them about the Reapers. "Sorry," he said meekly with head bowed. "I never thought those cowards would come after my friends."

After no one spoke for a while, I asked, "When did this happen to Freddy?"

"Just before dark," Cathy mumbled. "Haleigh wanted to say goodnight to him before I put her to bed. I looked out the window and saw him stumbling around the yard. Then he fell over and started twitching … hard, like a convulsion." She sniffled. "I barely grabbed Haleigh before she got to the back door. Told her she couldn't see Freddy tonight. He was already asleep. She started crying and threw a fit. When I finally got her to bed, I ran out and found Freddy like that. He tried to crawl into his house before he died."

Randal pulled her close as she wiped her eyes. "I don't know what I'm going to tell Haleigh in the morning. She loved that dog so much."

We stood quietly, nobody moving, nobody knowing what to say. "What are you going to do?" Randal asked Sam.

Uncertainty clouded Sam's eyes. "I don't know."

The next morning, Sam and I drove to Elliott Elementary School to talk to a group of third graders. Both of us were dragging from a lack of sleep the night before, but this was part of the team's community outreach program so we had to go. The kids stared in awe when Sam entered the room with his thick arms, long ponytail, dark shades, and backwards Giants cap. Though I did most of the talking, the young audience kept their eyes on my large companion.

After I finished my spiel about the importance of teamwork, the teacher asked her students if they had any questions for us. The best one came from a girl who looked like one of the Olsen twins. When she asked Sam what type of conditioner he used for his hair, he gave a one-word reply: "Rainwater." An undersized boy with a red butch asked me if I thought I'd make the majors someday. I told him anything was possible with hard work and perseverance.

Mrs. McMullan's class then presented us with their crayon drawings of the Giants players. After thanking them, Sam and I said goodbye and went out to the parking lot while the kids lined up to go to lunch. We'd barely left the building when I noticed an unwanted visitor in a tan suit leaning against my Buick. His grin widened as we approached.

"Somebody's gonna die," Sam muttered, quickening his step.

I hustled forward to block his path. "Sam, don't make this worse." I dropped the envelope of drawings and pressed both hands against his chest. "He's got some dangerous friends." Much to my surprise and relief, Sam stopped.

"That's right, Sammy," Merc said. "You got to be careful. It was with great effort that I convinced my bosses to give you another chance. They wanted to take you down, but I said, 'Sammy's a good boy. He just made a mistake.'"

"What kind of sick bastard kills a little girl's dog," Sam snarled over my shoulder.

"Now, I had nothing to do with that," Merc said. "Didn't even know it was going to happen. Remember, I'm just the messenger."

I removed my hands from Sam's chest and turned to face the little man. Merc grinned at me. "Boo, you pitched a heck of a game yesterday. Very impressive. Keep it up, you can get yourself a decent set of wheels and send this heap to the junkyard." He tapped the ashes from his Lucky Strike onto the hood of my car.

"You'd better get out of here," I said. "Unless you'd like to get stuffed into this heap's trunk."

"Boo." He snickered. "Leave the threats to Sam. He's better at it."

I continued to glare at him while Sam cracked his knuckles.

"I get it," Merc said. "No time for chit-chat. Fine. I'll get to the point." He sucked in more nicotine and exhaled a stream of smoke in our faces. "The Reapers are very displeased with you, Sammy. They lost a lot of money on that St. Cloud game. Not good. Not good." His grin slid into a frown. "As I mentioned earlier, I went to bat for you with my bosses. Got you a second chance. All you have to do to make things right is lose game one of the championship series."

"Your bosses got a problem with me, let 'em face me," Sam said. "Don't go after my friends like cowards."

"Oh, they will face you," Merc said. "If you disappoint them again, your baseball career is over. The world will know that you threw a ballgame in Pierre so you and your lady friend could collect. Remember we've got the tape of her placing the bet." His face darkened. "Unfortunately, the men I work for are a spiteful lot. Cross them one more time and they won't stop at ending your pitching career. Not with so many other ways to express their displeasure. Let's see, they could visit the skipper, the doper, the cowboy, or maybe your parents in Des Moines." He tapped a finger in his palm as he listed each potential target. "Then there's the professor. With that cough of his, it wouldn't be hard to make that look like natural causes. And don't forget sweet little Haleigh …"

Sam lunged forward and grabbed his neck. "You touch that girl or any of those people, I'll kill all of you. You understand?"

The little man's eyes bulged as Sam lifted him to his tip-toes. "Don't do this," he gasped. He tried to say something else, but could manage only a squeak.

I grabbed Sam's arm, which remained rock hard with tensed muscles. "Let him go, Sam. This won't solve anything."

He continued to squeeze until Merc's face turned red and then purple. Just when it looked like the troll was about to pass out, Sam dropped him down to the pavement. Merc rolled onto his knees and drew a series of deep breaths. When his quivering face finally lightened to pink, he stood and straightened his suit jacket. "You better watch yourself, Meat!" He jabbed a finger at Sam. "Here's the deal. You lose game one of the championship series. Period. No more warnings after this."

"Just get out of here," I said, fearing that Sam might strangle him here in broad daylight.

"Don't mess around with the Reapers," Merc said, still huffing. "Or your career is over and somebody close to you is dead!"

Sam stepped forward. "Get outta here, Merc," I said, trying to stop Sam's progress. "Or you're the one who's dead."

The little man stepped backwards. "You damn sure better lose this time. You can't protect them all." With that, he turned and scurried away.

Sam flung his cap to the ground and started cursing. I leaned back against the Buick, my eyes searching the sky above.

That evening, St. Joseph defeated Pierre to win the other playoff series. The Bandits would be our opponents in the finals. Their regular season record was identical to ours, but we had a better head-to-head record. That meant Lincoln held home-field advantage in the five-game series to determine the league champion.

Game 1 was Thursday night. An enthusiastic crowd jammed into Sherman Field. Among their ranks were a dozen big league scouts who'd arrived for what was maybe their last chance this season to see Sam Judge on the mound. They also wanted to check out Bandits right fielder Bobby Kalkwarf, who'd won the league triple crown with a .361 average, 34 home runs, and 103 RBIs. Much to the delight of owners, fans, and scouts, the two brightest stars in the Central States League would be facing each other head to head.

The Lincoln Star ran a feature earlier in the week about how the Giants were vying for the city's first professional baseball championship since 1957. Wright and Mendenhall brought in one of the stars from that team, Dick Stuart, to throw the ceremonial first pitch. Known as Dr. Strangeglove for his lack of fielding prowess, Stuart played first base for the Pittsburgh Pirates and Boston Red Sox after his days at Sherman Field. Many Lincoln fans still remembered the 66 home runs he'd hit in the 1956 season. When he stopped by our dugout to greet the Giants, I asked him to autograph a baseball for my dad.

The two managers exchanging lineup cards at home plate were a study in contrasts. On one side stood the rotund Angley, a grizzled veteran with nearly four decades of coaching experience. St. Joseph skipper Les Burton, on the other hand, was young, tall, and athletic. Not yet forty, he looked more like one of the ballplayers than a manager. This was in fact only his second year as the Bandits skipper. But having captured the league championship during his rookie campaign, he already owned one more ring than the venerable Angley. With St. Joseph again in the finals, Burton was a lock to be managing a Double-A or Triple-A team for a big league organization next season.

Our dugout buzzed in the final moments before the Giants took the field. Sam had faced the Bandits twice in the regular season, winning both times while surrendering only three earned runs in 17 innings. And he had limited Bobby Kalkwarf to a modest two hits in eight at-bats. Lincoln fans and players alike were expecting an emphatic statement from our ace to open the series.

Aside from Randal, Cathy and me, nobody in Sherman Field knew about the dark cloud hovering over the Giants that night. The players, fans, owners, scouts, and coaches were all unaware of the decision our starting pitcher had to make. So too were the newspaper reporters and the camera crew broadcasting the game live for Nebraska Public Television.

Having watched Sam brood, sulk, rage, and mope since our last meeting with Merc, I felt the weight he carried to the mound that night. Still, I did not know what he was going to do. The first clue came when he walked the leadoff batter on five pitches. A second base on balls put runners at first and second with Kalkwarf at the plate. Sam fired in a couple of wide ones before serving up a meatball right down the middle. Bobby airmailed the gift over the scoreboard above the left field wall.

When he returned to the dugout, Sam looked like he'd swallowed a bottle of turpentine. The guys tried to encourage him. "We're only down three," Matt said. "We'll get it back." Kenny lightened the mood by playing "Smoke on the Water" with his armpit. Unamused, Angley told him to knock it off.

Sam retired the Bandits in order in the top of the second and Lincoln got on the board in the bottom of the frame. In the third, Sam walked a guy ahead of Kalkwarf and then put another lollipop right in the big man's wheelhouse. The ball took forever to land. It finally hit the ground somewhere near the railroad tracks, a distance that may have surpassed the moonshot I gave up to the redneck Buddha earlier in the year.

After the inning, Angley asked Sam if he was okay. He nodded and sat next to me. With a sick feeling in my stomach, I hoped our guys would not score again so Sam didn't have to keep giving up runs. It felt strange not being happy for Vince when he knocked one over the fence to close the gap to 5-3 in the fourth.

Sam's slow trek to the mound in the fifth reminded me of a death row inmate heading to the electric chair. I knew he wanted to ensure that the Giants couldn't come back after Angley pulled him. He walked the number two hitter in the Bandits order and then drilled Kalkwarf in the back. That earned him a warning from the umpire and invectives from the St. Joseph bench. Myrtle Schultz tried to fire up a "FEE FI FO FUM" chant from the crowd to rouse our struggling hero. But Sam gave up a single and a double to plate three more runs. Waiting for Angley, he listed on the mound like a torpedoed battleship. A pall settled over the muted stands as he limped back to the dugout.

Kalkwarf later blasted his third dinger of the night—this one off Weed—to complete his Reggie Jackson-esque performance. He drove in eight runs in his team's 11-4 triumph. Shell-shocked Lincoln fans trudged to their cars as if being led away to a detention camp. My heart broke when I saw the boy I'd met at the car dealership earlier that summer walk by with tears streaming down his cheeks. Sam was already gone when the players entered the locker room. Our trainer Jerry told us Sam was sick and that Danika had driven him home. The team showered and changed in silence. Not even Angley or Tony had anything to say.

Though not in the mood, I went to JK's with the boys—more out of habit than anything else. Randal did not join us. Understandably still spooked, he wanted to take his wife and daughter home as soon as possible. Amid our sulking, Fender asked me what happened to Sam. "Eight earned runs in one game," he said. "Did he give up eight earned runs the entire season?"

"One of those nights," was all I could say.

Sam dragged me out of bed a little before 7:00 the next morning. Before I could figure out why he was up so early, we were downstairs at the kitchen table eating pancakes with the professor. Hornsby tried to encourage us by directing our focus to Game 2. "Burke is a good pitcher," he said. "The team will rebound. Baseball if anything is a game of renewed hopes."

After breakfast, Sam asked me to drive him to Sherman Field. He'd left his wallet in his locker. Still groggy, I stumbled up the stairs to get my keys. The cobwebs in my head finally cleared on the drive to the ballpark. Upon steering the Buick into the gravel lot, I didn't notice any other cars. Surprisingly though, the front gate was unlocked. Sam's gym bag was in his locker, just where he'd left it the night before. He made no expression upon flipping through his wallet, so I assumed everything was present and accounted for.

After exiting the clubhouse, he wandered toward the diamond. I figured he wanted to exorcize the demons of the previous evening. A faint mist hovered over the field, which murmured like a long-abandoned battleground. Our Game 1 defeat replayed in my head. I could only wonder what Sam was thinking as he gazed at the mound with a faraway look in his eyes.

"What are you boys doing here?" A voice snapped our heads to the right. Angley sat in the front row of the stands just behind our dugout.

"Skip," I said with surprise. "Just picking up something we forgot last night."

He nodded and stared out at the field. I expected him to say something more, but he didn't. Sam went up into the stands and stood in the aisle near Angley. I followed. Lines etched the skipper's downcast face. Even in front of two of his players he was too tired to summon his tough managerial demeanor.

"Did I ever tell you I pitched in those last two games at Yankee Stadium," he said, drifting back in his memories. "Forty-nine."

Sam sat next to him. I remained standing in the aisle a few feet away.

"Just needed to win one of those last two," Angley said. "The first game was tied headin' into the bottom of the eighth. McCarthy brought me in. That New York crowd was goin' crazy. I'm just a kid standing out there all by myself. But I had a cocky streak and nasty curve." He made throwing motion that ended with a twist of his wrist. "Got Berra on a pop out near the dugout and DiMaggio on a groundout to short." His lips formed a wan smile. "The crowd fell dead silent. I was high as a kite after gettin' those two guys. I was gonna shut the door and we was gonna win it in the ninth."

Skip stopped talking to admire the sight of Sherman Field bathing in the rays of the morning sun. "Yankee Stadium, you ever been there?" Sam and I shook our heads. "Majestic. A true cathedral. Second only to Fenway Park." A deep sigh followed.

"Johnny Lindell comes to the plate. He's a big guy, but only hittin' about two-forty for the year. I relax a little, thinkin' I'll slip a fastball past him to get ahead in the count. He was waitin' for it. Knocks it over the wall in left. The Yankees win." Skip coughed out a bitter chuckle. "Johnny Lindell." He shook his head in disgust.

"The next day," Angley continued, "we're down 1-0 in the eighth. McCarthy sends me in again. I don't get nobody out. The guy after me gets roughed up too. It's 5-0 when we finally get the third out. We scored three in the ninth but it was too little too late. And that was our season."

I wanted to say something, but couldn't find the words. Sam appeared to feel the same way. The skipper cleared his throat and gestured out to the field. "This game is beautiful. The grass, the chalk lines, the positioning of the fielders, the matchups ... but it'll break your heart. Some of us know plenty about that."

"Skip, I'm sorry about last night," Sam said with pain in his voice. "We'll get back into this. If I get another start, I'll shut 'em down." Wheels seemed to be turning in his head. "Let me start game three. I don't need the rest."

Angley tapped Sam's leg with his fist. "Judge, it's not your fault. Nothin' you coulda done. This is just my burden. I've given my life to this game and I've gotten a lot out of it. But I don't get to win the big one at the end. Not in forty-nine. Not today."

"Skip, that's not true." Sam's voice cracked like a teenager's.

"Just like Osborne and the Cornhuskers. One year it's a bad call against Penn State that costs him the championship. Then it's a failed two-point conversion. And last year in the Orange Bowl, he just needed a field goal to win it all. But of course it sailed wide left. No other result was possible. It's fate. Like what happened last night." Angley's sad face tightened in defiance. "But I accept it. I don't need a ring. What matters to me is teaching my players. Preparing 'em to go on to bigger and better things, whether they continue in baseball or not."

Sam's eyes met mine for an instant. It was hard enough for me to hear Skip talking like that, but Sam had spent countless hours working with Angley over the past two seasons. "Give me one more chance," Sam pleaded. "Start me in game three. I'll get the win."

"Can't do that, Kid. Not gonna blow out your arm here. You got a bright future ahead of you. This season brought you to the doorstep of the majors. You got nothin' left to prove as a Giant."

"That's not true, Skip." The morning breeze carried away Sam's mumbled words as the three of us returned to our contemplations.

Another lively crowd filed into Sherman Field that night for Game 2. Languidness, however, shrouded the players as we dressed in the locker room. And Angley lacked the energy to try to motivate us. Tony said a few words and Vince threw out some exhortations, but neither could prevent a flat group of Giants from taking the field. Burke didn't make it out of the third and the infield combined for five errors. Kalkwarf blasted two more home runs as St. Joseph cruised 8-0.

Saturday was an off day. Before the start of the championship series, when excitement still burned in us all, Wright and Mendenhall announced that we'd ride to St. Joseph on Saturday so the team would be fresh for Game 3 Sunday afternoon. Now that Burton's Bandits had us buried in a two-game hole, our owners decided not to pay for a hotel stay Saturday night. Their change of heart sent a clear message about what they thought of their team's chances.

The owners' popularity dropped even further with the spreading rumor that Angley would be sacked after St. Joseph finished us off. Skip, no doubt aware of these whispers, descended even deeper into a funk. Shocking us all, he announced after Friday's game that there would be no practice on Saturday.

Sam took off with Danika Saturday morning. I'd been wanting to talk to him about her, but the conversation would have to wait. My thoughts turned to my own plans for the day. Firing up the Buick, I headed to Mabel Lee Field on the UNL campus, where the Husker softball team was opening its fall season. My eyes immediately fixed on the curvy first baseman with the blond ponytail. Whether she was fielding her position, swinging the bat, or running the bases, her movements captivated me. I especially liked watching her jog from the dugout to the field.

In her first at-bat, she turned on a fastball and drove it to the fence for a double. I wanted to jump up shouting and clapping, but restrained myself amid the smattering of spectators in the stands. In the third, she struck out and in the fifth hit into a double play. She made an error in the sixth, allowing the visitors from Northern Illinois to take the lead. I wondered if the stink of failure I carried from the Giants had spread to the Huskers.

In the seventh she stepped to the plate with two outs and runners on first and second. Nebraska trailed by one. Three strikes later the game was over. Watching her drag back to the dugout with her head down sent a wave of sadness sweeping over me.

I remained seated in the fifth row as the fans around me migrated away. Even though there were no more than a couple hundred people at the game, I was sure she hadn't noticed me with my Giants cap pulled down low. My eyes lingered on the deserted field as daydreams of the past summer ran through my head. Then a voice called me back to the present. "Boo?"

She stood near the railing with a bat bag slung over her shoulder. I hadn't noticed her approach. I waved. "Hey, Eileen."

"I saw you up here during the game and wondered if it was really you. What are you doing here?"

"Giants need some help. Thought I might pick up some pointers from you guys." I stepped down toward the railing. "Nice double."

Her eyes dropped. "And then I blew the game."

"Nah. You did great. Made a bunch of nice plays."

She looked out at the field. "I sucked out there. Don't know what's wrong with me."

"I'll have none of that kind of talk, young lady."

A smile flickered before dissipating into a glum expression. It was a look I'd seen before. "Don't you have practice today?" she asked.

I shook my head. "Cancelled. They're pulling the plug on our life support machine. Do not resuscitate."

"What? You guys can still win."

"Maybe." Gazing into her blue eyes fired a bold impulse within me. "Hey, you want to go get a pizza? I found this great place. Best in town."

A look of surprise replaced the gloom as she examined me for a few beats. "Sure. Gimme about twenty to get changed."

While driving to Piezano's on South Street, I was embarrassed by the smoke wafting from the hood of my growling metal beast. She didn't seem to notice. Her distraction likely came from the softball game replaying in her head. At our table we started off with small talk—her classes, the baseball strike, Husker football, and her roommate's unfortunate fascination with Shawn Michaels. Happily, the name Chad did not come up. Not once. She later mentioned Freddy and how sad that was for Haleigh. Cathy hadn't told Eileen how the dog had died, and I said nothing to enlighten her.

After our pizza arrived, she asked, "So are you ready for your big start tomorrow?"

"I guess. Could be the final game of the season. Either way, it's probably my last start as a Giant."

She frowned. "You don't think you'll be back next year?"

"Doubt it. Team almost cut me in August. Wright and Mendenhall want younger pitchers."

"But you've been throwing great lately. A win tomorrow in the finals would get their attention, right?"

"I don't know … minor leaguers get shuffled around a lot. It's the nature of the business."

A melancholy smile appeared. "I would miss you, Boo."

My heart nearly thudded out of my chest. "I would miss you too," I stammered, before taking a drink of Coke to regain my composure. "You'll be too busy next spring to think about the Giants anyway. After leading the Huskers to the College World Series, the little people from your past will be a distant memory."

She lowered her head. "Right. Didn't you see what happened today? I'll be lucky if I'm still on varsity by then."

"Oh, come on. You're the best hitter on the team. One subpar game at the start of the fall season doesn't mean anything."

"I dunno. I've been sucking in practice too. Just not picking up the off-speed pitches. The coaches have really been riding me." Her voice wavered. "And I can't believe how much homework I've got this semester."

"Which classes?"

"Business Management, Business Calculus, American History. I have to write a ten-page paper on the causes of the Revolutionary War, and it's due in three weeks." She stuck her tongue out in disgust. "Haven't even started."

I swallowed a bite of pizza crust and pressed a napkin to my mouth. "I wrote a paper about that in college. I could help you. I mean, if you wanted."

Her face brightened. "Really? Oh Boo, that would be great. This thing's got me freaking out."

"No problem. Want to meet at the library tomorrow?"

She laughed. "You're funny. Gonna fly back from St. Joseph between innings?"

Oh yeah, I'm pitching tomorrow. "Eh, I'll just blow that off. Reed can take my spot."

"I don't think so. The Giants need you to kick-start their big comeback. Remember the sermon about Joshua last week? 'Be strong and courageous.' Tomorrow, you're the team's Joshua." She grabbed a slice of sausage.

"Right, Joshua. Too bad I'll be on the bus tomorrow morning and have to miss the rest of the story."

"Oh … well, I'll take notes for you. Then maybe I'll see you next Sunday. If you come to early service, we could sit together." She flashed me a look.

My body froze. I knew I should say something, but my brain wanted to hit the Pause button and savor this moment. "Uh yeah," I mumbled, "that sounds good."

"That'd be fun. Then maybe you could help me with my paper that afternoon. And you can tell me all about how the Giants won the championship."

"Sure." The recent turn of our conversation swept away the lingering depression I'd been feeling. A door finally appeared to be cracking open.

After I pulled up next to her car in the Mabel Lee parking lot, she touched my arm. "Thanks for hanging out with me, Boo. I really didn't want to be alone with my books this afternoon."

"It was a lot of fun," I said.

"Yeah, it was." Her mesmerizing eyes held me long enough to accelerate my pulse. "Hey, good luck tomorrow. I'll be listening." She said goodbye and got out. Best of all, she didn't say I was a good friend.

Sunday morning the Giants loaded their bags and equipment onto the bus. After hitting the road, it seemed like we were riding in a giant hearse. The dismal mood provided little indication that we were a team playing for the league championship. The few guys who did talk described their plans for the off-season and where they thought they'd end up next year. Even Vince seemed depressed. Going one for seven in the first two games of the series hadn't helped. A few miles down the highway somebody in back fired up a boombox. The first song was "Everybody Hurts" by R.E.M.

We arrived in St. Joseph, Missouri, around noon, two hours before game time. My thoughts had been with Eileen ever since we'd left Lincoln. I pictured her at church that morning and imagined me sitting next to her. As the team dressed for the game, it hit me that I was the most optimistic guy in the locker room. I never could've imagined that turn of events.

Angley tottered to the front of the room and tossed out some pebbles of encouragement. Few players seemed to notice. Eileen's words about me being the team's Joshua played in my head. I asked Vince if I could borrow his Bible. With a puzzled look, he handed his book to me. After flipping through the pages, I stepped up onto a bench.

"Guys, listen up." A room full of faces turned my way. "I want to read something to you. I know a lot of you aren't religious, but I heard some words recently that were kinda inspiring. Thought maybe they could apply to us." After taking a breath, I started reading from the first chapter of Joshua.

"No one will be able to stand up against you all the days of your life. As I was with Moses, so I will be with you; I will never leave you nor forsake you. Be strong and very courageous. Do not be terrified; do not be discouraged, for the Lord your God will be with you wherever you go."

Dead silence blanketed the room as all eyes, including Skip's and Tony's, remained on me. I closed the Bible. "All we have to do today is win one game. That's it. We can worry about tomorrow, tomorrow. Today we just need to win a single game against a team we beat several times during the season. I'm going to do everything I can on the mound to make that happen. I know you'll do the same. As a team, we've got a lot going for us. We've done some great things this season. We've played with confidence and we've played with courage. And that's what we need to do now, today."

Silence. Nobody said a word as I stepped down from the bench. All that was missing was the sound of crickets chirping. Even Vince just sat with his head down as I handed his Bible back to him. Feeling like an idiot, I left the locker room and headed to the bullpen.

Unlike Sam, I didn't have overpowering stuff. I survived on the mound by mixing pitches, changing speeds, and hitting the corners. My control was always best when I was calm and relaxed. And that's how I felt warming up. Nothing bothered me. Not the apathy of my teammates. Not the prospect of getting swept. Not even the teenagers leaning over the fence to heckle me.

My first fastball nipped the inside corner for strike one. My subsequent sliders, heater, and changeup went exactly where I wanted them to go. Two groundouts. *Maybe I am strong and courageous.* I needed to be because Bobby Kalkwarf was stepping into the batter's box. A baseball demolishing machine, he stood a couple inches taller than Sam and was almost as muscular. My first slider missed. Another got fouled back. I checked the sign from Sarge—fastball low and in. I let it fly, but the pitch sailed waist-high out over the plate. A thunderous crack from Bobby's war club blasted a one-hopper to third. Though Matt ducked and turned his head away, the white rocket lodged in the webbing of the glove he'd raised in a reflex act of self-preservation. Happy to be alive, he threw over to first to end the inning.

On the way back to the dugout, Vince slapped my back. "Hey, that was cool what you said before the game. It really moved the guys. Just what they needed to hear."

"I don't know about that."

"It's true. I wanted to say something to you at the time, but I was praying that the Lord would guide and sustain you during the game."

It did seem like the guys had a little more pep as they bantered in dugout. In the third inning we took the lead when Jamario singled, stole second, and came home on a hit by Willie Small. Though my control remained sharp, the Bandits tied it in the fourth when their cleanup hitter ripped a changeup into the gap to drive home a runner from first.

In the sixth, Lincoln DH Brad McGill homered with a man on to put us up 3-1. But the Bandits got one back with a couple of sharp hits in the bottom of the inning. In the top of the seventh, Randal drilled an RBI double down the right field line to push the lead back to two.

Trouble brewed in the bottom of the seventh. An infield single, a blooper, and a walk loaded the bases with two outs. The pesky Che Ramirez stepped to the plate. I needed to get him because the foreboding presence of Bobby Kalkwarf loomed in the on-deck circle. My first pitch to Ramirez, a slider, hit the outside corner for strike one. I then missed with a change and another slider. After Che fouled one off to even the count, my eyes blinked in disbelief when Sarge flashed the sign for a curve. *What is he thinking? This may have worked once before, but I haven't thrown a bender near the plate in weeks.* Visions of a wild pitch bouncing to the backstop flashed through my head. But Sarge nodded as if to reassure me that everything would be okay.

I checked the runner at third and thought of Eileen. *"You're the team's Joshua."* My foot pivoted to start the windup. My arm reared back and then whipped forward with a twist of the wrist. *Crap!* I knew immediately that the ball had no chance of reaching the catcher's mitt. But to Ramirez, who'd never seen a curveball from me, the pitch must've looked for an instant like a slider sailing into the strike zone. His bat swung around as the baseball flopped like a shot quail into the dirt in front of home plate. Sarge corralled the bounce and pumped his fist at the strike out.

Though my elbow twinged with pain, confidence coursed through my body. It came as a disappointment when Angley congratulated me and said my work for the day was through. The Giants scored one in the eighth to increase the lead to 5-2. In the bottom of the frame, Kalkwarf smashed a towering solo shot off Weed to narrow the gap. In the ninth, the Bandits tagged Fender for three hits to score again and put the tying run on third. With tension thick in the air, the Texan then slammed the door shut to preserve a 5-4 victory.

The guys treated me like a hero after the game. Several teammates even told me that my pregame speech had inspired them. Chip interviewed me for the postgame show. I kinda felt like Sam, soaking in the accolades and attention. Sipping a beer at the bar afterwards, I let my thoughts drift back to Eileen. A smile crossed my face as I thought about her listening to the game on the radio.

The victory seemed to remove a 500-pound gorilla from the team's back. At practice the next day, the guys were back to their confident, wise-cracking, selves. Reed Perry got the start in Game 4 and brought some decent stuff. The Bandits' starter, on the other hand, had nothing. Vince's grand slam in the third highlighted a 14-hit barrage as the Giants prevailed 9-3. The series was tied and heading back to Lincoln for the deciding game. And for that contest we would be sending a fully-rested Sam Judge to the mound.

The trip home Monday evening was a complete contrast to the ride into St. Joseph. The jovial bunch clowning around on the bus barely resembled the mourning brood I'd sat with a day and a half earlier. We pulled into the Sherman Field parking lot around 11:30 p.m. After Sam and I tossed our bags in the backseat of the Buick, I noticed an envelope tucked under the windshield wiper. My spirits leapt, thinking it might be from a Husker softball player. Reading the note within, however, immediately doused my optimism.

"What's that?" Sam asked.

"It's from Merc. He says we have to meet him tonight." The not-so-veiled reference to Eileen in the note left me barely able to speak. "Or there will be consequences."

Chapter 14

"Let me see the note."

Saying nothing, I steered the Buick out of Sherman's gravel lot and onto South Street. A tempest swept through my head.

"Brian?"

"Yeah. Here." I handed over the sheet.

Sam reached up and turned on the dome light. It didn't take long for him to comment. "A meeting … and we both have to be there."

"Yeah."

"If we don't show up, people we know could get hurt, including a certain blond softball player." He paused for a second. "Is that supposed to be Eileen?"

"Sounds like it." A sick feeling formed in my gut.

"Why would he mention her? We broke up two months ago."

After stopping at a red light, I glanced over at him. "Well, it could be because—"

"You're kidding," he interrupted, his eyes fixed on the note. "The meeting is at one o'clock tonight at a warehouse. Unbelievable." He then read aloud Merc's closing line. "And boys, you do not want to miss this appointment. Trust me."

"What do you want to do?" I asked.

Sam scratched the side of his scruffy chin. "Let's meet him. You know how to get to this place?"

I hesitated. "Yeah, I know the general area. You really think this is a good idea?"

"If we're gonna have a meeting with him sometime, might as well get it over with. We got time to go home first, right?"

"Yeah." I glanced at my watch. "We got over an hour."

"Good. Let's go drop off our bags."

We whiled away the time at Hornsby's kitchen table finishing off a package of chocolate chip cookies that had been sitting on the counter. Sam said something about hitting the can and went upstairs. Minutes passed. At ten till 1:00 he was still up there. I paced at the base of the stairs. I still wasn't sure we should be going to this meeting, but if we did I wanted to be on time.

Finally the stool flushed and Sam clomped down the stairs.

"Thought you might have fallen in."

"Let's go." He brushed past me to the door.

The warehouse was located a few blocks west of downtown in an industrial area near the Salt Creek. After the Buick crept over some railroad tracks, my eyes scanned the boarded up brick building described by Merc. With great reluctance, I steered into the dark lot and stopped in front of a loading dock.

"The note said the west side. Here we are."

"Yep."

"Really want to do this?"

Sam eyed the warehouse before us. "Yeah. We need to do this."

We got out and stood before two huge rusty metal doors that had once served as loading bays. They looked as if they hadn't been opened in years. I held a faint hope that we wouldn't find a way to enter. A squeak drew our attention to the left. About thirty feet away, near the corner of the warehouse, a walk-in door opened. Sam headed in that direction. I followed. With no hesitation, he entered the building. I poked my head in and then hurried to catch up before I lost him in the darkness.

A musty stench invaded my nostrils. Though walking into total blackness, I sensed we were in a large open chamber. A single light bulb clicked on about fifteen yards ahead. In the cone of light below sat Merc at a small wooden desk. "Right on time," he said. "This way, boys. Front and center."

Sam stepped forward. I remained at his side, matching his slow gait. When we were about halfway to the desk, the door slammed shut behind us. Both our heads jerked around to see nothing but darkness. As we turned to face Merc again, something struck Sam in the stomach with an echoing thud, and three masked figures descended upon him. A battering ram then smashed into my gut, doubling me over. As I struggled to draw painful gasps of air, strong hands pulled me forward and forced me down into a hard chair. One of the assailants handcuffed my wrist to the leg of the chair. The metal dug into my skin, cutting off the circulation to my hand.

"Sorry about the impolite greeting," Merc said. "But I like a captive audience." A goon wearing a ski mask patted all around my torso and then slapped up and down my legs. "Just a formality," Merc continued. "Gotta make sure you fellas ain't miked … or packin'."

My chair was at the farthest extent of the bulb's glow, where light faded into darkness. Looking to my left, I could barely see Sam handcuffed to a chair about ten feet away. Behind us lurked several goons. Five, maybe more. Their heavy breaths provided a disturbing reminder of their proximity. My stomach still throbbed.

"I didn't want to meet like this," Merc said. "But Sammy's inability to control his temper left me with no choice." Tendrils of smoke swirled from the cigarette between his fingers up into the light. "So here we are." The echoing of his voice through the vast chamber added to the malevolence of its tone.

Again turning to Sam, I noticed that both his wrists were cuffed to the legs of his chair. My left arm for some reason was unbound.

"First, let me offer my congratulations to the Giants for coming back to tie the series. A job well done." Merc tapped his cigarette into an ashtray on the table. "Unfortunately Lincoln's return from the dead creates a bit of a problem. Hence our meeting here tonight." His fingers shifted the knot of his navy blue tie slightly to the left.

"See, my bosses wagered vast sums of money not only on game one, but also on the outcome of the entire series. After Sammy's defeat in the opening game, the Giants were supposed to collapse. But they didn't." His eyes moved back and forth between Sam and me. "So that brings us to game five on Wednesday for all the marbles. And guess who's going to be pitching." An ominous grin formed.

"You said I only had to lose one game," Sam barked with disgust.

"Indeed." Merc rose and strolled around to the front of the desk. "But, as you recall, you did not lose the St. Cloud game like we asked. Very bad. That cost my bosses a lot of money."

"I lost to St. Joseph, just like you wanted."

"Yes, you did," Merc agreed, leaning back against the desk behind him. "And that did help atone for your earlier transgression. But you see, that just puts us back at square one. You still owe us. And, as you know, the championship rides on this last game. My bosses *cannot* lose the bets they placed on this series." His expression dropped into a chilly glare. "Plus, they will be wagering even more money on the outcome of game five itself. With Sammy pitching for Lincoln, the odds for a St. Joseph bet are very nice."

"Forget it," Sam snapped. "I already rolled over for you scumbags."

Merc sighed. "Sammy, please, I'm trying to have a conversation with you like a gentleman. And I just explained, very politely, why you must lose again." He turned to tap his ashes into the tray. "Consider the big picture, Sammy. This is the LAST time we will ask you to take a dive for us. On my honor." He raised a hand. "You just have to lose one more game in this bush league. I mean, come on, how many yokels show up at your games? Two thousand. Three thousand, tops. That's nobody." He elongated the vowels of his last word. "Whether the Giants win or lose will mean nothing to your career. Think about it. Do you know Greg Maddox's minor league record? How about Roger Clemens? Did he ever win a title in the minors?"

Merc grinned at Sam before turning to me. "Do you know, Boo?" He shook his head. "No, you do not. Nobody does. Cause what they did in the minors doesn't matter!" He held his palms out to Sam. "Be smart about this, Sammy. You lose one little insignificant baseball game on Wednesday. By Friday the people in this football-crazy town will have already forgotten about it. And the scouts, they already know what you can do. You're gonna have offers up the wazoo. Your ticket to the majors has already been punched. You'll be making millions, Sammy. You'll be famous, pitching in front of fifty thousand every start. The playoffs. The World Series. Cy Young Awards. You can have all that." The grin on his face then tightened into a frown. "But if you win this next game, it's all gone. We've got the tape. Your big league career will be over before it even starts."

"Yeah, you've mentioned that a few times," Sam said.

"You're right, Sammy. I have indeed mentioned that a few times. And I've also described what could happen to you and your friends if you disappoint us again." Merc directed a grim look at Sam while slowly shaking his head. "Yet, we still don't know if you appreciate the gravity of this situation." He sauntered back around the desk and returned to his chair. "So my bosses have asked me to demonstrate to you just how serious they are about this issue."

The creepy gaze that followed sent chills down my spine.

"See, you hear the words I say to you about the consequences of your actions, but do you really understand? So I repeat, if you win on Wednesday night, we will inform the commissioner's office about the games you have thrown in the past. We will cause bodily harm to someone close to you. And—pay attention now Sammy, this part's new—we will disable that million-dollar pitching arm of yours. Your career in baseball will be over. For good."

He gestured in my direction. "And now for a demonstration to make this last point crystal clear."

Two powerful hands gripped my shoulders from behind and pressed down hard. Another strongman grabbed my left arm and pulled it straight out to the side.

"I'm sorry, Boo," Merc said. "I really wish this wasn't necessary." A hammer tapped my forearm, before resting its chilly metal head on the middle of the radius bone, halfway between my wrist and elbow.

"Okay," I shouted, struggling to move. "You've made your point. Sam will lose." Beads of sweat rolled down my back.

"But we have to be sure Sam understands. He needs to see with his own two eyes what will happen. For you Boo, it's just your left arm. With Sam, it will be his pitching arm."

"Stop," Sam yelled. "I'll lose."

"Yes, you will," Merc said. He then nodded at the man behind me.

The cold metal left my skin. An instant later, an explosion of searing pain detonated in my left forearm. My lungs emptied into a scream. My stomach lurched with nausea. The room spun.

"Shut him up, will you." I barely heard Merc's command.

Someone shoved a rag into my mouth. I gagged at the foul taste of the oily cloth as tears rolled off my cheeks. Blood trickled from the trauma point on my destroyed limb.

"Look at him, Sammy. That will be you if you don't comply." Doubled over in the chair, I saw only my brown boat shoes as Merc spoke. "Good night, gentlemen."

The handcuff fastening my right wrist to the chair clicked open. An instant later Sam was at my side pulling me to my feet. "You'll be alright, Brian. We're gettin' outta here."

I spat out the rag and cradled my broken arm against my stomach. The light above the desk went out, bringing complete darkness. The door behind us opened to create a dimly lit rectangle in the wall. Sam held me up as I staggered toward the egress. The flaring pain pushed me to the edge of unconsciousness.

A grandfather clock chimed ten times. My brain emerged from its fog to explore the world around me. Books. A large globe. *I'm sitting in Hornsby's study.*

A large presence appeared before me. Sam. "Here," he said, handing me a glass of milk. "Doc says you're supposed to drink plenty of this."

I sipped the cold white liquid and set the glass on an end table. "The professor here?"

"Just took off." Sam sat in the armchair across the room. "How ya feelin'?"

"Kinda mellow."

"I'm surprised you're awake."

"Maybe I'm not. That stuff they gave me makes it hard to tell."

"Does it still hurt?"

I ran my fingers over the hard white plaster encasing my left forearm. "No, not really. Kinda itches though."

He nodded, his eyes fixed on my cast.

"What did you tell the ER nurses?" I asked. My memory of the past several hours was a blur.

"Told 'em we had some drinks. Then we started goofin' around climbing trees in Cooper Park. You got yourself way up and then fell out."

"Sounds like something Fender and Weed would do." I chuckled. "Not a bad story, I guess. Hope Skip and Tony buy it. Guess it doesn't really matter at this point."

His face dropped into a somber look. "Brian, I'm really sorry. This is my mess and you shouldn't have gotten dragged into it. I …"

"Forget it." I waved a hand. "Neither of us saw this coming."

He nodded and glanced out the window. The clock ticked away the seconds.

"What are you going to do tomorrow night?" I asked.

"What choice do I have?" He shook his head. "What would you do?"

I drew a deep breath. "Guess going to the cops wouldn't help. We've got a dead dog and a broken arm, but can't prove who did either."

"And talking to the cops would reveal my involvement with gamblers. I'd never pitch again." His words echoed with defeat.

"Same thing happens if you win tomorrow. Your career is over and probably worse." I rapped my knuckles on the cast.

"Bastards," he said under his breath.

"I hate the idea of giving in to them just as much as you do, but you really don't have much of a choice. It's one minor league game against a career in the majors." I watched him thinking. "Sam, you'll be in The Show next year. If not then, the year after. Definitely. You'll be making millions."

"Poor Skip. It kills me to let him down again."

"Yeah, it sucks Skip won't get his title. Neither will our teammates. But if they knew the situation, they'd understand. Every one of 'em would do the same thing in your shoes."

"I'd rather eat a roll of barbed wire than give in to those scum gamblers." Sam's voice dripped with contempt.

"I know, but the Reapers are dangerous. They won't stop at wrecking your career. People will get hurt."

A string of profane invectives rolled off his tongue.

"Look at the bright side," I said. "It will be nice to see Wright and Mendenhall lose."

That brought a sneering smile. "Yeah. I will enjoy watching those guys end the season as losers."

191

More time evaporated before I spoke again. "What does Danika say about all this?"

His eyes darted from me to somewhere else. "She says I have to lose. I've come too far to blow my shot at the majors now."

"Do you trust her?"

A hard gaze fixed on me. "What do you mean? You just said the same thing."

"I'm talkin' about the big picture. Lookin' back. How she kept pestering you to give up three runs in a game so she could win a bet. Then, when you finally agreed, her call to Uncle Turk just happens to get taped."

"Turk did that without her knowin' about it. He's the backstabber."

"Okay, but remember when Merc showed up at the school? He listed off the people in your life who could get hurt. Skip, Hornsby, your parents. But he didn't mention Danika. Your girlfriend. The woman closest to you."

"What are you sayin' Brian?"

"I'm saying she could be working for the Reapers. Her, Uncle Turk, they could all be in on it. What if they set you up?"

His countenance darkened. "No. Danika loves me."

"It all fits, Sam. Why do you think she was so persistent about getting you to give up runs? That's what got you into this whole mess."

He sprang from his chair and aimed a finger at me. "Brian, you're still doped up. You're not thinkin' straight."

He stomped away, leaving me alone with the globe, books, and grandfather clock.

I was still in the same chair when a calmer Sam woke me up hours later. "Goin' to practice?"

"Yeah." I grabbed the hand he offered to hoist me to my feet. The room wobbled around me.

"Want me to drive?"

I nodded. Everyone at Sherman Field was suitably surprised when I showed up with my left arm in a sling. Sympathetic as ever, my teammates howled with laughter when I told them I fell out of a tree. Kenny said something about me being a monkey and started jumping around like a primate.

The guys of course wanted to sign the cast. Vince was first, writing "Joshua 1:9" next to his name. Weed added a marijuana leaf to his signature. Sarge wrote something in Spanish under his name. Kenny drew a picture that I'd be crossing out later.

Angley shook his head when he saw the sling. I braced for a lecture, but he just shot me a look that said "idiot" and sent me to the team offices. I spent the next hour filling out paperwork under Mendenhall's disapproving glare.

As the sedatives wore off, my mind darkened. Thinking about the Reapers and what they were capable of created a bolus of dread in my gut. Thoughts of Eileen materialized. The line in Merc's note about "a certain blond softball player" gnawed away at me. Even though Sam was planning to comply with the gamblers' demands, I feared for her safety. *What if the Giants stage a late rally and win despite Sam's efforts? Would the Reapers blame me and go after her?* My anxieties multiplied as I sat in the stands watching the last half hour of practice. I had to talk to Eileen. I had to warn her.

About fifteen minutes after Sam drove us home from practice, Danika pulled up in her Pinto and they took off. After deflecting a few queries from the professor about the previous evening's mischief, I called Eileen. Nobody answered. I called again a half hour later. Nothing. My thoughts churned. *What if the Reapers took her hostage? What if she's out with Chad?* Hornsby fried pork chops for supper. He asked what was bothering me. I told him I was stressed about the final game. That I really wanted the Giants to win for Skip. The professor said Angley was a tough cookie and would be okay either way.

After we'd finished eating, I called again. Eileen's roommate answered and said she was studying at the university library. Off I went. Steering the Buick with one hand required more labor than I'd anticipated. My right arm ached from all the cranking and twisting, but I finally made it to campus.

Upon entering Love Library, I realized I had no idea where to look. There were several different levels in both the north and south buildings. Some desks were out in the open, while countless others hid in nooks and crannies. My head on a swivel, I started wandering. After twenty minutes of searching, I crossed the link and spotted a table near the history stacks where three girls sat. A familiar blond ponytail beckoned. She didn't notice me until I stood right next to her.

"Boo." Her face brightened. "What are you doing here?"

"I, uh, wanted to …"

"Oh my gosh, your arm. What happened?"

"Had a little accident. Kind of a long story." The two other girls at her table—probably softball teammates—examined my cast.

Eileen glanced at her friends. "I'm gonna take a walk," she said to them. "You're gonna be here a while, right?" They nodded.

Upon exiting the library, we decided to go to the Student Union, where we ended up in a booth at the Burger King inside. "So what's the story?" She gestured at my arm.

"What I told the guys is that Sam and I were drinking and horsing around at Cooper Park last night. I climbed a tree and fell out."

"A tree?" Her brows rose with skepticism. "You and Sam were climbing trees? Did anybody believe that?"

"Actually, they did." I downed a swig of Coke. "I think everybody's just happy it was me and not Sam with the broken arm."

"Oh Boo." She shook her head and sipped her coffee. "So what really happened?"

I scanned the sparsely populated tables in the restaurant. "Gamblers."

"Gamblers?" Her blue eyes narrowed in puzzlement.

"Actually it was the thugs working for the gamblers who did this."

Her mouth fell open. "What? Boo … what is going on?"

I told her the story, everything from Danika's bet to my late night visit to the ER at Lincoln General. Her face was pale by the time I had finished.

"There's one more thing," I said. "In that note Merc left under my windshield last night, he mentioned a blond softball player."

She blinked a couple times. "Me?"

"I don't know who else it could be."

"But I'm not in Sam's life anymore. Why would—"

"I think they're watching both me and Sam. Since I've been present whenever Merc showed up, the Reapers must consider me a person of interest too."

"Think they saw us at Piezano's last Saturday?" Concern strained her voice.

I nodded.

Her eyes darted around the restaurant and out at the Student Union concourse. Both hands gripped her coffee cup before raising it to her lips.

"I'm really sorry, Eileen. This is the last thing I wanted. But I thought you should know what's going on."

"It's not your fault. This is Sam's problem. You just got caught up in it. Apparently I did too."

I rolled the wrapper from my straw into a little ball. "When Sam loses tomorrow, that should take the heat off. But if something goes wrong—if the Giants come back and win or something, the Reapers are going to be pissed. Merc said they'd break Sam's arm. I don't know who else they'll target." I searched her face. "Is there any way I can see you tomorrow night?"

Her eyes widened. "You want to see me?"

"I know you aren't planning to go to the game. That's probably a good idea. But afterwards, I want to make sure you're safe. I may be down an arm, but I've got a can of Mace."

She smiled. "My hero."

"I'm sorry to bother you like this, but after everything that's happened I have to know you're okay." My voice cracked.

She looked touched. "Boo, of course you can see me tomorrow. Where do you want to go?"

I leaned back. "I dunno. Anywhere. As long as we're …"

"Together?" She flashed a coy look.

My face heated as I looked away. "Yeah."

We remained at Burger King a while longer talking about nothing in particular. When we approached the library entrance she checked her watch. "It's getting late. I don't feel like studying anymore."

"Oh. I'm sorry I took up so much time."

She waved her hand like it was no big deal. "I've got to go in and get my books and backpack."

"I'll wait."

"'Kay." She disappeared into the building.

When we reached her car a few minutes later, she turned to face me. "Thanks for coming out here tonight. I'm glad you're looking out for me."

My heart rate accelerated. "Uh, yeah."

"So, you'll pick me up after the game tomorrow?" Moonlight gleamed in her eyes as the wind sent an alluring fragrance in my direction.

I nodded. Then my brain, probably still loopy from painkillers, issued a sanity-defying message that propelled my body to action. Sliding my good arm around her back, I pulled her in and pressed my lips to hers. My nervous system nearly shut down at the overload of sensations. For an instant, terror seized my body at the realization of what I was doing. But the fear dissipated when she wrapped her arms around me and returned my kiss.

At some point we parted and said goodnight. I finally knew what it was like to fly.

The atmosphere at Sherman Field Wednesday night reminded me of the other big games we'd played that season: opening night, Fourth of July, the first game of the playoffs. And with a championship on the line, there was an extra charge of electricity in the air. Before the game, the Giants held a pregame ceremony honoring the players. We all formed a line across the infield and tipped our caps when our names cracked from the PA system. Then it was time for the team awards. Flashbulbs popped when Sam stepped forward to receive the Giants pitcher of the year plaque from Wright. Vince won the team's offensive MVP award.

The final award was for most popular player, an honor decided by the fans. I figured either Sam or Vince would win, but following a dramatic pause, the name "Dallas 'Fender' Bender" echoed through the park. Fender and Weed traded smirks. Earlier in the season they had talked about stuffing the ballot box. I assumed they were joking—I was wrong. The PA system revved up "Cotton Eyed Joe." With a whoop, Fender sauntered forward, hooked his thumbs in his front belt loops, and started dancing. The crowd clapped along with the beat as his feet stepped forward, back, and side to side. Several fans jumped up to join in with the dance.

Adding to the excitement among players and spectators was the ESPN2 crew sent to cover the game. With the big league games cancelled, network executives hoped the nation's baseball-starved viewers would be drawn by the opportunity to watch a league championship game featuring two potential major league stars. So not only would a few thousand fans at Sherman Field watch Sam roll over again, but also a TV audience of hundreds of thousands across the country.

My eyes roamed the crowd during the national anthem. Several scouts claimed spots in the front three rows behind home plate. Looking higher in the stands roiled my stomach. Flanked by two goons, Merc sat in the top row just below the press box. They reminded me of vultures. My discomfort turned to sadness as I scanned the surrounding fans, young and old, proudly clad in Giants purple. This feeling multiplied when my gaze fell on Angley. The spark had returned to the old man's eyes since we tied the series. He really believed we had a chance.

The crowd cheered as the Giants took the field. I couldn't bear to watch Sam warm up, so I stared at the horizon beyond the centerfield wall. A bag of sunflower seeds lay beside me on the bench. With only one functioning arm, I couldn't open the package. And I didn't feel like asking anyone for help.

Sam rocketed the first pitch, a 95-mph fastball, over the plate for strike one. Our fans roared and kept on roaring as he mowed down the first three Bandits, including Kalkwarf who struck out chasing a filthy slider low and away.

St. Joseph sent its ace Quinton Murphy to the mound. His twelve wins and 2.78 ERA in the regular season made him one of the top starters in the league. He came out throwing smoke, sending Jamario, Willie, and Brad down in order.

And that's how the game progressed. Sam retired the Bandits in the top of an inning; Murphy retired the Giants in the bottom. Neither team managed a hit until Willie's broken bat blooper in the bottom of the fourth. Even though Vince walked later that inning, the Giants couldn't push across a run. Sam surrendered a base on balls in the fifth, but gave up nothing more in the frame. The score remained 0-0 after six. I couldn't see Merc from my seat in the dugout, but I imagine he wasn't pleased.

Between innings Sam sat by himself at the end of our bench. All things considered, he looked rather content—much more relaxed than the 3,000 spectators on the edge of their seats. In the top of the seventh Kalkwarf drilled a slider between first and second to notch the first St. Joseph hit of the night. I figured Sam had decided it was time. With Murphy pitching so well, at least he wouldn't have to give up a barrage of runs. Two or three should do it. My jaw dropped when Sam struck out the next two batters to end the inning.

During the seventh-inning stretch, the crowd rose to sing "Take Me Out to the Ballgame." Stilted Lincoln pranced around before them. He then pulled a long-barreled fake pistol from his black overcoat and fired blanks at the Bandits players. The crowd loved it, finally showering our much-maligned mascot with cheers.

As the Giants batted in the seventh, I sat next to Sam at the end of the bench. "How ya doin'?"

His expression remained stoic. "Not bad. You?"

"Got things under control out there?"

"Yep." An ESPN camera appeared at the end of the dugout, bringing an abrupt end to our conversation.

In the eighth, Sam gave up a walk with one out. The runner stole second as the next batter went down swinging. With two outs, the Bandit shortstop hammered a hard grounder to third that went through Matt's legs into left field. The crowd groaned as the runner on second raced around third to score. Sam pounded his fist in his glove. A fly out to Randal ended the inning.

Sam dropped onto the bench muttering to himself under his breath. With the cameraman gone, I leaned over to him. "An unearned run. Might not have to give up any more. You'll still look good when this is over."

"Yeah, right." His cold gaze roamed the field.

Salazar flew out to start the Giants eighth. Sarge followed by fouling off a succession of pitches. Then, completely fooled, he swung wildly at a curve in the dirt for strike three. But the ball skidded past the Bandits catcher to the backstop, allowing Sarge to take first.

That brought Kenny, our number nine hitter, to the plate. Skip scanned the bench, contemplating which pinch hitter to summon. It made sense to bat for Kenny, who hadn't hit much in the playoffs and was 0-2 on the night. Yet Angley, for reasons known only to him, made no move. He just turned and yelled, "Make solid contact, Haldeman. Solid contact."

Kenny went after Murphy's first offering and hammered it to deep left center. The Bandits centerfielder, who'd been playing shallow for this at bat, raced back in a dead sprint. He closed the gap so rapidly, it looked like he'd make the play. But the ball barely cleared his glove and struck the base of the wooden wall with a loud knock.

The centerfielder crashed into the Barbers on Arapahoe sign and flopped backwards onto the warning track. The baseball ricocheted back into centerfield, far away from the left fielder now chasing it. Kenny meanwhile motored toward second. By the time the St. Joseph outfielder reached the ball, Tony was waving Kenny around third. He crossed the plate standing up. His first home run of the season had put the Giants ahead 2-1.

The stands erupted. In the dugout Kenny's ecstatic teammates batted him around like a ragdoll. As the ovation continued, he escaped to tip his hat to the cheering throng. That had to be his first ever curtain call. Sam remained expressionless sitting at the end of the dugout. If the Giants were to lose, he'd need to give up more runs.

Sam stalked to the mound to pitch the ninth. He stood impatiently waiting for the first batter to dig into the box. The Bandit managed a check swing roller to third, which Matt easily turned into out number one. The second batter hit a lazy fly ball to shallow right for out number two. I watched in confusion, wondering what was going through Sam's head.

Kalkwarf stepped to the plate. The crowd tensed, awaiting one final matchup between the two titans. Sam unleashed a 96-mph fastball that flashed over the inside corner. He then conjured a changeup 30 mph slower that clipped the outside corner at Kalkwarf's knees. Down 0-2 in the count, Bobby paced out of the box as the crowd broke into a thunderous "FEE FI FO FUM" chant. The batter finally stepped back in, his devastating bat raised high above his shoulder. Sam went into a slow windup and cut loose an unholy curve that held Kalkwarf motionless.

Strike three. Game over.

Because of my arm I couldn't join in the dog pile of Giants on the field. Players jumped, wrestled, and hugged each other in a big scrum near the mound. Fans clapped and yelled. A few of them ran onto the field to congratulate their heroes. Angley and Tony remained near the dugout watching their players celebrate.

"How about that," Tony said. "You did it."

Skip gazed out at the chaos. "*We* did it." His countenance brightened as ancient demons were cast from his presence.

At last my teammates unformed their pile. Children crowded around anyone in a Giants uniform, including myself, to ask for autographs and souvenirs. Signing was tricky for me since the requester had to hold the object on which I tried to scribble my name. I still enjoyed the attention.

A group of reporters surrounded Sam. As he answered their questions, Springsteen's "Glory Days" blared from the PA speakers. Shouting and revelry filled the air. Fireworks lit up the sky with colorful brilliance. The fey atmosphere produced an ebullience unlike anything I'd ever witnessed on a baseball field.

Then my eyes passed over the spot in the stands where Merc and his henchmen had sat. They were gone, but the danger they represented lingered. My nerves tensed as I looked around for anyone suspicious.

The Giants finally waded through the fans to file into the clubhouse. Champagne flowed, though somewhat sparingly since Wright and Mendenhall had sprung for only three bottles. Angley tried to deliver a speech, but got choked up. He managed to rasp out how proud he was of us and how this was his happiest moment in five decades of baseball. His players responded with whoops and hollers before the plentiful cans of beer started popping open.

Bobby Evans helped me pull my shirt off over my cast. Then, for the last time, I removed my spikes, belt, stirrups, and pants—each article soaked with alcohol. Memories of the past season floated by as I ran my hand over the purple 21 stitched into the back of my uniform. This reminiscing quickly turned to thoughts of Eileen. Even though she said she wouldn't unlock her door for anyone but me, I wanted to get to her apartment as soon as possible.

After dressing and making sure my can of pepper spray was still in my gym bag, I burst out of the clubhouse into a small group of lingering fans. Plastering on a fake smile, I signed my name a few more times. Just when I was almost in the clear, a reporter for the *Lincoln Journal* cornered me. So I had to spend another five minutes describing how great it felt to help bring a championship to the city.

At last, I broke free and exited the front gates of Sherman Field. A line of cars waited to leave the lot. I stopped to scan for any sign of the Reapers, even though I didn't know what they drove. A hand gripped my shoulder.

"I need your keys," Sam said.

It took a few seconds for my fried nerves to settle. "You won," I stuttered. "You won."

A few passing fans congratulated us. Jamario, Willie, and Bobby then strutted by and asked about our postgame celebration plans. After they went on their way, Sam pushed me back into the ballpark. Next thing I knew, he'd ushered me into the equipment shed just inside the front gate. He pulled the swinging wooden doors shut, leaving us in the dim glow of a hanging bulb.

"I need your car, Brian."

"What happened to the plan? You know, the one where you lose the game and none of us gets murdered?"

"Plans changed. I need your keys."

"Why? I have to get somewhere too." My grip tightened on the key ring in my hand.

"This is really important." His stare bored a hole through me.

"I need to go warn people," I said. "Merc and two of his thugs were here tonight. You see them?"

"Yeah, I saw 'em."

"We have to move fast. Before they strike."

"I'm going to strike them first." His tone darkened.

"What? You don't even know where they are."

"Yes I do."

"How?"

"At the warehouse when they were wrestling me into the chair, a hotel key fell out of one of their pockets. It was the Cornhusker."

My eyes drifted to a riding mower as I pondered his revelation. "That was two nights ago. You think they're still there?"

"Yeah."

"How do you know?"

"Brian, I don't have time for all these questions."

"You also don't have a car."

His face tightened in frustration. "I used some of the money I won from the Pierre game to bribe a clerk at the hotel to tell me their room numbers and the nights they're booked. Once I described Merc, he knew exactly who I was talking about. There's five guys with him and they're stayin' in three rooms on the ninth floor. They're probably there right now planning what to do. That's why I've got to move fast."

"These guys have guns, Sam. You can't just kick down their door and start swinging."

"Don't worry about it. I've got a plan." His eyes squinted with a wild look.

"This is crazy. I can't let you do this."

He exhaled in exasperation. "Brian, I'm really sorry about this." He spun me sideways and slid behind my back. One thick arm wrapped around my neck while another pressed against the back of my head.

"What the hell? Let go!" I tried to escape, but my movements sent jolts of pain shooting through my broken arm. "Ow!"

"Just relax. This won't hurt."

"You stupid oaf! I can't breathe! Let go … I'm not going to sleep I'm …" My world went dark.

Sometime later, I awoke lying on the floor. A fuzzy light above me grew brighter until it hurt my eyes. Rakes, clippers, gas cans, and other objects slowly came into focus. I was unsure how long I'd been out, but it didn't seem like too much time had passed. Scrambling to my feet, I burst out of the equipment shed and ran to the parking lot.

My Buick was gone.

Chapter 15

I stood in the gravel lot processing the situation. Taillights of exiting cars glared like red eyes. A second glance at the spot where I'd parked hours earlier still revealed nothing but an empty space. It didn't seem real. This night. This week.

"You lost?" Lugging a stuffed gym bag, Kenny approached from the front gate. "C'mon, Boo, you forget what your pile of junk looks like?"

"My car's gone. I need a ride."

"What? Who'd want to steal that old piece of—"

"Sam took it. We need to go. Now!" I grabbed his arm and pulled him toward his car.

His grin became a frown. "Hey! What's going on, Boo?"

"Keep moving. I'll explain in the car."

We climbed into Kenny's Escort hatchback. "Alright," he said, fastening his seatbelt. "Just where is it we gotta get to so fast?"

Good question. I wanted to try to stop Sam if possible. But I *needed* to get to Eileen. I had to know that she was safe. "Eileen's. We're going to Eileen's."

"Eileen's? Why? Hey, are you two …"

"Yes. Now get moving. I'll give you directions on the way."

His mouth curled into an adolescent smirk. "All right, Boo. Ooh, does Sam know?"

"Just drive, Kenny!"

I explained the situation to him on the way. Gamblers. Thrown ballgames. Threats of violence. Sam on the loose with a crazy plan. Kenny didn't believe me at first, but the urgency in my voice and frantic admonitions to drive faster eventually convinced him.

"But if you want to stop Sam from getting himself killed," he said, "why are we going to Eileen's?"

"I told you. The Reapers listed her as a target. I have to make sure she's okay." My mind swept aside a fearful thought about what might be happening at the hotel. "Sam can take care of himself." *I hope.*

After Kenny pulled into a parking spot in front of the apartment complex, I gripped my can of Mace and darted into the building. Seconds later I pounded on the door to Eileen's second floor apartment. Nothing. My body tensed. *Please let her be okay.* More knocking. Kenny scooted down the hall and stood at my side.

Finally, a lock clicked and the door cracked open as far as the chain would allow. Eileen peeked through the narrow slit at me. She then slid the chain loose and opened the door. "Boo ... Haldeman?" She looked confused.

"Are you okay? Has anybody come here?"

"Yes ... no. I'm fine."

We stepped into her apartment and locked the door behind us. "Sam won," I said.

"I know." Anxiety flashed in her eyes. "Now what's gonna happen?"

"He took my car. He's going to the Cornhusker Hotel to confront the Reapers."

"Huh? How does he know they're there?"

"He found out. Says he's gonna hit them first before they can hurt anybody."

"That's crazy. That big idiot's going to get himself—"

"I know. We have to try to stop him. If it's not too late."

She nodded.

"Are you kidding me?" Kenny threw up his arms. "Haven't you seen *GoodFellas*? Those mafia guys have guns. And all we've got is Boo's can of pepper spray."

"Sam's our friend. He'd do the same for us."

Kenny sputtered a few expletives. "This is just great. I'm finally the big hero and ten minutes later I'm gonna get killed by mobsters."

"You won't get killed," I said, moving to the door. "You just need to drive me over there. Besides, the Reapers are only concerned about Sam."

"Is that what they told you when they were breaking your arm?"

"We have to do this, Kenny. If we don't, something very bad could happen."

The three of us hurried down the hall toward the stairs. "Oh aren't we cool," Kenny quipped when we reached his Escort. "The Hardy Boys and Nancy Drew comin' to save the day."

"Shut up, Haldeman," Eileen snapped.

We got in the car, none of us convinced this was a good idea.

Eileen's apartment was only a couple minutes from downtown. When we arrived at the Cornhusker, a prickling nausea germinated in my gut. The sight of my Buick parked nearby on the street turned this nausea into a flaring ulcer. Kenny slowed in front of the hotel's main entrance on 13th Street.

"There's nowhere to park," he said.

"That's fine." I reached for the door handle. "Just drop me off. Then drive somewhere safe." I opened the door and got out.

"I'm going too," Eileen said, pushing the passenger seat forward and crawling out from the backseat.

"No. Stay with Kenny."

"Boo, you have one arm." She slammed the car door shut. "I'm not letting you go in there by yourself."

"No. You need to …"

She marched halfway toward the hotel entrance before looking back at me.

"Guess she's going in," Kenny said through the open window.

Cursing under my breath, I caught up with her. "When we get up there, stay behind me."

We passed through the glass doors into the hotel lobby. Everything seemed normal. The lone clerk behind the counter was busy assisting a young businessman. An older couple leisurely descended the spiral staircase. Eileen and I veered left toward the three elevators. After I pushed a button, the middle doors slid open with a ding. We entered and pressed nine.

Two horses inside me galloped in a desperate race. Adrenaline-fueled courage drove one of the animals, while a fearful dread jockeyed the other. They raced forward neck and neck. I turned to Eileen, her brow creased with determination. Or concern. She moved in close and grabbed my arm. The courage horse nosed ahead.

My nerves shuddered when the elevator stopped at the ninth floor. Stepping in front of Eileen, I raised my spray can and waited for the doors to part. They opened to reveal a carpeted space, empty except for a table and a gold-colored lamp. My lungs exhaled in relief. Crouching, I crept forward and peered left down the hallway. Nothing but closed doors. Looking the other direction around a corner, I saw more of the same.

Though I didn't know which way to go, I headed to the right. About halfway down the corridor, I heard voices from one of the rooms. The words were muffled, but the tone rang with truculence. Eileen nudged me and pointed to the door handle. It had been bashed loose, leaving the door slightly ajar.

Then a noise made me flinch. It was like a discharge, something I'd heard before on television. *A gun with a silencer.* Someone groaned. Then someone else said, "I'm going to enjoy watching you die. Where should the next one go?"

Casting fear and prudence aside, I sprang forward. Driving my shoulder into the door, I burst into the room. In a flash, my eyes took in the scene. A man in a suit was splayed face down across the near bed. Another was strewn over the dresser. Sam sat on the floor between the beds, his hand clutching the left side of his chest. Merc stood over him with a pistol aimed at his forehead. His head jerked toward me to reveal a red face contorted with rage.

"You," he snarled. "Fine. I'll kill you both." The gun barrel swung around to point directly at me. His eyes squinted, freezing me with terror. Then his body lurched from the impact of Sam's foot driving into his knee. The gun went off. I charged forward. Behind me, Eileen screamed.

Merc regained his balance and raised the gun again. I pressed the button on the can I held, sending a stream of liquid into his face. He yelled and fell backwards onto the far bed. Dropping the pistol, he rubbed frantically at his eyes while shouting and kicking.

A cry turned my attention back toward the door. Eileen knelt on the floor pressing a hand against the side of her face. I dropped the pepper spray and ran over to her. A crimson drop trickled through her fingers. My soul collapsed. "No! Eileen!" I fell to my knees and tried to cradle her with my one working arm. Thoughts in my brain collided violently with each other. Amid the confusion, a coherent statement formed. "Don't move. I'll call an ambulance."

"I don't think the bullet hit me."

Hearing her voice brought a wave of relief. "Really," I stammered.

She pointed to a jagged hole above us. "I think a piece of the wall flew out and nicked me." She moved her hand. "How does it look?"

An inch-long cut marked her right cheek. It was red, but not bleeding much. "It's just a cut," I said. "Thank God."

A metallic thud drew my attention back to the interior of the room. Merc lay motionless on the bed. Above him stood Sam with a bloodstained tire iron in his hand. He raised the weapon again.

"Sam, no!" I yelled. "Don't kill him."

He stared at me with glassy eyes. His tottering body then dropped onto the bed next to Merc. A red spot the size of a grapefruit blotted his shirt just below the left shoulder. As he sat in a daze, I noticed another dark mark on his right thigh.

"Sam." I ran over and grabbed his arm to steady his swaying. "Sit tight, man. We'll get help."

"The little bastard shot me," he mumbled.

"I know. I'm going to call an ambulance." I turned to the nightstand, where Eileen had already grabbed the phone.

"Busted up two of 'em." He gestured at the goons sprawled out in different parts of the room. "Then the troll shot me in the leg."

"You're gonna be okay."

"Then he did it again." He placed his hand over the chest wound.

"Did you just burst in here swinging the tire iron from the trunk of my car? I thought you had a plan."

"That *was* my plan." A slight grin formed, before he coughed out a spray of blood.

"Easy man. Just keep breathing. Help is on the way."

"There's more to it," he said with a wince. "My plan. You'll find out."

"Okay." I glanced at Eileen, now describing the situation to the 911 operator.

Sam gripped my shoulder. "You were right about Danika."

"We can talk about it later. Save your strength."

"The bitch was in on it the whole time." His eyes moved to Eileen. "I had a good thing and threw it all away.... Treat her right. She's special."

"You know about us?"

"Yeah, I know." He managed a faint smile.

I again examined his bloodstained shirt and the oozing hole in his jeans. "Maybe I should get some washrags to apply some pressure." I didn't know if that would help, but it sounded like a good idea.

He nodded. "You're a good man, Brian. I was lucky to have you as a friend."

In the bathroom, I ran water over three white washcloths. It couldn't have taken me more than thirty seconds, but when I came out, Sam was gone. I checked the floor on each side of the beds. Eileen hung up the phone.

"Where's Sam?" I asked her.

"He isn't in the bathroom? He got up and limped after you. I figured you guys were both at the sink."

"Oh no. He took off."

"He couldn't have gone far."

As I moved toward the door, the man sprawled across the dresser stirred. With a moan, he rose to a sitting position and blinked a couple times. His blood-caked face formed a scowl and he slid a hand inside his blazer. Not waiting for it to reemerge, I reached for the pepper spray lying on the floor. By the time my hand clutched the can, I was once again looking down the barrel of a revolver.

As my brain scrambled to find words that would convince him not to shoot, Eileen sprang forward, smashing her fist into his jaw. His head snapped back from the impact. A pair of glazed eyes returned to me just in time to receive a blast of burning spray. His head again jerked back, this time crashing hard into the mirror. Leaving a spider web of cracks in the glass, he flopped forward off the dresser and landed face first on the floor.

I turned to Eileen. "Nice punch."

"Thanks."

"The police are coming, right?"

"Yeah."

"Let's get out of here and look for Sam."

I scanned the hallway carpet for a trail of blood but found nothing. We opened the door to the stairwell. Nobody was there. I listened for footsteps, but heard only sirens echoing through the streets below. Eileen and I hurried down the hallway to the elevators. During the ride down, my mind struggled to process what had just happened. And what was still happening. The doors opened to the lobby as two police officers entered the hotel. More were on the way.

With red and blue lights flashing through the front windows, Eileen and I sat in the lobby of the Cornhusker answering questions. While we gave our statements, Merc and two semi-conscious Reapers were wheeled past us to ambulances waiting outside. Throughout my testimony, I emphasized the need to find Sam. Six officers scoured the building while a half-dozen more combed the surrounding blocks.

The police weren't the only ones searching for Sam Judge that night. After I told the head detective about Merc's threats to people we knew, he dispatched squad cars to residences throughout the city. Officers arrested two Reapers staked outside Hornsby's house. That left one more thug out there somewhere in Lincoln.

When the sun rose the following morning, Sam was still at large. But that afternoon a package from him arrived at the police station. Mailed a day earlier, before the final game, it included two tapes. One of them contained Sam's testimony about everything— giving up runs, throwing a game, Merc's blackmail, and the Reapers' threats. The other tape was a recording of the events at the warehouse the night the Reapers broke my arm. Sam had used a Sony M909 recorder for this tape. Police later found the device when searching our room at Hornsby's. Though very small, the M909 should've been detected when Merc's men patted Sam down. Investigators asked me where he could've hidden it. I thought of only one answer—he must have tied it into the thick mane that hung down behind his head and neck. I recalled how long he'd spent in the bathroom before we left for the warehouse. Sam had apparently put some thought into his plan.

The tapes provided authorities exactly what they had been looking for. The FBI had been investigating the Reapers' activities for more than two years. With Sam's recordings, my testimony, and the documents seized from Merc's hotel room, the Feds were able to lower the boom on the illegal gambling syndicate. After his indictment, Merc turned state's evidence. His testimony revealed that the organization's tentacles stretched across the Midwest and included meth-trafficking and money-laundering operations. The entire crime network came crashing down into a pile of rubble.

The local media immediately made Sam's attack on the Reapers their top story. This news spread and reporters from all over descended upon Lincoln. All three major networks, along with CNN and ESPN, featured the story on their nightly broadcasts. It was beyond bizarre hearing Tom Brokaw utter my name on the NBC Evening News. Sam's disappearance elevated the story into a national phenomenon. He became something of a vigilante folk hero. Bogus reports of Sam sightings were reported from coast to coast. I waited anxiously for a real announcement that he had been found alive and safe. It never came. The police searched for weeks, but the trail grew cold. He had vanished.

It seemed like everybody had a theory about Sam's fate. The most popular explanation among people familiar with the case was that the Reapers or their allies had grabbed him. There was at least one more of Merc's thugs in Lincoln that night who was never arrested. And the Reapers had ties to powerful mobsters in other parts of the country. These men possessed the resources to quickly find a guy and make him disappear.

Investigators questioned me repeatedly about Sam's wounds. They found one of the bullets in the hotel room lodged near the base of the wall between the beds. That was likely the one Merc fired from above into his chest. Since the shot apparently passed cleanly through Sam's body, it may not have been life-threatening. Especially if it hit high, near his shoulder. But if the bullet passed close to his heart, his prospects were less promising, regardless of who may or may not have found him.

In November I drove to Des Moines to visit Sam's parents. His father stared at me with vacant eyes, never altering his stoic expression. His mother tried to have a normal conversation, but eventually broke down. She nonetheless still believed her son was alive. They hired a private investigator to continue the search.

Weeks passed. The leaves blew away and snow covered the ground. Still nothing. Finally in April, there was news. Police in

Tucson picked up Merc's fifth man. He told investigators that after Sam disappeared from the hotel, the Reapers' mob allies sent six hitmen to Lincoln that night to look for him. A couple of these guys found him hiding in an empty railcar outside town the following afternoon. The hitmen put a bullet in his head and then burned the body. At first, nobody believed this creep. Everything about him—especially the frequent blinking and lopsided smirk—suggested he was lying. But he passed a polygraph test. The news was devastating.

The Judges ended their search and held a memorial service for their son in Des Moines. Nearly all of our Giants teammates from the previous season showed up, as did Angley, Tony, and Hornsby. Also present were two FBI agents, in case the people who had ended Sam's life decided they wanted even more revenge. Pictures of Sam covered a large bulletin board at the church. The photos charted his growth from a surprisingly bald baby to a muscular hairy man. It was easy to identify Sam in his baseball team photos. From Little League through college, he was always the big guy with the dark mane flowing down from his cap. One of the recent snapshots showed just the two of us. He had his arm draped over my shoulders. Randal had taken the photo in his backyard while we were hamming it up after a few beers. The only other time I remembered Sam putting his arm around me was when he helped me stagger out of the warehouse.

During the service, the pastor invited friends and relatives to come up and say a few words about Sam. Angley fought off his emotions to talk about Sam's greatness as a pitcher—the best he'd ever coached. Randal, Weed, Fender, Kenny, and Vince shared some memories from the '94 season. Then it was my turn to speak. After I said a few words about our friendship, I talked about Sam's character: "He could've taken the easy road. He could've thrown that last game and gone on to a successful career in the majors. He probably would've been rich and famous. But he took a stand against something he knew was wrong. And when the people closest to him were being threatened, he sacrificed his career and ultimately his life to protect us. That was Sam Judge."

Life went on. It had to. The Giants opened the 1995 season at Sherman Field on May 18. For the first time in more than two decades, Don Angley was not in their dugout. After all that had transpired the past six months, he decided to retire and pass the managerial reins to Tony. The new Giants skipper asked me to come back as a starting pitcher. I declined. I just couldn't wear that uniform again. Plus, I had a new job that, unlike baseball, could turn into a career for me. A couple months earlier, an editor for the Lincoln newspaper had asked me to write a guest column about the Giants '94 season. He liked what I wrote and I ended up with a job as a local news reporter.

Eileen had her best season yet for the Nebraska softball team. An all-conference selection, she led the team in home runs and RBIs, helping the Huskers set a school record for victories. In the final game of the NCAA Regional, her bases-clearing double sent Nebraska to the College World Series, where the Huskers finished third. After graduating from UNL in May, she took a job as a claims examiner with American Family Insurance in Lincoln.

Neither of us made it out to Sherman Field during the '95 season. It was just too weird. But Randal talked us into going to the final game on Labor Day. He had spent the season as a pinch hitter and backup outfielder for the Giants. He was no longer the everyday right fielder because Tony had hired him as his assistant coach. In what would be his last game as a player, Randal got the start in right field.

Eileen and I sat in the second row behind the home dugout. As stilted Lincoln staggered before us, I reviewed the Giants program. Fewer than half the names on the roster were familiar. Weed, Matt, and Brad were back. So too were Charlie Christianson and Bobby Evans. Ted Pottebaum and George Lazzeri were the only pitchers I knew, besides Weed. Tony and Randal had guided the '95 Giants to a winning record, but they were four games out of a Wild Card spot with one left to play. It was actually an impressive showing, given the talent that Lincoln had lost. The core of the previous season's championship team was now playing elsewhere. That's the way it is with minor league baseball. Players are always moving around, trying to climb the ladder to the big leagues.

Vince had signed with the Royals, splitting the season between AA Wichita and AAA Omaha, where he batted cleanup behind Bobby Kalkwarf. The San Diego Padres signed Sarge, assigning the young catcher to its minor league team in Rancho Cucamonga,

California. Fender joined the Red Sox organization, finishing the season as Les Burton's closer at AAA Pawtucket. Willie, Jamario and Burke had also moved on to big league farm teams.

Kenny was at Sherman Field for the season finale, but he wore the uniform of the visitors from Colorado Springs. Even though he was the offensive hero of last year's championship game, Wright and Mendenhall had traded him to the Pikemen. Although he took this as an insult, Kenny was thrilled to be back in his home state.

The sights and smells at Sherman brought back happy memories of toeing the rubber for the Giants. Scanning the stands, I spotted Angley in the top row of the section behind home plate. His eyes focused intently on the field. According to rumor, the St. Louis Cardinals had hired him as their scout for the Central States League. Hornsby sat beside him. The professor had finished another book about baseball history a few months earlier. I thought about that upstairs bedroom in his old Victorian house and wondered which two Giants were living there.

At some point in the middle innings of the game, the little girl sitting beside me started playing with my ring. "Where did you get this?" she asked, spinning it around my finger.

"Haleigh, you know where I got it. Your dad has one just like it."

"Oh, from baseball." She examined the details of the ring.

"Yes. We got these rings for winning the championship last year."

She scooted in front of me to Eileen, who sat to my right talking with Cathy. "What about this ring?" Haleigh asked me, grasping Eileen's left hand. "It sparkles."

"I don't know about that one. It might mean she's gonna get married."

The girl's doe eyes widened. "Really?" She tugged Eileen's arm. "Leenie, are you gonna get married?"

Eileen lifted Haleigh onto her lap. "I am. Can you believe it?"

"To Boo?"

"Yep."

"But I wanted to marry Boo." Her bottom lip poked out.

"I thought you wanted to marry Kenny." Eileen pointed to the Colorado Springs second baseman.

"Oh yeah." Haleigh giggled. "I'm gonna marry Kenny!"

"Your dad will be so pleased," I said.

After the game, Kenny came to JK's with the Van Dykes, Weed, Eileen, and me. It was sort of like old times. Though goofy as ever, Kenny seemed a little distracted. I figured it may have been because he only had an hour before his team's bus departed for Colorado Springs. When the time came, I drove him to the motel where the Pikemen had stayed.

"All right, Kenneth," I said, pulling to a stop near the idling bus. "Try to stay out of trouble. At least until the wedding. I don't want to have to find another groomsman."

"Yeah, right." He chuckled and then drew a deep breath. "Hey Boo, I gotta tell you something."

The serious look on his face bothered me. "What?"

He fidgeted with his watch for a few seconds. "The middle of this season, my team signed this kid from Mexico. Can't be more than eighteen years old. Nineteen tops. Pitcher. Average fastball, but a wicked curve. Just a nasty thing. I tried to talk to him when he joined, but he didn't speak any English. Then as the season goes on, he picks up a few words. So on this last road trip, I tried again. I ask him how he learned to throw a bender like that."

"And?"

"Kid tells me he played in southern Mexico, like on a semi-pro team or something. Sounds like a dirt league in the middle of nowhere. Well, one day his team plays this other team with a big gringo pitcher nobody can hit. Strikes out at least twenty batters every game. Almost never gives up a run. That's the guy who taught him the curveball."

"Did the kid tell you this gringo's name?"

Kenny shook his head. "Didn't know his name. But get this, he said the locals down there call this guy ... it's some Spanish phrase. I had no idea what it meant, so I asked the kid to write it down."

Kenny pulled a crinkled scrap of paper from his pocket and handed it to me. On it was scrawled, "*El hombre fuerte del pelo largo.*"

I shook my head. "Sorry, man. I can't read Spanish."

A grin spread across Kenny's face. "I looked it up."

"Well, what does it mean?"

"The strong man with the long hair."

About the Author

Kent Krause writes content for online high school history courses and social studies textbooks. He holds bachelor's and master's degrees from Iowa State University, and a doctorate from the University of Nebraska-Lincoln. In addition to his four books, he has published articles in *Great Plains Quarterly* and *The International Journal of the History of Sport*. USA Book News selected his first novel, *The All-American King*, as a category finalist for the National Best Books 2009 Awards. Kent lives in Nebraska with his wife Jill.

Visit Kent online at: **kentkrause.com**

www.ingramcontent.com/pod-product-compliance
Lightning Source LLC
Chambersburg PA
CBHW060212180626
46813CB00007B/2805